CAT-HOUSE SHOWDOWN!

Raider leapt off the bed, grabbing the robe to cover his nakedness. He picked up the freshly oiled Colt and started through the dim shadows of the brothel. Again the woman cried out, but this time her voice was smaller than before.

Wan Chur slide beside him, clutching a silk robe to her neck. "It's Madam Wu," the girl cried. "I know it."

"Where is she?"

"In the back, where she prays."

Wan Chur led the way, taking him through the house. The door to Madam Wu's chapel was locked. Raider opened it with a hard shoulder.

The assassin wheeled around when the door splintered. Raider lifted his Peacemaker, but the man was too fast. He moved toward the open window where he had entered. The fiery discharge from the Colt missed him by inches.

"Raider!" Wan Chur screamed and pointed to the left.

A second man ran out of the shadows . . .

Other books by
J. D. HARDIN

RAIDER

J.D. HARDIN

BERKLEY BOOKS, NEW YORK

RAIDER

A Berkley Book / published by arrangement with
the author

PRINTING HISTORY
Berkley edition/July 1987

ISBN: 0-425-10017-0

A BERKLEY BOOK ® TM 757,375
Berkley Books are published by The Berkley Publishing Group,
200 Madison Avenue, New York, NY 10016.
The name "BERKLEY" and the "B" logo
are trademarks belonging to Berkley Publishing Corporation.

PRINTED IN THE UNITED STATES OF AMERICA

10 9 8 7 6 5 4 3 2 1

*This book is dedicated
to the late* John D. McDonald,
creator of Travis McGee
and a great writer.

CHAPTER 1

A hot, sandy Nevada wind blew in off the plain, dusting Raider with a thick layer of ghostly white earth. As the tall Pinkerton agent listed in the saddle of the gray gelding, he resembled a specter, a spook in faded denim jeans and Justin boots. The big man's chalky Stetson had been pulled down to shield his black eyes from the flying grit. A weathered duster coat hung on his broad shoulders, with the right tail of the coat pulled up to allow quick access to the Colt .45 Peacemaker that was strapped to Raider's side.

As he headed steadily northward, Raider reached down to touch the wound on his thigh. One bullet, that was all it had taken to put him out, to allow the Comancheros to capture his partner, Doc Weatherbee. The rifle slug had only dealt him a glancing blow, but it had been enough to send him over the edge of a cliff, crashing into a deep Colorado River hole. Raider managed to climb out of the river, but it was too late. The Comancheros had Doc and were driving north.

Raider grunted when he thought of the Comanchero gang. They were mostly renegade Comanche Indians, joined up with border-jumping Mexican bandits and other drifters, territorial outlaws, lawless scum. A shiver went through his shoulders. He wondered if Doc was still alive. He speculated as to his chances for bringing in some help, either more Pinkerton agents or some men from the territorial marshal's office. To request aid, he'd need a town with a telegraph office. And there didn't seem to be much chance of that, not in the wilds of the Nevada desert.

The gelding whinnied and almost stopped. Instead of spurring the lathered animal, Raider reined back and stepped out of the saddle. He cupped his hand in front of the horse's mouth and poured a short drink of water from the half-full canteen. When his mount had enough, Raider took a swallow himself. He then turned back and looked north.

What if Doc was dead? The Comancheros didn't have much reason to keep him alive, unless it was for pure damned meanness. They'd probably be torturing the well-dressed gentleman from Boston. Doc was tough, but Raider figured the Comancheros might be too much for him. Even if Doc was still alive, what was left of him might not be worth saving.

Raider swung back into the saddle. He had been lucky to find the gray. A sodbuster had sold it to him, along with the saddle and the canteen. The sodbuster was heading back east, after having lost his family during the attempt to farm the poor land of the Arizona plain. Raider wished the farmer had had a rifle to sell, but he had had to settle for the mount.

Raider urged the gray forward. With tireless legs, the horse plodded on, obeying the rider as best he could. The sun fell to Raider's left, bringing on a hostile night. Raider figured to ride straight through the darkness. It no longer mattered to him if Doc was dead or alive. The big man was going to find the Comancheros, and he was going to kill them all if he got half a chance.

At dusk, Raider stopped and withdrew a pouch from inside his slicker. The pouch contained an old compass and a weathered map. Raider tapped the compass, which did not seem to be in working order. His rugged countenance slacked into a frown.

"Gadgets," he muttered, lofting the compass into the breeze.

The directional instrument shattered against the hard ground of the plain. It had gotten wet when Raider had gone into the Colorado. So had the map, but it was made of cloth and was already too faded for the wetness to make a difference. His black eyes fell on the thin lines of Nevada.

Was he south of Carson City? Southeast, maybe. Hard to say. He looked up at the sky, fixing on a few early stars that glowed in the purple firmament. If he was southeast, that meant the Comancheros would be somewhere away from Carson City. Too much law for them to run to a big town.

Why the hell were they heading north, anyway? Comancheros rode the southern territories. What the hell did they want in Nevada? Unless there was something big for them to steal. Silver?

He peered toward the darkening horizon. "And me without a rifle," he muttered to the night.

He nudged the gray. "Don't hate me, boy. I'm as tired as you are."

As he rode on, the desert began to come alive. The night animals were on the prowl, hunting each other for a dinner meal. Raider's own stomach reminded him that he had not sat down to a plate of beans and bread for three days. His last piece of beef jerky had disappeared the day before. He considered shooting something, a rabbit or a bird, but then he knew he would have to stop to cook it. Best to keep riding if he was going to find Doc.

Ambling through the darkness, Raider had time to brood, to think. A man could think himself up some real misery, he pondered. The worst was second-guessing—like wondering why he and Doc had decided to try to infiltrate the gang instead of waiting for reinforcements from the marshal's office. Were they getting old and stupid? Reusing too many ploys that had worked before?

What if he found Doc dead? Would he have to report it to Allan Pinkerton and Wagner? Doc always did the reporting. What would Raider say? *Doc's done dead and I'm sorry as hell*. Sometimes, the big man from Arkansas thought that the only reason Pinkerton kept him on in the service was Doc's intervention every time Raider broke procedure. But hell, there were just certain times when a man couldn't rightly follow the rules.

Like when a gang of Comancheros captured your partner.

Raider slapped his thigh—the wounded one. He gritted his teeth, sucking air, whistling through the gaps. He accepted the pain like a man who thinks that, because of something he has done, he deserves the sting.

In the abyss of the plain, it was easy for Raider to reckon that he had been responsible for Doc's abduction. They should have had more sense than to waltz into the Comanchero camp, Doc perched on the seat of his Studebaker wagon, his mule Judith leading the way. Doc didn't look like a man who would ride with Comancheros, even in his cleverly crafted disguise. Raider figured he should have gone in alone. That would have been better. At least his partner would still be alive. Even if Doc Weatherbee was a pain in the backside, he didn't deserve to die at the hands of trash like the Comancheros.

Best not to kick yourself too much, he thought. Besides, Doc could still be alive. The fancy-pants magician from Massachusetts had come through some cases that were almost as bad as his current plight. Doc had ways of talking himself out of things. Maybe Doc was the very reason the Comancheros had come north in the first place.

The gray snorted, as if to tell Raider that he was dead wrong about everything. Raider shook his head, trying to force some pleasant thoughts into his brain. He remembered the girl in Tucson, fat and sassy, smooth skin, a willing disposition, satin sheets. He saw her lying on the bed, stretched out, huge breasts heaving to both sides, a dark patch to match the blackness of her thick curls. He couldn't even remember her name, but he saw that.

Then the scene seemed to shift a little, but not through a voluntary vision on Raider's part. The girl was suddenly gone and Doc was lying there with his hands and feet staked out. Blood gushed down Doc's cheeks, flowing onto his bare chest. Two Comancheros were lowering torches to ignite the crimson stream of—

Raider's head snapped up. He had fallen asleep, lolling like a drowsy bear in the saddle. His eyes lifted to the heavens. The stars were bright without a moon. After marking a few heavenly guideposts, he reached down to pat the animal's neck. The gray had held on a dead northeast path away from Carson City. At least something had gone right.

If he had figured the course correctly, there would be mountains ahead pretty soon. By morning maybe. More hiding places for Comanchero guns. Raider reached to his side, hefting the weight of the Colt .45 on his hip. His Peacemaker had gotten him out of some bona fide logjams in the past. Two dozen or so Comancheros certainly qualified as a jam. If he could just make himself believe that the .45 would be enough.

The gray suddenly startled, lifting its forelegs from the ground. Raider eased the animal back down. He peered out into the dark plain, wondering what had spooked his mount.

"What do you see, boy? Or do you smell it?"

Probably a coyote prowling for its dinner. Maybe a cougar, if he was close to the mountains. Raider drew his pistol, wishing he had a torch. He wasn't afraid of the dark, but he sure wanted to be able to see anything that might rush out of it, attacking him and his gray. Did wolf packs still venture this far south?

A howl went up in the distance.

The gray spooked again.

Raider got down, holding the Peacemaker, staring into the blackness ahead of him. Again the howl rose up, low and throaty. Raider listened, thinking the cry didn't belong to a coyote or a wolf. It was a domestic animal, a dog that slept around a campfire.

A twinkling jumped out at him from the distance, like a star that had fallen too close to the horizon. A man-made light. He started forward, walking the gray. A crescent moon had begun to rise on his right, so by the time he had gone a hundred yards, he could make out the dull shape of the building where the lone light burned.

He heard the howl and then the barking of a dog. It was probably an old prospector's outpost. He smelled a fire on the breeze. Maybe there'd be food and drink. He had a few pennies left. He could pay for something.

His pace quickened. He holstered the Colt and fixed his

gaze on the twinkling light. Suddenly it wasn't as dark as it had been. And his chances of finding Doc were looking better and better.

The gray snorted, jerking its head toward the water trough. Raider swung into the saddle and gave the animal full run. The gelding romped at a surprising pace. Raider had to rein back when he saw the shack in the glow of the crescent moon.

A hitching post held three mounts outside the dwelling. Raider climbed out of the saddle and let go of the gray. The horse ran immediately to the water trough and dipped its muzzle into the cool liquid. Raider stayed in the shadows, watching the small, oil-paper rectangles that served as windows.

As tired and hungry as he was, it took all his willpower to slide up next to the casement. When he peeked inside, he saw five men. The storekeeper had to be the skinny, bearded man with a white apron covering most of his body. A portly man appeared to be a gentleman of sorts, clad in a black suit and a broad, black Stetson. The other three men were huddled around a wooden table, eating from tin plates.

Raider's black eyes flared. "Sons of bitches."

His hand came up with the Colt.

He saw the dusty, pearl-gray derby sitting on the head of a rat-faced Mexican man who was spooning stew meat into his brown mouth.

"Ambushin', gopher-faced . . ."

He started slowly for the front door, his Colt ready.

The big man from Arkansas wanted to find out why the rat-faced man was wearing his partner's derby.

When Raider's boot shattered the rickety planks of the door, the five men froze inside the dimly lit recesses of the shaded enclosure. Two oil lamps burned over a store counter that served as a bar for the man in the Stetson and string tie. The three diners and the storekeeper were rigid in their different poses, the diner's forks lifting or falling in the various gesticulations of eating.

Raider thumbed back the hammer of the Peacemaker, making sure they all heard the threatening click. Easing

into the musty shadows, he kept his black eyes trained on
the dinner table, anticipating the slightest twitch of movement from three pairs of hands. Their eyes were burning
through Raider as well, sizing up their chances, three to
one, deciding on the odds of the intruder getting all three of
them.

Raider studied them carefully, wondering if he had seen
their faces during his brief time in the Comanchero camp.
"Stay real still," he urged, "and you'll stay alive."

The diners did not move, even to continue chewing on
the tough stew beef.

The well-dressed, round-faced man in the Stetson gave
a forced but hearty laugh. "No need to pull iron, stranger.
Holster that hog-leg and have a shot of red-eye on me.
Clarence here don't water it too much."

Raider ignored the man's attempt to be cordial. He
looked at the pearl-gray derby that sat atop the pointed
head of the rat-faced man. It was dusty, but unmistakably
Doc's hat.

The thin, bearded proprietor of the outpost shifted
against the store counter, dropping his hands toward the
shelves underneath. "Look here, mister, you can't come
bargin' in here and—"

"Hands on the bar or I'll have to drop you!" Raider
barked, keeping the storekeeper in the corner of his eye.

The man's hands fell on the wooden counter.

The rat-faced man's beady eyes glared out from under
the brim of the pearl-gray derby. "Señor, we eating. *Co-
midas!*"

Had he seen those faces before? Two burly Mexicans
flanked the man in Doc's derby. Did Raider see recognition
in their eyes? He had to make sure they were the ones he
wanted. No need to kill them if they were innocent.

Raider gestured with the barrel of the Peacemaker. "I'm
a Pinkerton agent, lookin' for a band of Comancheros what
kidnapped my partner."

The rat-face broke into an ill grin. "Señor, we are not
Comancheros. No." He entreated his men to agree with
him. They laughed and nodded. "I tell you, we are good
men."

"That hat," Raider offered. "Where'd you get it?"

The smile disappeared from the man's face. He shrugged. "It is only a hat, señor. I do not remember where I bought it."

"He does not remember," echoed the other two men.

Raider kept the Colt ready. "My partner wore a hat like that," he insisted. "He'd never sell it. Somebody would have to take it from him. Like the Comancheros that were ridin' this way. Either you boys are ridin' with the Comancheros or you seen 'em to buy that hat. Which one is it?"

The rat-faced man laughed, starting to lean back. "It is just a hat. Here, you take it. I do not want it anymore."

It was a variation on an old trick. The rat-faced man grabbed the brim of the derby and skimmed it toward Raider. Even before he let go of the hat, Raider had begun his drop. A knife, taken from a neck sheath, flew past Raider's head, thudding into the wooden wall behind him.

The two compatriots were moving as well. They reached for old, rusty pistols at their sides. Raider thumbed the hammer of the Colt as soon as his belly hit the floor. The sound from the Peacemaker was deafening inside the cramped shack.

Both men fell backward, clutching their bloody chests, dying before their fingers reached the butts of their pistols.

The rat-faced man lifted the wooden table, tilting it toward Raider, who rolled twice, coming up with the barrel of the Peacemaker in front of him.

The hammer fell on the Colt, but the cartridge fizzled harmlessly.

Raider stared back at the shiny barrel of a new .38 Diamondback.

He was going to be killed with Doc's gun.

"Adios, lawman."

Raider thumbed the hammer again, but another explosion preceded the blast from the Colt's barrel.

The rat-faced man buckled, his eyes slanting inward, his mouth forming the last syllable of death.

As the bandito fell, Raider wheeled back to see the smoke rising from a gun in the hand of the portly, well-dressed man. A large-caliber derringer had saved the big man. The gentleman had discharged both barrels.

He nodded at Raider, tipping his hat. "Hall's the name. Cleveland Hall."

Raider shook his head, exhaling. "Much obliged to make your acquaintance."

The gentleman pointed toward Raider's weapon. "Dud, huh."

Suddenly the proprietor leaned over the bar. "Uh, Mr. Pinkerton fellah, I reckon I ought to tell you that—"

Raider was way ahead of him. He lifted the Peacemaker, hoping his next shot hadn't been ruined by the waters of the Colorado. The man in the black Stetson gaped at the big man from Arkansas.

"What the hell are you—"

Raider fired the Colt in the direction of Mr. Cleveland Hall, sending a slug just two or three inches over Hall's shoulder.

A loud chortle resounded from behind Hall. Stumbling on the wooden floor. Gurgling sounds, a throat with a hole in it, gasping for air. A fourth man fell out of the shadows, slamming at the feet of Cleveland Hall.

"I'll be damned!" the portly man shouted, sweat dripping off his chubby red face. "I thought for a minute there you were going to shoot me!"

Raider shook his head. "Three horses. Musta been ridin' double."

"That's what I was about to tell you," the proprietor offered.

Raider glared at the thin man. "Anybody else hereabouts?"

The beard went back and forth. "Nope, not that I know of."

"Go through their pockets," Raider insisted.

The proprietor hesitated. "Dead men?"

"You can keep any money you find," Raider offered. "I just want to see if they've got any of my partner's belongin's."

At the sound of money, the proprietor hurried to his task.

Cleveland Hall was shaking his head, almost smiling. Raider had seen dudes like Hall before. Texas sharpies, drummers, preachers. He slid next to the gentleman and reached over the counter for the bottle of red-eye.

"Hey," came a protest from the storekeeper.

"I'm payin'," Raider barked.

"Oh." He went back to the pockets.

Raider poured a shot of whiskey and threw it back in a hurry. The second and third gulps went down as quickly. The rough whiskey burned, but it took the edge off a little. No matter how many gunfights he had been in, Raider had never gotten used to killing. He accepted the fact that killing was needed, but it never made it easier.

"You look like a man who knows how to drink," Hall said, pouring one for himself. "You from Texas?"

"Arkansas," Raider replied.

"I reckon they know how to drink up that way too."

Raider turned full front, staring into the portly man's pale blue eyes. "What's a dandy like you doin' up this way, Hall? How'd you come to end up in this hole, with these men?"

Hall bristled a little. "I ain't as dandy as you think, boy. You saw how I delivered that 'un there into the hands of his Maker. Didn't flinch either."

"Killin' don't make you a man," Raider replied, scowling at his drinking partner. "And it don't explain what you're doin' here or why you're wearin' them fancy clothes."

Hall straightened himself as if he was invoking the last shred of his dignity. "I am a businessman, Mr. Pinkerton. Not that it's any of your never mind. I sell things, guns mostly."

Raider gestured back to the fallen men, whose belongings had formed a pile next to the storekeeper. "You doin' business with them four?"

Hall's face flushed even redder. "I ain't obliged to be tellin' my dealin's to the law." He lifted the shot glass toward his mouth.

With a bear-paw backhand, Raider knocked the glass from Hall's hand. He grabbed the lapels of the fancy suit and drew him in face to face. "Now you listen to me, Hall. I don't give a damn if you're armin' the whole Comanche nation to rise up and kill every white man in this territory. I need information about my partner. If he's still alive, he's ridin' with the amigos of them dead ones. I got to find him if he's still breathin'."

Hall was trembling. He swallowed, reaching up to pull

at his starched collar. "Please, let me go, I'll tell you everything. You're choking me. I'll tell you everything."

Raider dropped the gasping arms dealer.

When he had recovered, Hall outlined the deal for the big Pinkerton. One of the Comancheros, a half-breed named Tal, had approached him offering to pay top dollar for guns. There was a wagon out back filled with Winchesters and Colts. Raider could see for himself. And Hall had no knowledge of Doc's whereabouts. Tal had not mentioned him or anything else except the guns.

When Hall accused Raider of blowing the deal for him by killing them, Raider only laughed and reminded Hall that his derringer had done some of the dirty work.

"Besides," the big man offered, "I saved your ass, Hall."

The pudgy man raised an eyebrow. "How you figure that?"

Raider looked back at the storekeeper. "Find any money, hombre?"

The proprietor shook his head. "Only a silver dollar and a couple of Mexican pesos."

Raider turned to Hall. "How much was the deal for?"

"An even thousand."

"They weren't plannin' on payin' you," Raider insisted. "After they ate, they were probably going to kill both of you and take everything here."

Hall clutched his throat in an involuntary motion. "Land o' Goshen, I reckon you did save my dadburned hide. Unless they got the money in their saddlebags."

"Ain't no money no where," Raider replied.

"I found this," the storekeeper said, holding up a shiny object.

Raider recognized the rectangular shape. It was a silver matchbox. Doc always used it to light his cigars. Raider could not stand the smell of the Old Virginia cheroots, but he would have given anything to see Doc torching the end of a stogie.

"Can I keep the dollar and the pesos?" the storekeeper asked.

Raider nodded. "You got to bury them."

"All right."

He tossed the matchbox to Raider.

"This partner of yourn must be somebody special," Hall offered.

Raider scowled at the matchbox. "He's worse'n a week-old saddle sore. Never stops talkin'. Always gettin' us into trouble with some highfalutin notion. Thinks he's better'n everybody else."

"Can't agree or disagree," Hall replied. "Don't know the man. Well, I reckon I better be gettin' on my way."

Raider grabbed his shoulder as he tried to slide away from the counter. "Stay put. I might need you."

Sweat beaded on Hall's forehead. "But I—"

"Ain't no buts," Raider said. "You're stayin'."

"See here!"

Raider grabbed Hall's lapels. "Only *see here* is this. I *see* you *here* in Nevada talkin' to the marshal about illegal guns that came in over the border. How's the marshal gonna take to a Texas sharpie runnin' guns to a band of Comancheros?"

Hall eased back a little. "And if I stay, you won't tell the marshal?"

"Won't tell a soul."

"I found this," came the storekeeper's high voice.

A gold watch dangled from his hand, swinging on a gold watch fob. Doc's timepiece. It had stopped running. Raider wondered if time had also run out for his partner.

"Bring me some stew," he ordered. "And put the oat bag on that gray out there."

The storekeeper's thin face had broken out into a nervous smile. "Are you goin' after a whole gang of Comancheros by yourself?"

Raider just snatched the watch from his hands and told him to get about his business.

The stew meat was tough and tasteless, but Raider ate every bit of it, swirling stale fry-bread in the gravy. When his stomach was full, he asked for coffee and another bottle of whiskey. The proprietor of the solitary outpost had been studying the big man with furtive eyes.

Raider glared at him as he poured the coffee. "Somethin' on your mind?"

The man blushed behind his beard. "Well, I was just wonderin' if you was maybe wantin' to—"

"To pay?" Raider said cynically. "Sure as hell." He reached into his pockets and dropped every bit of money he had on the table. "Ninety-six cents, pilgrim. That cover it?"

The storekeeper raked the money off the table. "Thank you kindly, sir. This will be fine. But I was wonderin' somethin' else."

Raider lifted the steaming tin cup to his lips. "Spill it. We ain't got time for you to be shy."

"Well," the skinny man started, "I was wonderin' if you might want a . . . well, a woman. I mean, my wife's sister is upstairs with my wife. They're squaws, and the sister gets lonely, see, and she . . . "

Raider shook his head.

"No charge," the proprietor insisted. "Here, let me call her. Flower!" He smiled back at Raider. "Little Desert Flower's her name. She's a plain sort of gal. Flower! . . . Here she is."

She was prettier than the storekeeper had let on. A round, dark face, flirting doe eyes, thick mounds of firm bosom. When she smiled at Raider, she showed a mouthful of white teeth.

Raider was tempted to run his fingers through Little Desert Flower's coarse black hair. He felt the need, stirring in him like some long forgotten dream. But he had other things on his mind and he didn't need the distraction. Women could go a long way toward making a man weak, and Raider needed all his strength if he was going to face a whole camp of Comancheros.

"Get her out of here," he commanded. "And you stay gone for a while. I want to talk to the gun seller alone."

"Okay," the skinny man replied, "but she'll be upstairs if you want her. And like I said, no charge."

He disappeared into the back, pushing the girl ahead of him.

Raider turned to see Cleveland Hall's pale blue eyes staring at him from under the black Stetson. "What you lookin' at, Hall?"

A short, nervous laugh from the fat gentleman. "She

was a pretty little thing. Reckon he had her hid from them Comancheros. Probably offered her because you saved his bacon."

Raider leaned back in the wooden chair, pouring red-eye into his coffee. "I ain't the kind to turn it down most of the time. But right now I got other things to think on."

Hall cleared his throat. "Speakin' of time. Ain't you worried that the Comanchero gang will be long gone from here by now?"

Raider shook his head, gesturing toward the back of the dwelling. "They're waitin' for what you got out there. They ain't gonna leave until they get it."

Hall nodded. "Been thinkin' about that. You was right to say that I done wrong by—"

"I never said nothin'."

"All right, then I'll say it. I was wrong. I reckon I never figured on what these boys was goin' to use them guns for. I ain't as young as I once was and—"

Raider waved him off. "Save it. I ain't the one to pass judgment on you."

Hall tipped back his Stetson. "Well, I can thank you for that."

"Save your thanks, too."

"Consarn it, Pinkerton, ain't you gonna give me a chance to say what I want to say?"

Raider's rugged face slacked into a half-smile. "I reckon there ain't no way of stoppin' a man who's ready to flap his lips. Just make it short and sweet, gun seller. If you know how."

Hall removed his hat and twirled it nervously on his fingers. "It's just that, well, like I said, I ain't as young as I once was. Can't cover as much territory. I never took much to sellin' my wares to the outlaw kind, but of late, I've had to take on any customers what was willin'."

Raider grimaced, pouring another shot into the tin cup.

"Go on," Hall said, "give me that disgusted look. I s'pose I deserve it. But just let me say this. If there's any way I can help you square things, I'm willin' to do it. Is that understood?"

Raider nodded. "I hope you're not just payin' lip service, fat man. I was gonna make you help me anyway. But just remember, if you try to back-shoot me, I'll plug you just as dead as them Comancheros. Is that understood?"

They were quiet for a while.

Hall stuffed tobacco into a corncob pipe, keeping his pale eyes trained on Raider. "Where you think they're hidin'?"

Raider stood up, staring out the open window. "The mountains are close by. There's a hundred ravines and holes where a varmint can hide." He sighed deeply. "Only one thing is botherin' me."

Hall glanced up. "What might that be?"

"Why the hell did they run north? What are they lookin' for up here?"

Hall shrugged. "Maybe they just wanted to get away from you."

"Maybe. But they wouldn't be lookin' for guns, a lot of guns anyway." He spun around, focusing his black irises on the portly gun dealer. "How long ago did you meet up with this Tal?"

"Day before yesterday. But it was more like he caught up to me. I was in Elko, waitin' for a train. Said he had heard of me, that I was a man who could get guns for him. But I don't see how that makes any difference. If he was . . ."

Raider turned away from him, taking out his map and laying it on the table. "Come here and look at this."

Hall ambled to his side and peered down at the map.

"Here's Elko," Raider said, pointing to a fuzzy dot on the map. "You got any notion where we're at right now?"

Hall indicated the approximate location with a weathered finger.

Raider looked up, nodding. "Then they're closer than I thought. If Tal could come into Elko and then send his men here, he'd have to be holed up in the closest range of mountains."

Hall agreed. "Probably no more than a day's ride."

Raider began to fold up the map. "Timin'. It's got to be right. Tal is gonna be expectin' his men to come back. But when?"

"What's to stop him from sendin' somebody to look for 'em?" Hall asked.

Raider shrugged his shoulders. "Nothin'. That's why we can't wait around here too long."

Hall tapped his pipe on the counter. "Tell me somethin'. How do you expect to find this Tal?"

"I don't. He's gonna find me." Raider grinned. "Or should I say, he's gonna find you."

Hall licked his lips, staring at Raider from the corners of his eyes. "Me?"

Raider frowned at the gun dealer. "Where'd all that righteous talk go? A second ago you were tellin' me how you want to set things right."

"Well, I do," Hall replied. "But I don't know if it's too smart to ride into a Comanchero gang and hand over a whole wagonload of rifles."

"Yeah, well, that's the quickest way to get to Tal." He hesitated before adding, "And my partner, if he's still alive."

"Them kind can make a man wish he was dead," Hall rejoined. "They'll kill me once I hand over the rifles."

Raider glared at the portly gentleman. "You shoulda thought that through before you offered to help."

Hall's nerves, or the lack of them, were taking over. He began to pace back and forth. "I don't like it, big man. What do I say to them?"

Raider exhaled impatiently. "Just say that Tal's boys got themselves into a little ruckus and never showed up. So you decided to come lookin' for Tal himself. Then you give him the wagon and the guns. If he don't want to pay, you just ride on out and leave him be."

"I still don't like the idea of handin' over them rifles, not after what I seen tonight."

Raider grabbed up the whiskey bottle and sat down in the wooden chair. "You won't be givin' him anything that shoots."

Hall raised an eyebrow. "Come again?"

"Before that wagon rolls out of here, we're gonna take out all the firin' pins, just break 'em off so the guns won't work."

Hall frowned. "Destroy all my rifles? But what if Tal decides he wants to shoot one of them?"

Raider tossed back a shot of whiskey before the reply. "Then we leave a ringer on top, a good rifle."

Hall nodded reluctantly. "I s'pose you're onto somethin'. But look here, my life won't be worth a plug nickel if he finds out I'm rookin' him."

"It ain't worth that now . . . if you decide to cross me, I mean." Raider watched from the corner of his eye, half expecting Hall to draw the derringer again. "Look here, gun seller, if you're gettin' a yellow streak, just try to think about spendin' your last days in a territorial prison. An old buzzard like you won't have a chance. At least if you cash in this way, you'll be goin' out like a man. You'll have a better chance with Saint Peter."

Hall sighed. "I ain't never been one for religion, but I reckon you do make some sort of sense. God help me."

They were quiet again. Both of them visited the bottle of red-eye. Raider was thinking, trying to get everything straight. He could have used some sleep, but he knew he would never be able to close his eyes, not with Doc out there in the wilderness.

"Hadn't we better get started?" Hall asked finally.

Raider shook his head. "Not just yet. We got to bust up them rifles. How many you got out there?"

"Twenty-five or so."

Raider sighed. "I reckon it is a shame to break good iron, but we got no other choice."

Hall stood up. "Wait here for a minute." He started for the door.

Raider lifted his Peacemaker from the holster. "Where you aimin' to go?"

Hall smiled foolishly. "Don't worry, pardner. I ain't gonna try nothin'. You're too damned fast with that thing."

Raider kept his hand full of the Colt while Hall went outside into the darkness. In a few minutes, he came back inside holding a shiny new Winchester in hand. Raider thumbed the hammer of his .45.

"No need for that," Hall said. "I just wanted you to have this."

He held out the rifle for Raider. The big man holstered the Colt and took the Winchester into his hands. He had seen one like it in Tucson, just before he and Doc had took off after the Comancheros.

Raider looked down the straight sights of the barrel. "Model 1876," he said. "Just come out of the oil cloth."

"Forty-five caliber," Hall said proudly. "Three hundred grains of lead and a hundred grains of powder. It'll stop most anything short of an elephant. You know what an elephant is?"

Raider shook his head. "Not today, I don't."

"Well, it's a big damned critter," Hall rejoined. "I can tell you that."

Raider levered the Winchester, dry firing. He nodded appreciatively at the gun dealer. "When this thing is over, I'll see to it that you get full payment, Hall."

The portly man dropped a box of cartridges on the table. "Don't fret none about the price. It's yourn to keep."

"Much obliged," Raider replied. "But you'll get your money. How many cartridges will she hold?"

"Fourteen. Fifteen if you keep one in the chamber."

Raider began feeding the brass bullets into the side load. The food and whiskey had brought him back a little. Things were looking better, if not good. Did he really have a chance against two dozen renegades? Hell, it was really only twenty if he subtracted the four dead ones.

"We better jury-rig those rifles," Hall said.

Raider started to get up. He heard a noise behind him. He jacked a cartridge into the chamber of the '76 and leveled it on a pair of dark eyes. The squaw only giggled at the sight of the bore.

"Looks like she don't want to take no for an answer," Hall said, smiling.

Raider felt the jolt running through his body. He wanted her, needed her. And there she was, laughing at him.

Hall puffed on his pipe. "I can take care of the firing pins."

Raider hesitated.

"Go on," the portly man urged. "It might be your last chance."

Raider felt the heat of his own breath. Hall was right. It might very well be his final opportunity to be with a woman.

He turned to regard the gun seller. "You sure you can rig them repeaters by yourself?"

Hall nodded. "As much as I hate to, yeah, I can do it."

The girl was giggling, pursing her lips at him.

Raider pointed a finger at Hall. "You go on and do your

business, old man. But keep this in mind. If I hear one wagon wheel turnin', I'm gonna be up in the window, cuttin' you to ribbons with this seventy-six. Savvy?"

Hall winked at him. "Savvy."

He turned and went out the door.

Raider took another shot of whiskey and then followed the squaw into the loft above.

The room was little more than a planked enclosure with a cornhusk pallet spread out on the wooden floor. Raider leaned his new Winchester against the wall. He took off his hat and then reached for his gunbelt. The girl's hands stopped him. She wanted to undress him herself.

"So they call you Little Desert Flower, huh?"

But she didn't want to talk. His gunbelt landed on the floor, followed by his shirt and his boots. She made him lie down on the pallet, tugging at his pant legs. The night air felt cool on Raider's skin.

"You got a blanket, honey?"

But she did not reply. When her flour-sack dress hit the floor, Little Desert Flower stretched out next to him. He caught the scent of her in his nostrils, sweet and delicate like a blossom after a fresh rain.

His hands entangled in her thick hair. She pressed her body against him, rubbing her firm nipples on his hairy chest, laughing as if she had found a new toy. Her hands were all over his torso, tracing the bumps and knots of his rippling muscles.

He put his hand behind her head, trying to pull down her face. "Come here and give me a kiss, honey."

She didn't want to be kissed either.

Her tiny hands groped for the massive erection between his thighs. A gasp escaped from her lips when she stroked the fleshy length of him. Her fingers seemed to measure the thickness, and she laughed again.

She said something in her native tongue that Raider had heard before, something that amounted to calling him a horse.

He ran his hand down her smooth back, cupping her buttocks. "I'll show you horse, lady. Git over on your bottom so I can . . ."

He tried to roll over, but she wouldn't let him. Instead,

she urged him back on the mattress, pulling at his cock all the time. She was as spry as a desert fox, straddling his crotch, hovering over the head of his prick.

Raider reached between her thighs, fondling the wet lips of her cunt. Both of them were fighting for breath, unable to find enough air in the musty enclosure. Raider thrust his hips upward, trying to impale her with his throbbing member. Little Desert Flower only laughed, teasing him, rubbing her wetness over the tip of his manhood.

Raider grabbed her hips. "I've had about enough of this game, little lady. You gonna let me have it?"

She guided his prick into the opening of her cunt. They both shivered as she sat slowly on his length, taking in half of his cock. Her hips began to work, rising and falling, bringing an anguished expression of pleasure to her full, brown lips.

Raider cupped her ass helping her along until she was able to receive his entire offering.

He felt his sap begin to rise, but then she was off him in an instant.

Raider looked up, fearing some sort of trap. But she had only gotten off so she could stretch out on her back, spreading her thick little thighs, beckoning him to settle into the notch of her cunt.

"Now you want to do it my way, huh?"

She giggled, groping for his prick, trying to pull him down on top of her. Raider lowered his mouth to the firm mounds of her breasts, licking and sucking, tickling her with his thick mustache. He finally collapsed between her legs, and she guided him in for another round of pleasure.

Raider lost himself, abandoning all sense of mission, driving his cock in and out of her. She vocalized her lust, almost screaming at the top of her lungs. When he felt his discharge rising again, he fought it off, trying to prolong his ecstasy. She was only an Indian girl somewhere in the dark of the Nevada wilderness, but he had never felt anything better, not even in the best brothels of New Orleans or San Francisco.

She wrapped her legs around his waist, trying to keep him imprisoned between her thighs. Her teeth bit his shoulder; her tongue licked the ridge of his chest. Like the man on top of her, she didn't want it to end.

But Raider grunted and his body buckled. He drove his cock in as far as it would go, releasing most of the hostile energy that had haunted him for nearly a month. He pressed his mouth to hers, finding her willing to kiss him now. Her skin was prickled with chill bumps. When he tried to pull out, she begged him not to.

"More," she whispered. "More for me."

Raider withdrew and stretched out beside her. His finger went down to the crest of her cunt. He began to manipulate the part of her that always made women crazy, a trick he had learned from a dozen different whores. Little Desert Flower lay back and enjoyed his ministrations until he was erect again. He rolled over and penetrated her, achieving the desired climax in several heated minutes. Again she tried to stop him when he wanted to vacate her body.

"No!" she said into his ear. "Stay. Don't go."

Raider sighed. "I can't, honey."

"A little while," she pleaded. "I got no man."

Raider shook his head as she buried her face in his chest. The big man listened in the darkness, straining to hear the night sounds. Somewhere in the outpost shack, low moans rose from the mouth of another woman, no doubt the storekeeper and his wife engaged in similar love-play. Outside, he heard the clicking of soft metal as the gun seller disarmed the two dozen rifles that were meant for the Comancheros. It would take a while for Hall to knock out all of the firing pins, he told himself.

The girl was so soft and warm and sweet. Even the cornhusk mattress felt like a cathouse featherbed. What would it hurt to close his eyes for a couple of minutes? Little Desert Flower would wake him up. Or Hall would call him from downstairs.

The world went black on him.

Then he felt a gentle tugging on his cock. He intended to roll over and impale her again, until he heard the rooster crowing somewhere near the house. He looked up to see the first glow of sunrise on the oil-paper window.

"Son of a bitch," he cried, jumping up.

As he fought with his pants, he knew he had made a big mistake. The girl, the sleep, trusting the gun seller. He hadn't really hurt himself, but he just knew that he had all but ruined his partner's chances for survival.

CHAPTER 2

As he pulled on his boots, Raider heard the chinking rattle of harnesses below. He grabbed his gunbelt and the new rifle, stepping up to the small window. Unlatching the crude casement, he swung open the oil-paper rectangle and looked down.

Hall had all the horses, including his gray, tied to the back of a rickety buckboard. He seemed to be getting ready to flee. Raider levered a cartridge into the chamber of the Winchester and then took a deep breath. With a powerful sound from his lungs, he leapt feet first from the second story of the house.

Raider's feet hit the tight canvas tarp that covered the gun seller's deadly wares. The big man bounced forward, which prompted him to tuck and roll, coming up on his feet with the Winchester aimed right at the pudgy gentleman's white face.

Raider peered down the sight at the black Stetson. "Goin' somewhere, Cleveland?"

Hall pulled back on the reins of the buckboard, fidgeting from the scare Raider had inflicted. "Dad blame it, boy, you oughta try sayin' hello sometime without a gun."

Raider kept the '76 at eye level. "You was back here tryin' to get away, Hall. Don't deny it. You was gonna take all the mounts with you so I wouldn't have a chance of catchin' you."

Hall fumbled nervously with his pipe. "Wasn't goin' to do no such. Had some oats back here and I figured to dose 'em all before we lit out, so they'd be fresh and ready to run."

"You sure you wasn't plannin' to leave me high and dry while I was upstairs sleepin'?"

"You think I'd wait till just before dawn if I was gonna leave you?" Hall replied. "Nosiree, if I was boltin' on you, I'da gone as soon as you and that squaw started makin' all that ruckus. Hell, they could probably hear her all the way to Carson City."

Raider lowered the gun to his hip. "Why the devil didn't you wake me if you wasn't plannin' to run out?"

Hall chortled derisively. "Now that's a pretty sight. Me traipsin' up a flight of stairs to wake up a trigger-happy Pinkerton and his squaw. Yes sir, that makes a lot of sense, don't it? I mean, you got to ask yourself, would you have done it? Huh?"

Raider exhaled, lowering the '76. "No, I reckon I wouldn't at that." He laughed a little. "I reckon that's the way it musta looked from your side."

Smoke rose from the pudgy gentleman's pipe. "Damn right, that's how it looked. I wasn't goin' nowhere, I can tell you. If I figured to run, you'd figure to find me. And if you didn't roll out soon, I was gonna make some kind of noise to roust you."

Raider threw his gunbelt around his waist and fastened it tightly. When he was armed, he looked up at the sky. "Sun's on the way." He rubbed his chin. "This don't look too bad after all. We can think up somethin'."

Hall puffed at the pipe, wondering what he had gotten himself into.

Raider looked up at the window above them. "Storekeeper!"

After a few moments, the window swung open and the

beard protruded from the aperture. "What is it?"

Raider gestured to the north. "How far to the mountains?"

The storekeeper cogitated for a while. "Well, if'n you ride till the sun is on your shoulder, you ought to start seein' them by then. Reach 'em by noon, maybe later. Depends on how hard you want to work them horses."

"Thanks," Raider replied. "And bring me down my Stetson and my duster."

"Sure 'nough." He hesitated. "And good luck to you." The window swung shut.

Raider peered north at the shadowy horizon. "We'll ride till we see the mountains, and then we'll decide what to do."

Hall nodded. "If you say so."

Raider untied the horses from the back of Hall's wagon and fixed the Comanchero ponies back to the hitching post.

Hall eyed the three mounts.

"Somethin' on your mind?" Raider asked.

Hall shrugged. "Just wonderin' how I'm gonna explain to Tal that his boys didn't come along with me. I mean, I just can't up and tell him that a Pinkerton shot 'em."

Raider swung into the saddle of the gray. "You shot one of them."

Hall laughed nervously. "I can't tell him that, for certain!"

Raider tried the reins of the gray. The animal felt strong, ready to run. Hall had been true to his word, feeding the gray from an oat bag. Maybe Lady Luck was finally starting to look his way.

What was it Doc always said about luck? That it was for losers. A professional didn't need luck. Raider figured to take all he could get.

"What's on your mind?" Hall asked.

Raider shook his head. "Nothin' you want to hear."

They were turning north when the squaw came running from the shack. She was completely naked, save for Raider's Stetson, which covered her thick hair. He reached down and grabbed his hat. She laughed at him, offering his duster and a brown sack.

The sack was full of fry-bread and cold potatoes.

Raider looked down at her and smiled. "Thank you, Little Desert Flower."

She raised her arms, grinning at him. "Come back."

With a single motion, he lifted her from the ground, kissing her soft mouth. He immediately felt like staying for more, but there just wasn't time. Gently, he lowered her to the ground, thinking he had never seen a woman with a prettier face.

"Let's ride, gun seller."

They started north at a slow pace.

Raider reached into the bag and took out a handful of food. He threw the sack to Hall. "Here. Breakfast."

Hall dug in appreciatively. "Sure could use some coffee with this."

"Can't have everything," the big man replied. "Just be thankful for this and hope a few other things fall our way."

Hall frowned suddenly. "How many men you say Tal has ridin' with him?"

"Two dozen," Raider replied with a full mouth.

Hall coughed, like he was choking.

"Don't die on me," Raider said. "I'm gonna need you if we got a chance in hell."

The gun seller seemed to recover. "Two dozen to two. Them ain't my kind of odds, big man."

"Me neither, gun seller. Me neither."

"Seems like we're ridin' straight to our deaths," Hall offered.

"Put a cork in it, Hall. I got to think."

As they rode on, Raider tried to figure a way out of it. But the image of Little Desert Flower kept intruding on his thoughts. He couldn't help but think about her nubile body and how much better he had felt after sharing the corn-shuck mattress.

"Mountains."

Hall had said it. He sat on the seat of the buckboard, drawing off the pipe. As the storekeeper had predicted, the sun was on their shoulders, rising higher in the sky.

Raider's head snapped up. He saw the vague apparition against the horizon. Rounded sandstone peaks jutted up out of the plain. He wasn't sure of the range, or if it even had a name.

"Whatta we do?" Hall asked.

Raider drew his Colt, checking the full cylinders. "Nothin'. Yet." He touched the '76 Winchester on the saddle's sling ring.

They kept on until they could see the whirls of smoke that rose from the peaks. Raider reined back. A camp. He reached into his duster and took out a long, cylindrical object.

Hall's brow fretted curiously. "What's that?"

Raider pulled open the cylinder until it had telescoped into a spyglass. "Used to belong to my partner," he said gruffly, raising the glass to his eye. "If we don't find him, it'll be the last thing I have to remember him by."

"Musta really liked him," Hall offered.

Raider laughed cynically. "Tell you the truth, I couldn't stand him."

He scanned the hills, looking for signs of movement. Nothing except the lazy curl of the smoke. He snapped the glass back into a compact tube.

Hall was glaring warily at the big Pinkerton. "What do we do now, Raider? Or have you thunk of that yet?"

Raider scowled at him. "I thunk it."

"And?"

He gestured toward the mountains. "You just keep right on ridin' till you find the leader. Or until he finds you."

Sweat broke out on the pudgy man's upper lip. "Ain't you comin' along?"

Raider shook his head. "Nope."

Hall's face turned beet red. "I thought we was in this thing together!"

Raider pointed to the right, to a lower rise in the foothills to the east. "Don't fret. I'm gonna be close by, watchin' everything. You just do your part and let me worry about the rest."

The gun seller stood up on the buckboard, demanding vehemently, "And what might be my part!"

"Deliver the guns," Raider replied. "I don't care how you do it. If you have to lie, cheat, or steal, it don't matter to me."

He turned the gelding to the east.

Hall took off his Stetson and waved it in the air. "Consarn you, Pinkerton, you're danged and determined to get me killed."

"I saved your bacon once," Raider replied. "You owe me."

"Can't repay nothin' if I'm dead!"

Raider took a deep breath, waiting for Hall to cool off a little. "Okay, gun seller, here it is. If Tal wants to know about his boys, you tell him this. Say they was drinkin' and whoopin' it up at the store back there. Tell him there was a couple of squaws and his boys decided to take turns. Then they all passed out and when you couldn't wake 'em, you decided to deliver the guns yourself. That oughta make him happy. For a while."

"Then he kills me and takes all the guns!"

Raider turned the gray east, calling back over his shoulder, "Just deliver the guns, pardner. I don't care how you do it."

Hall shook a fist at the big man. "Yeah, well, if I see a way to keep my owndamnedself out of the noose, I'm agonna take my best chance."

"You do that," was Raider's only reply.

"What if they already seen *you!*" Hall cried.

Raider stopped and looked back. "Just say I was a drifter ridin' along, and when I heard there was Comancheros hereabouts, I didn't want any part of it. That makes sense, don't it?"

"Big 'un!"

"Yeah, gun seller?"

"Good luck."

Raider grimaced, shaking his head, turning the horse east again.

Hall picked up the reins. "Giddayup."

The buckboard eased toward the mountains. Hall considered turning around and hightailing it in the opposite direction. But then he saw the telltale flash in the hills, a triangle of broken mirror used for signaling. They had seen him, which meant that they had probably seen Raider, too. There wasn't much else to do but keep rolling for the mountains.

Then it hit him, an idea to deliver the guns and to save his own hide. The Pinkerton probably wouldn't like the notion. But then again, Hall thought, he didn't much care what the Pinkerton liked. It was every man for himself now. They were both on their own, trying to stay alive as best they could. The portly gun dealer from Texas had decided he was in love with his life. He planned to do everything he could to keep it going.

Raider spurred the gray toward the foothills, kicking up a trail of dust behind him. The animal was strong, asking its rider for a full head of steam. Raider let it go, knowing that he had been seen by the men in the mountains. Even at a headlong gallop, he saw the flickering mirrors that they were using to signal the arrival of the gun seller.

Did Hall have a chance against the Comancheros? Or would they just kill him and take all the weapons for themselves? Maybe the slippery little arms dealer would slide out of it. Raider couldn't blame him if he found a way to save his own hide, as long as he delivered the merchandise. The altered rifles had to be in Tal's hands, to keep him from backtracking and discovering his dead compadres.

Raider grinned at the thought of the four slain outlaws. An eye for an eye. Even if Doc was already dead, the score had been partially settled. It would never be right until they were all six feet under.

He guided the gray into a pass between the foothills. The vantage point had to be right. He wanted to see everything without being seen. The Comancheros had spotted him, so he had to lay low if they were going to believe Hall's story about him just being a drifter.

Tying the gray to a clump of dried vegetation, he grabbed his rifle and Doc's telescope and climbed up a sandstone incline to the dull point of a ridge. He positioned himself on the south side of a rocky protrusion in order to use the telescope without the reflection from the glass being seen by the Comancheros.

When he was flat on his belly, he lifted the lens to his eye and peered down on something he had not expected to see.

"Damn it, Hall, what the hell do you think you're doin'?"

The gun seller wasn't exactly sticking to the plan. He had stopped the buckboard about a mile from the foothills and climbed down out of the seat. His hands were busy unhitching the harness of the draft horse. He appeared to be leaving a little early.

Raider swung the glass to his right. He really didn't need the telescope to see the cloud of dust from the ten men who rode out of the hills. They were heading straight for the gun seller.

Raider looked back at Hall. The portly man was swinging onto the back of the harness-bred. Suddenly Raider was rooting for Hall to get away, to outdistance the onrushing hoard.

"Come on, fat man. Come on!"

Hall dug his boot heels into the harness-bred, loping away from the murderous band. He was less than a quarter mile from the wagon when the Comancheros surrounded the buckboard. Two of them started after the gun seller, but a grunt from their leader called them back. Tal no longer cared about the messenger. He had what he wanted.

Raider focused the glass on the broad-shouldered half-breed. Long hair, scarred face, half of one ear missing, corded arms, the hateful scowl of perpetual rage emblazoned on his face. He wore ragged buckskin pants, moccasins, and something else that made Raider cringe: Doc Weatherbee's silk vest covered his torso. The vest was stained with blood.

Tal's face lifted, looming in the telescope lens, steely eyes glaring straight up at Raider.

The big man dropped the telescope, wondering if the reflection had been detected in the rocks. Best not to use it, he figured. It didn't matter, though, because he could witness the rest of the spectacle with the naked eye. Tal's performance was much like that hot-air actor in the stupid play that Doc had forced Raider to see in Austin.

The Comanchero leader bounded effortlessly out of his saddle. He strode to the back of the buckboard, thumping his chest. His men also dismounted and circled around him, awaiting their booty. When Tal threw back the canvas tarp, the others gave a savage cheer. The gun boxes were stacked neatly in the wagon, crates full of salvation and vengeance.

Raider shook his head, thinking the scheme could still fail. If Tal discovered that all but one of the rifles were inoperative . . .

"Come on," Raider growled under his breath. "Don't pick the wrong one."

Tal's hand lifted a '76 Model Winchester into the air. Raider held his breath as the Comanchero madman slipped several rounds into the side loader. The echo of the rifle lever reached the foothills, followed by the blast of the first test shot. Again Tal's followers gave a primitive hurrah.

Raider had a glimmer of hope until the savages swarmed over the wagon like ants on a dead prairie dog. They were young boys at Christmas, joyous at receiving their first squirrel guns. Raider gritted his teeth as one of the Comancheros lifted his rifle toward the sky, aiming at the slow, deliberate circling of an eagle.

The big man figured that was that. As soon as he fired, they would all know that one of the guns was bogus. Then the rest of them would discover that Hall had knocked out all the firing pins. The gang would go after Hall and then after the storekeeper. They wouldn't leave much standing in their path after they learned the truth.

Raider held his breath as the rifleman followed the eagle with the barrel of the weapon.

The man gave a grunt, but his leader stepped up next to him, knocking the rifle barrel down.

Tal shouted at him. He didn't want him to kill the eagle. He didn't want them to waste ammunition.

Raider exhaled, relieved for the moment.

Then he realized what Tal had said. *Save your ammunition*. Something big was coming. The Comancheros were going to ride, and they needed their guns.

Raider looked up at the eagle, which still circled lazily over the plain. Tal hadn't wanted his man to kill the bird. Maybe Tal felt a kinship with this bird of prey. Tal. Wasn't that short for Talon?

A shiver rode down Raider's spine, in spite of the mid-day heat. Things were in motion, he felt it in his aching gut. He had to take it slow, but he was starting to believe he might actually get a chance—if Doc was still alive.

He leaned back against the rock, peering away from the sun. No matter what transpired, he'd have to wait. There wasn't a thing he could do until the sun went down. Then Mr. Talon might be in for a few surprises himself.

CHAPTER 3

A light afternoon wind blew along Fifth Avenue, cooling all of Chicago with fresh air from Lake Michigan. The carriages seemed to slow, the pedestrians eased their gait, the entire city paused, taking a collective breath, enjoying the end of the summer day. William Wagner, assistant director of the Pinkerton National Detective Agency, sat back in his chair, hands folded into a steeple, eyes staring over the steeple into the street. Unlike the other residents of Chicago, Wagner was worried and had no intention of delighting in the balmy dusk.

Wagner's main concern lay many hundreds of miles west, with two of his best agents—Doc Weatherbee, the well-bred, well-studied gentleman detective from Boston, and Raider, the ill-bred, rough-and-tumble agent from Arkansas. Company files were full of the exploits performed by the unlikely pair. And if the records, which spoke the truth, were not enough, word of mouth among the other agents had cemented Doc and Raider as legendary in the myth and lore of Pinkerton's finest. They were indestructible, never left a case unsolved, mastered even the most difficult quandaries.

Wagner sighed deeply. He took off his spectacles, pulled a handkerchief from the pocket of his tailored suit-coat, and wiped the lenses, which in fact were clean from the same nervous procedure performed ten minutes earlier. For, unlike the other associates of the detective agency, Wagner did not, could not, believe in Doc and Raider's invincibility. They were just men, after all, bullet-stopping, blade-catching flesh and blood. And they were getting older. Not ancient or decrepit, but old in the way of men who had been on hazardous duty for too many years.

Wagner had seen it before. There was no name for it: a man simply quit, hung it up. He became leery of turning the dark corner, of rooting into the pits of humanity for a single clue. His eyes tired of treachery, his ears grew squeamish at the sound of deceit. Good men, big men, strong men simply ceased to function without any fore-warning. Well, the assistant director thought, retiring was probably better than dying in an explosion.

The bell on the front door jingled as a foot messenger returned from the Western Union office. Wagner looked up expectantly, catching the lad's eyes. The boy shook his head and turned away. He knew what Wagner had wanted —a wire from Doc and Raider—but it had not arrived.

Wagner dipped into his vest pocket and took out a gold timepiece. Six o'clock. The summer sun had not yet de-scended below the horizon. Perhaps a walk along the lake-front. He sighed. A walk would only leave him distracted and probably lost in an unfamiliar neighborhood.

Another messenger rushed past Wagner's desk, heading straight for the office of Allan Pinkerton.

"Boy!" Wagner cried.

The lad stopped and turned his freckled face toward the agency's number-two man. "Yes, sir, Mr. Wagner?"

"Nothing from Weatherbee?"

The boy lowered his eyes. "No. And I was hopin' too. You see, I never met Raider, but I did meet Mr. Weather-bee once."

Wagner nodded. "Yes, yes, I know. You want to be just like him when you grow up. A big detective."

"That's right," the lad replied with due respect. "Doc Weatherbee is the best ever." His brow wrinkled. "Why'd they ever put him to work with Raider?"

A wry smile crossed Wagner's thin lips. "Why? Because Allan Pinkerton is a genius, my boy. Never forget that."

"No, sir."

Wagner eyed the missive in the lad's hand. "Were you taking that in to Mr. Pinkerton just now?"

"Yes, sir, if he's still here. Arrived today, from Nevada."

Wagner's ears perked up. Doc and Raider's last communiqué had been from Arizona, but that never mattered. It was just like them to turn up in a place where they were least expected.

"I'll take that, son."

The lad gave Wagner the report without hesitation. Wagner dismissed him and gazed toward Pinkerton's office. The light was still on. The old boy usually burned the midnight oil. Wagner's eye fell on the report. It wasn't uncommon for the second-in-command to screen papers meant for the head man. That way, Pinkerton dealt only with the most important matters.

Wagner opened the message and began to read. After ten minutes, he got up from his desk and went to knock on Pinkerton's door. A gruff voice bade him enter.

Pinkerton was ensconced behind his desk, poring over volumes of case-related material. Wagner wondered where he found the time and energy to be the hardest-working member of the company. Pinkerton was a marvel.

"Ah, yes, William, come right in." Pinkerton offered the chair where Wagner always sat. "You're workin' late on such a fine evenin'."

Wagner smiled. "I could say the same about you, sir."

Pinkerton nodded. "And you'd be right."

Wagner's smile disappeared as quickly as it had come. "Sir, I just received a request from the territorial marshal's office in Nevada."

Pinkerton did not reply, but his expression urged Wagner to finish his speech.

"Comancheros, sir," Wagner said prosaically. "Territorial vermin pushed up from the borderland. They were spotted north of Carson City, heading for the mountains. It seems the marshal's office is short-handed, and Nevada doesn't really have much of a militia as yet. They're requesting help, at the usual rate, of course."

Pinkerton frowned. "Comancheros. Weren't Weatherbee and Raider chasing a gang of men like that?"

Wagner sighed. "At last report, sir. But I haven't heard from them in more than a month."

Pinkerton rubbed his chin. "Strange. Weatherbee is usually on top of things. You don't suppose they're in trouble?"

"With Raider along . . ."

"Now, now, don't go runnin' down Raider." Pinkerton waved a finger at his associate. "He may be unorthodox, but he gets results. You can't argue that point. Why, in the old days, a head-crushin' lad like Raider would have been the toast of the police force. Now . . . ah . . . I suppose that's why we sent him out west with Weatherbee."

"Yes, sir."

Pinkerton got out of his chair and strode over to a huge map on his wall. He pointed to a place in the Nevada Territory. "No agents nearby. Have to send them from San Francisco or Denver. Maybe both." He looked back at Wagner. "Send the best we've got. If Weatherbee and Raider are mixin' it up, I want our best boys in their corner."

Wagner nodded like a man who had just garnered the desired result. He started to get up, but something stopped him—the question the messenger boy had asked him earlier.

"Sir," he said to Pinkerton, "if I may be so bold as to ask you a simple question . . ."

Pinkerton shrugged. "Be as bold as you like."

"It may sound ridiculous, sir, but I was wondering what ever possessed you to assign Doc and Raider to be partners in the first place."

Pinkerton laughed, almost fondly. "It was more like the last place. You see, Raider came into the agency like a wild bronco, full of fight but no brains to be found. He needed to be tempered. He needed to learn that a six-shooter isn't always better than usin' your head."

Wagner nodded appreciatively. "I had thought of that myself."

"I needed a team of troubleshooters," Pinkerton went on. "And Weatherbee was free then, his last partner havin' been killed. They hated each other at first—probably still do sometimes. But they're good. And that's all that matters

when you're dealin' with the criminal type." He caught a
look of doubt in his associate's eyes. "Ah, William, I know
you've never much taken to Raider's way of doin' things,
but the western provinces are still as rough as ever. We
need him there."

"Yes, sir, but I wasn't thinking about Raider, I was
considering Doc. Why would a man like him become a
detective? He has everything—breeding, intelligence,
eloquence . . ."

Wagner hesitated when he saw the fiery look in Pinkerton's eyes. Clearly he had pushed too far. Pinkerton did not
like it.

"Some things you'll just have to ask Weatherbee himself," Pinkerton said curtly. "There's a great deal under
God's heavens that's none 'o my concern, William. Good
night."

Wagner rose and nodded. "I'll dispatch the other agents
to Nevada in the morning, unless I can get to the Western
Union office before it closes."

"Do that."

Wagner hurried back to his desk. What had brought on
Pinkerton's sudden ire? The question about Doc. Wagner
had never thought to inquire as to Doc's background before. Doc had always been a fixture at the agency, someone
to be depended on and often taken for granted.

Why had Doc Weatherbee become an agent? Wagner
pored over Doc's file, but there was nothing beyond the
sketchy information—Harvard graduate, Boston born, age,
case reports, etc. Suddenly Doc loomed over his head like
a mystery man.

Wagner began to worry about the man from Boston. He
even had concerns for Raider. Their presence and well-
being became the foremost thing in his mind. Had Doc's
reports been slipping lately? Raider's influence, perhaps?

Wagner decided to try the Western Union office. As he
pushed out the door, he discovered that the gentle wind had
stiffened into a storm gale. A thundercloud was blowing
down from the north. An eerie feeling of premonition filled
William Wagner. He decided not to go back for his um-
brella. He'd rush straight for the telegraph office. And if it
was not open, Wagner planned to make a fuss until it was.

CHAPTER 4

While the sun was falling steadily toward the western horizon, Raider made good use of the time. He found a deposit of dark, claylike soil and dug out a few handfuls. Mixing the dirt with water from his canteen, he worked up a brown, soupy paint to use as camouflage. Removing his shirt, he slathered the concoction all over his torso, arms, neck, shoulders, and finally his face. He needed to move unseen in the mountains, circling the rocks and crags like a silent wind.

When he had finished, he leaned back, waiting for the paint to dry. He couldn't see a sign of the Comanchero camp from his vantage point, with the exception of the thin wisp of smoke that rose toward the red and orange sky. The flickering from the signal mirrors had stopped completely.

Tal was drawing in all his compadres, readying them for the big strike. But where? Carson City seemed an unlikely target. There wasn't much at Elko or anywhere else within a hundred-mile range. Maybe somebody had been whispering the wrong information in Tal's greedy ears. Either that or Tal was onto something that nobody else knew about.

Maybe the half-breed was a lot smarter than Raider had figured. Look at the way he had stolen himself a wagon-load of guns.

Raider lifted the canteen to his lips and took a long, cool drink. He silently thanked Cleveland Hall for filling it. The gun seller, despite his cowardly exit, had really done pretty good. Besides taking care of the horses, he had acted as closely to the plan as his lack of bravery would let him. Raider wasn't going to miss the portly arms dealer, but he might think of him again someday if he ever got out of Nevada alive.

Raider ate the rest of the fry-bread for dinner. He had one or two fleeting thoughts about the squaw, but decided it was best not to work himself up too much. He'd need all his energy for later, when the sun went down.

He got up and tied a piece of cloth around his head. Then he filled the loops on his gunbelt with extra cartridges for the Colt and the Winchester. Hunting knife in the boot sheath, derringer in his back pocket. The Comancheros might kill him eventually, but he was going to take a few of them with him before it was time to go.

His black eyes peered to the west. Another hour until dusk, but it was best to get started a little early. He had a long way to wind through the mountains, and all of it would have to be on foot. Untying the gray, he set it free with a slap on the flank. It would be better if the Comancheros found the mount and figured the drifter had met with some unfortunate accident. And unless a miracle happened, he probably wouldn't need a mount again. Hall had said it—two dozen to one was damned bad odds.

The going was easy while the sun still hung low in the sky. He followed a narrow trail between the hills, keeping his eyes cast upward for signs of furtive movement. A Comanchero could get you and you'd never see him coming. *Whoosh!* An arrow in the back, a knife in the throat. If Raider was going to die, he wanted to face it head on at least.

He had been on the trail for about an hour when the light began to fade, rendering deep shadows around him and on the slopes above. Raider had to make a quick decision—stay in the foothills or climb higher. He had guessed that Tal's men were somewhere in the lower hills, otherwise they never would have rallied so fast to meet the gun seller. If he took the low path, it would mean walking straight into the Comanchero camp. Higher up, he could look down on them and assess the situation, even it meant climbing in the dark.

Raider took in a deep breath, lifting his eyes to the craggy peaks. He knew very little about the terrain. He might climb all the way up, only to find that he couldn't see a thing. What was it that Doc always said? Caution? How many times had caution saved their lives?

He decided to climb.

The handholds were firm, and the rocks weren't too sharp. After several hours of grunting, during which time the stars gathered in the sky, Raider lifted himself onto a flat ledge about a hundred feet above the rounded summits of the foothills. He caught his breath, turning in a circle, gazing out over the thick demon-shadows of the plain. Had he not been in search of a murdering horde, he might have thought the view beautiful. As it was, however, he saw only the bright glow of Comanchero fires below him.

He couldn't see clearly, so he followed the ledge for several hundred feet. His eyes and ears were ready for the ambush from one of Tal's men. It made sense that the half-breed would put a man or two on the ledge, to keep a lookout. But no one greeted him as he stepped around a boulder and stared down at the unholy spectacle taking place in the Comanchero camp.

Three huge bonfires raged in the opening of a ravine, the flames licking and lapping at the angles of the rocky slopes. Tal's men danced and hopped around the fires, lifting whiskey jugs as they moved with their strange steps. Someone pounded a drum in a primal beat.

Then Raider saw it. "Son of a bitch!" His foot slipped, sending a few loose stones down the slope. Raider caught himself before he fell headlong into the revelry. No one took notice of him as he leaned back against the rock, his lungs sucking for air.

His eyes focused again. He saw what the Comancheros were feeding into the flames. Even from his elevated view he could make out the shape of Doc's Studebaker wagon. The gutted frame sat beyond the fires, lying naked as if it had been stripped like a carcass by Mexican red ants.

If he hadn't been sickened by that sorry sight, the next tableau would have done the trick. Two Comancheros led a mule toward the flames. Raider could hear the braying over the din of the drum.

"No," he whispered, his eyes wide, "you can't do it."

He levered the rifle.

It was Doc's mule, Judith.

One of the Comancheros raised an ax over the animal's head.

"No!" Raider cried.

He sighted in on the ax man's chest.

The rifle's sound reverberated through the ravine, stopping all action below. The ax man fell, clutching his chest, missing his mark. Judith ran away from the fire, but no one tried to catch her. They were all looking up at the ledge, where Raider stood with a smoking Winchester.

Another guttural cry resounded in the heated night air. Raider saw the flash of polished steel as the Comanche warrior bounded over the boulder. The knife blade was coming straight for the big man's heart.

Raider lifted the bore of the Winchester, driving the barrel into his assailant's chest. Using the rifle like a pike, Raider vaulted the man over his shoulder and sent him flying headlong onto the ledge. He landed on his back with a grunt, and then, with surprising agility, he sprang to his feet and spun toward the big Pinkerton.

As he made his lunge, Raider jacked a cartridge into the chamber of the '76. The burst from the Winchester caught the Comanche in the chest, where blood erupted in random streaks. Diverted by the power of the blast, the man's flight took him falling into the ravine below, crashing headlong into one of the fires. His brothers stood there for a moment, stunned by Raider's unexpected entrance.

The big man took aim on a bare chest and fired, buffeting a third dead man to the ground.

The Comancheros returned fire, chiseling the rock next to Raider's head.

"That woke 'em up."

Raider started back on the ledge, the Comanchero guns chasing him. He had to wonder how many firing pins Hall had removed. There seemed to be a whole lot of lead in the air.

He didn't hear the rush of air as the man fell toward him. Another Comanche landed on his shoulders, knocking him on his back. A hatchet raised high against the stars. Raider managed to catch the man's wrist as he dropped the iron club.

They wrestled on the ledge, teetering there on the brink of falling. Raider put a hand into his back pocket and brought out the derringer. He shoved it in the Comanche's gut and fired twin .32 slugs into the soft portion of the man's belly. The Comanche drew air, but he never cried out. Not even when Raider dumped him over the side into the rocks below.

He staggered to his feet, sweat pouring from his body. "By God, I reckon they know I'm here."

He had to stay in the shadows of the peaks. If he could just pick them off one at a time, peppering them like an angry hornet on a bear's nose, he might have a slim chance.

He started climbing, disappointed that he hadn't seen Doc among the Comancheros.

His hand struck a rock and he drew it back with blood flowing down his forearm.

"God Almighty," he muttered to himself, "this might be a lot tougher than I thought."

Raider held his breath, leaning back against a wall of stone, clutching his hunting knife in the white knuckles of his right hand. He heard the man coming toward him, moving slowly like a lizard on a cold day. The cat-and-mouse search had been going on all night. Raider had been able to kill two more of Tal's men, adding their number to the two he had dumped off the ledge.

The dark shape slid around the corner, his ghostly breath fogging the cool night air.

Raider struck like a rattle from under a rock. His fingers dug into the fleshy quick of the man's throat. He swung the hunting knife in a short half-circle, driving the blade in from the back, splitting ribs, sinking the point into the man's heart. The Comanchero would have cried out if Raider hadn't crushed his windpipe.

The hideous lump collapsed at Raider's feet.

"Nine," the big man muttered, recounting the bodies

that had begun with the slaying of the four men at the outpost. He gazed up into the heavens. "How long you gonna let me keep this up?"

A breeze stirred around the mountain. Raider looked down at the fallen man. A quiver was fixed on his back, and there was a Comanche bow strung over his shoulder. Raider picked up the primitive weapon and the quiver. It might come in handy later.

As he moved down through the rocks, his senses were as keen as a wounded cougar on the prowl. He wondered if he might eventually be able to kill *all* of the Comancheros. They weren't anything more than flesh and blood—just like him.

He continued the descent, his eyes and ears aware of any movement in the shadows. A morbid humor had overtaken him, giving him an unnatural energy. The night no longer held anything to frighten him—not even the sight of the Comanchero encampment below, where they were starting to build a new fire.

Raider hunkered on the ledge where he had been before. The flames from the other fires had died in the camp, but the crescent moon was returning to illuminate the dreadful scene. The marauders were stacking anything that would burn, including the bogus rifles. Tal knew they weren't any good.

Raider grinned. Score one for him and Hall. Score ten if he counted all the dead men.

As he continued to watch the encampment, the smile contorted into an expression of rage and horror. The words came from deep in his gut. "No. You can't. You bastards."

But they could and they were. Tal, his body painted with Comanche war colors, lurched toward the pile of kindling. The Comanchero leader dragged a sandy-haired man alongside him. Raider was pretty sure the man looked like Doc Weatherbee. Tal was going to tie Doc to the stake and burn him like a witch. Even in the moonlight, Raider knew it was Doc.

Raider put down his rifle and picked up the Comanche bow. He couldn't let them finish his partner like that. Not even if it meant giving up his own life.

He notched the Comanche arrow and let it fly. The shaft fell harmlessly behind Tal, but it was close enough to make him look. When the Comanchero leader turned, Raider delivered another arrow, aiming straight for Tal's broad torso. The rocky point of the shaft lodged in the sinew of Tal's shoulder. The cry echoed through the ravine, horrible to the night animals, but music to Raider's ears.

The big man's eyes grew wide as he watched Tal trying to wrestle with himself. Raider had found the right weapon. He reached for another arrow, but his arm went numb.

Raider spun around, but the man hit him again with the stone Indian club, catching the hard part of his skull.

His hand groped for the Colt at his side, but he was unable to grip it before he lost consciousness.

When Raider finally woke up again, the Comancheros were all around him and he was tied to the stake in back of his partner.

CHAPTER 5

"Pinkerton! Ha!" Tal, the half-breed Comanchero master, spat straight into Raider's face. He laughed, harsh and loud, exhorting the same reaction from his hideous band of followers. Tal moved backward and grabbed a torch from the hand of a Mexican man. Raider took a certain amount of satisfaction in the fact that Tal didn't reach for the torch with the arm on the wounded side of his body. The arrow had been removed, but the blood was still caked over Tal's dark skin.

Raider looked away from the torch, trying to see his partner. "Doc? Are you all right? Doc? Say somethin'."

Silence from the man on the other side of the stake. Did it matter either way if Doc was alive? The torch in Tal's hand would soon fix that—for both of them.

"Doc? I'm sorry I couldn't do better, Doc. You won't hold this agin me will ya? Doc, I—uhh!"

Tal had slapped him hard across the mouth. Raider spat blood back at the half-breed. Tal hit him again.

"Pinkerton!" He spat. "You could not catch me. No white man can catch Tal. White men are like the coyote

47

without ears or nose. He cannot hear, he cannot smell. He can only see, and not that far."

Tal's men found his speech exceedingly funny.

Raider gritted his teeth. "I caught nine of your boys. I almost got you. You untie me and we'll go round and round, man to man. Think you got the guts for it?"

The Mexican man stepped forward. "You could never bet Tal, gringo. He would kill you easy."

Raider's black eyes gleamed in the torchlight, possibly the last light he would ever see. "Is that so? You just cut me loose and we'll see who's the best! You hear me, Tal, I'm ready to—"

The Mexican slammed a rifle butt into Raider's gut, and Raider vomited up a bilious liquid. Tal just stood there with the torch, leering at him. Raider's head came up, and he glared at the half-breed.

Tal's eyes narrowed a little. "You are a brave white man. Ride with me. We can drive out the men who make the laws."

Raider lowered his head. "I am the man who makes the laws. Men like me and Doc. You might be able to kill us, but you can never kill the law. They'll get you no matter where you go."

"Ha," the Comanchero commander replied. "I will have silver today. My men and I will go back to Mexico. No one will find us."

This time it was Raider's laughter that reverberated through the rocky ravine. "No, Tal. Somebody'll find you. My boss will keep sendin' men till you're hangin' from the end of a rope."

Tal drew a hand across his chest, the signal that the fireworks were about to begin.

Raider gaped as the torch came down toward the kindling below his feet.

Tal smiled. "No one will catch me, white man."

The flames licked at the wood.

"Tal!"

The torch lifted as the half-breed looked back at one of his men.

"Sun!" He pointed upward, to the east.

Tal gazed at the sky. When he turned back to Raider,

there was a strange expression on his face. He started to lower the torch again.

"You must go!"

The cry had come from Doc Weatherbee, his first words since they had fixed Raider behind him on the stake.

Tal lifted the torch again.

Raider grimaced. "Ain't got the guts?"

"You will die," Tal replied with a laugh. "When we return. *Hombres! Vamanos!*"

To Raider's amazed black eyes, it appeared that Tal's men had begun to disperse. Dawn had called them. They had a rendezvous at daybreak. Had Doc been working on them?

Tal swung into the saddle of a black stallion. "Enjoy your last moments of life, Pinkerton. When I return, you will burn. It is your Hell, no?"

He laughed again and spurred the black to the head of the column of men. Raider was sure he heard Judith braying somewhere in the gang. They had decided to ride her instead of eating her. A wise choice, even for a Comanchero.

The big man watched as Tal led his men under the natural arch of rock at the entrance to the ravine. The Comanchero leader left only one man to guard them. A Mexican bandito hid under the wide brim of his sombrero—awake or sleeping, Raider could not be sure.

"Doc? Doc, talk to me. What the hell was all that about silver?"

The voice was weak, feeble. "I told them . . . Bardy mine . . . silver . . . payroll . . ."

"Hell," Raider replied, "the old Bardy mine's been closed for a couple o' years."

"I told them on purpose . . . hoped you find . . . tall tales about silver . . . money . . . augh . . ."

He began to cough uncontrollably. Was that really Raider's partner talking? Doc never lost his strength. Even when he was wounded he was still a pain in the ass. It scared Raider to hear him speaking so sick-like.

"Don't give up, Doc, you Boston-bred bastard!" Raider tried to look back at him. "You hear me, Weatherbee? We still got time to get out of this."

With that comment, the Mexican's eyes came up from under the sombrero.

Raider glared at him. "Hey, tortilla bender. You speak English?"

The Mexican nodded. *"Sí, señor.* Only I do not like to."

If Raider could just goad him into losing his temper. "Hey, bean-mouth, when was the last time you and your momma-cita made a baby? Does your daddy know you screwed her?"

Ordinarily an insult like that would have sent the guard climbing the rock wall, but he only sat still.

"Oh, I see," Raider continued, "you don't even like girls. You like the little boys, *sí? Maricone!"*

Raider made an obnoxious sound with his lips.

The Mexican stood up, raising an old breech-loading .50-caliber.

Raider had to get him going. "Maybe your father was a *maricone,* boy. You were born from your mother's—"

"No more, gringo!"

He was staring down the barrel of the breech-loader.

"Come closer," Raider entreated. "Let me get my hands on you, you Mexican piss-ant."

"Shut your stinking mouth, gringo!" He thumbed the hammer of the rifle. "Tal told me to kill you if you made trouble. One more word and I'll shoot you in the chest."

Raider thought it over. Maybe it was better to catch a slug than to die in the fire. Some men said they couldn't even feel it when the bullet entered. Dying was supposed to be peaceful, angels and everything.

His upper lip curled in a hateful snarl. "Hey, Pedro, why don't you use my dick for a piece of beef jerky?"

"Adiós, gringo."

Raider closed his eyes, anticipating the explosion of the .50-caliber. Instead, there was a smaller blast, from the muzzle of a tiny weapon. When he opened his eyes, Raider saw the Mexican man staggering forward, holding the rifle in his limp hands. He fell flat on his face. The .50-caliber exploded into the ground.

Raider's eyes opened wide. "You!"

Cleveland Hall, gun seller, stood over the body, holding his derringer in hand. "Damn, hate to shoot a man in the back. Didn't want to take no chances."

Raider laughed, whooping like a Rebel running into battle. "You done good, Hall. Hell, cut me loose."

The gun seller ambled toward them, reaching for a knife in his coat pocket. "I thought they'd kill you afore I got a chance to help. A blessin' when they left. God's watchin' over you, Raider."

Raider felt his hands free. He lifted them to the heavens. "Let me shout Amen and Halleluja for that!" He gave the gun seller a hug.

"Git off'n me, you big ape."

Raider grinned at the portly gentleman. "Hell, I figured you was gone for good, Cleveland, when I saw you high-tail it like that."

"I ain't gone," Hall replied. "Here, let's see to your partner."

"Doc!"

They cut him loose and laid him on the ground. Raider wasn't sure he recognized the man in front of him. Doc's face was a dull purple color. His nose had been broken. A couple of teeth were missing in the back. His eyes were a lifeless blue. Raider had seen dead men who looked better.

"Here, try this." Hall handed him a flask of whiskey.

Raider had put a few drops on Doc's lips, but it didn't make a difference. "He needs water."

Hall rounded up a canteen. "Ain't much in here."

Raider had poured the water into Doc's mouth. The man from Boston began coughing again. Raider turned back to Hall. "We better get movin'."

Hall nodded. "Maybe."

Raider glared at him. "Hell, man, are you loco? It ain't gonna be too healthy to stick around here. My partner's been fillin' Tal's head with stories about a pay-dirt mine. Only thing is, that hole in the ground has been dry for a dog's age. When Tal gets back here, I don't want to be the one to greet him."

Hall gestured to the entrance of the pass. "I don't want to be his welcomin' committee either. But I got a pair of horses stashed back in them rocks that might make the difference."

Raider's eyes narrowed. "What the hell are you talkin' about?"

"Dynamite," Hall replied. "Two boxes. Bought it off'n a prospector what needed the money. About ten miles from here. He was comin' this way to work, but he wasn't so eager when I told him about the Comancheros."

Raider still couldn't believe his good fortune. "Why are you doin' this, Hall? Tell me quick-like."

The gun seller shrugged. "Well, I couldn't bear the thought of leavin' you alone out here, boy. Wasn't the manly thing to do. But I didn't have a clue how I could help you. Then I run into that miner."

"And you just thought you'd waltz into the Comanchero camp and blow them all to hell by yourself?"

Hall shook his head, his hands trembling. "Partner, I wasn't sure what I was gonna do. I rode in after them boys got this spook party goin'. Otherwise I reckon they woulda caught me easy. Now, I don't have a notion why things worked out this way, but they have."

Raider exhaled, looking back at his partner. "No, I can't risk it. Doc is in too bad a shape. I got to get him where he can—"

"Raider . . ."

The weak voice again. The big man leaned down.

"Do it," Doc said. "Use the dynamite."

"But Doc, you're—"

Doc grabbed his arm, squeezing with the last ounce of his strength. "If you don't, they'll catch us anyway . . . augh . . . Do it."

Raider stood up. A tear rolled down his cheek. He was glad to see that all of Doc's spirit wasn't gone.

"What'll it be?" Hall asked.

Raider knocked away the tear. "You got fuse or blastin' caps?"

"Both," Hall replied.

"I'll have to find some rope. And there'll be a lot of climbin'. We only got about four hours."

Hall nodded. "I'm with you, boy."

A weird, coyote smile appeared on the face of the big, black-eyed man. "Let's get 'em."

"Kill them all," moaned Doc Weatherbee. "Kill every one of them."

• • •

Cleveland Hall leaned over the precipice, peering down at the big man who hung from the rope. "I can see their dust, Raider. Better get back up here while the gettin's good."

Raider eased the cluster of dynamite sticks into the hole in the rock, wishing that Doc was in better shape to help him. Doc always knew how to set a charge so it would explode and bring about the desired effect. As it stood, Raider could only guess where to place the explosive.

"I mean it," Hall called from above. "Tal and the boys are headin' back this way. Fast."

Raider attached the fuse, one of four lengths, the last one to be set.

"Big 'un . . ."

"I hear you, gun seller!"

Raider started to pull himself up, dragging the spool of fuse behind him. Tal was coming home mad as a nest of hornets in a rainstorm. He was expecting to barbecue a couple of Pinkertons in the bargain. But if things went right, the Comanchero leader might just be the one to have his feet in the fire.

Raider swung over the ledge, throwing the spool to Hall. The gun seller clipped the fuse and secured it with the three others, holding them in place with a small rock. Raider stood up and glanced to the north, toward the cloud of dust that stirred on the still plain.

"That's them all right," he muttered.

Hall nodded. "Gonna be tricky lightin' them fuses. Long ones. If they go off too soon or too late . . ."

"Yeah, yeah, I know."

Raider looked back at his partner, who was lying on the ground covered with an Indian blanket. It had been rough getting Doc to the summit of the rise. He seemed even worse in the bright daylight. Raider bent down and nudged him lightly.

Doc stirred a little, lifting his head. "Water," he moaned.

Raider gave him a couple of swallows from the canteen. Sweat beads broke out on Doc's head. His eyes were dull and lifeless. Raider hated to bother him in his present condition, but the question had to be asked.

"Doc, them fuses. How long will it take them to burn?"

Doc licked his dry lips. "Time short section yourself. Figure it out. You can . . ." He dropped his head and closed his eyes.

"Good thinkin'," Hall said. "Here, let's try it."

He cut off a foot of fuse and torched the end. Raider counted the seconds it took to burn. Then he estimated the length of the fuse from the ledge to the holes in the rock.

Hall was looking at Doc. "He's damned bright."

"Even when he's sick he's twice as smart as most men," Raider replied. "Come on, we got to get back some. If this rock goes, we might just go with it."

They carried Doc up into the rocks and left him lying as comfortably as the terrain would allow. When Doc was safe, Raider and Hall went back down to the ledge. Tal and his men were closer now, approaching the entrance to the ravine. Raider picked up the four remaining sticks of dynamite and started to lash them together.

Hall eyed the big man. "What are you up to now?"

"Little cover, just in case," Raider replied. "If them fuses ain't figured right, I can send Tal in whichever direction he ought to be goin'."

He turned and started south along the ridge.

Hall gaped at him. "Where you goin'?"

"Just keep a lookout, gun seller. When I drop my arm, you put the fire to them fuses."

"Then what?"

"Then you run like hell."

Hall sweated bullets as he turned back toward the fuses. Tal and the Comanchero gang were not in sight now. They had entered the pass, heading for the ravine. Hall spun around, searching for Raider in the rocks. The big man was standing high on a boulder. He lifted his arm and then dropped it down.

Hall cursed as his nervous hands fumbled with the matches. "Consarned bushwhackin', no-account . . ."

Horses' hooves resounded through the craggy peaks. The fuses burned slowly, heading for the ledge on a fiery trail. Hall did exactly what Raider said to do. He turned away and ran toward the rocks where Doc was lying.

Raider, however, did not run. He stood up on the

boulder, watching the fuses and the entrance to the pass. The fuses were slower than he had figured. Tal turned the corner, leading his band into the ravine. If they passed through without the charges exploding, they might be home free.

Smoke seemed to issue from the rocks as the fuses sparked their way toward the red clusters below. Tal went through the entrance to the ravine, heading for his camp. There was only one thing for Raider to do. He struck a sulphur match off his thumbnail and put it to the short fuse of the charge in his hand.

"Adios, Comancheros."

He launched the dynamite into the ravine.

The charge exploded over Tal's head, driving him and his men back under the rocky precipice. Their horses reared, throwing many of them from the saddle. Some turned to run, but it was too late. The concussion from Raider's grenade ignited the clusters in the rock, sending tons of debris down on the outlaws below. Raider would have witnessed the whole thing, but the force from the explosion sent him flying backward.

When he finally raised his head, the smoke was clearing in the ravine. He peered down on the lifeless remains of Tal and his gang. Something moved behind him, prompting the big man to turn around. Doc and Hall were standing there, gazing down as well.

"Doc, you oughta be layin' down!"

Hall shook his head. "I couldn't stop him. When he heard the explosion, he was on his feet."

An eerie gleam burned in Doc's eyes. "We have to go down there," he said. "We have to make sure none of them are alive."

Raider grabbed his partner's arm. "Doc, you better..."

Doc shrugged away. "Let's go. Now."

With a newfound energy, Doc followed them down the slopes. When they were in the ravine, he began searching the rocks, trying to find the bodies of the fallen Comancheros. His head snapped up when he heard the doleful braying of a mule.

"Judith!"

Raider was the one who found her. She had been

trapped beneath a huge boulder, her back legs shattered. Her head thrashed up and down; her mouth was emptying blood onto the ground.

Doc knelt and touched her snout. "She's not going to make it," he said softly.

Raider lifted a rifle he had found in the rocks. "Get away, Doc. I'll do it. No need for you to—"

The man from Boston turned toward his partner with a vengeance in his expression. "You! You killed her!"

Raider felt his stomach flipping over. "Doc, I—"

"Weren't his fault," Hall said. "This had to be done."

Doc snatched the rifle from Raider's hands. "Both of you get away from me. I'll do what has to be done."

"I'm tellin' you," Hall rejoined, "it couldn't be helped."

Raider motioned for the gun seller to follow him. They turned their backs and started through the rubble. Tears were flowing down the big man's rugged face.

Hall tried to console him. "Raider, it weren't your fault. You was just doin' what—"

"Shut up, Hall."

They leaned back against a rock. Raider was sure he heard Doc talking to that lame critter. His body flinched when the rifle went off. They waited for Doc to join them, but he never came.

Hall looked in every direction. "I wonder where he went?"

"Give him a few more minutes," Raider replied. "If he don't come, we'll go find him."

Doc did not come. Hall and Raider set off in different directions. Raider searched until he heard Hall screaming like he had seen the devil. The big man ran toward the sound of the gun seller's voice. When he came up on Hall, he saw the look of horror in the man's pale blue eyes.

"He's . . . your partner . . ." Hall held his stomach and stumbled away from the horrific scene.

Raider squinted at the sight. "Doc. Doc, don't. You don't have to . . ."

The man from Boston was hunkered over the body of Tal, the Comanchero leader. Doc had a knife in his hand. He was hacking at Tal's chest, opening up the dead man. Raider did not turn away, but stood there, watching as Doc plucked the man's heart from his lifeless chest. Doc lifted the bloody tissue and heaved it into the rocks.

"God almighty," Raider muttered. "Forgive him."

Doc turned, his eyes wide, his mouth agape. He stared at Raider, a savage look on his countenance. "They do things to a man," he said in a low voice. "They do things no man should have to endure."

Doc lifted his hands to look at the bloody mess. Then he began to laugh like a madman. Raider watched him, hoping he would pass out. Doc reeled, stumbling forward. He fell at his partner's feet, unconscious.

Raider called to the gun seller. "Find us some horses, Hall. Find 'em now."

Hall offered a weak reply. "I'll do my best."

Raider reached down and lifted his partner into his arms, carrying him away from the rubble, taking him into the sun. He couldn't blame Doc for what he had done, nor could he judge him. He could only raise the canteen to Doc's dry lips, offering him a taste of lukewarm water. But Doc would not drink. So for one of the few times in his life, the big man from Arkansas lowered his head, sending up a short but heartfelt prayer.

CHAPTER 6

When the door flew open, the storekeeper's head bobbed up, his frightened expression barely visible in the shadows of late afternoon. The Indian sisters were standing next to the table, watching the storekeeper as he counted his money. No doubt the proprietor of the outpost thought the big man in the doorway was going to steal his life savings. He hurried to put the money back into a strongbox.

Raider stepped into the room, his face drawn up in a disgusted scowl. "Ain't nobody gonna take your geetus away from you, storekeep."

The proprietor hesitated, the end of his beard trembling. "That you, Pinkerton?"

Raider grunted. "Ain't nobody else."

Little Desert Flower giggled at the big man's return, whispering into her sister's ear. They were laughing at the dark pigment of Raider's naked torso. His body was as brown as theirs.

The big Pinkerton gestured toward the doorway. "Got a sick man outside. Needs food, drink, and a place to sleep. Pronto."

The storekeeper's weak face was uncertain. "Well, I reckon I can oblige you. 'Course, if you want it . . ."

"We'll pay," Raider said impatiently, "if that's what you're frettin' about."

He stroked his pointed beard. "Ain't worried none about money. It's just that I heard all that commotion north of here, from the mountains. Sounded like thunder. Me and the women was plannin' to clear out before there was any more trouble. Don't want no truck with them Comancheros."

Raider laughed a little. "Ain't no more Comancheros. That commotion was the gates of Hell openin' and swallowin' 'em up. Savvy?"

The proprietor was agape. "You sayin' you killed all of them?"

"He says so."

Cleveland Hall had come in behind Raider. Doc hung on Hall's shoulder. The man from Boston was barely able to walk. His body was black and blue from the beatings and tortures inflicted by his captors.

Hall glared at the storekeeper. "He needs to rest."

The man nodded, sending the squaws to prepare a place for Doc to lie down. He turned back to look at Doc. "Half dead, ain't he?"

Raider glanced toward the counter. "You got any Injun medicine around here?"

"No," the storekeeper replied. "But if you can wait, I'll get my wife to start up a fresh batch. She makes a right good elixir."

"We ain't goin' nowhere," Raider replied curtly.

The storekeeper lowered his eyes. "About the money."

Raider glared right through him. "You're just gonna have to trust me, pardner. I done give you my last penny."

"I got money," Hall chimed in. "You're welcome to it."

Raider squinted at the gun seller. "You willin' to make good for us?"

Hall grinned. "Reckon I'll just have to trust you for it. Come on, help me get this boy into bed before he passes on."

They carried Doc to a room in the back, where he stretched out on a cornshuck pallet fixed by the squaws. Raider spoon-fed him some whiskey as the storekeeper's wife removed his clothes. Little Desert Flower brought a bowl of cool water and some liniment for his bruises. Despite their attentions, Doc just lay there, his eyes closed, his body limp

Hall clapped Raider on the shoulder. "Come on, big man. We done all we can. He's gonna have to sleep it off."

They went back to the counter, where they found a bottle of whiskey.

Hall downed a shot and sighed deeply. "Think he's gonna make it, Raider?"

Raider threw back his own shot of red-eye. "Cleveland, me and that Yankee boy have been from one end of this territory to the other. We been shot at, beat on, cut up, bitten, drowned, and just about anything else you can think of." He exhaled and washed down his next breath with another drink. "Damn it all, gun seller, I ain't never seen him this bad. What he did to the body of that Comanchero . . . And his mule. God, he loved that animal. I reckon I did too." Again to the bottle, knocking it back, slamming the glass on the counter. "Is he gonna make it? Hell, your guess is as good as mine. I hope he does. I pray he does. But I seen stronger men destroyed by a whole lot less. He lost his damned wagon, too. And there ain't no tellin' what them Comancheros did to him."

Hall shook his head. "Well, can't say that I know him, rightly, but I'm hopin' he pulls through."

"So do I, pardner. So do I."

Raider stepped back from the counter and looked at himself. "Hell, I coulda been wallowin' down with a razorback sow. Storekeeper! You got a bathtub around this place?"

The proprietor peered around the corner, stroking his pointed beard. "Ain't got no tub. Couple of buckets out back. Well's kinda low, but there should be enough water for you to clean yourself."

Raider drank one more shot of red-eye before he stumbled to the back porch, leaving Cleveland Hall to find his own resting place.

Filling two buckets from the well, Raider stepped up onto the porch and disrobed, too weary to entertain any thoughts of modesty. After pouring one bucket of water over his head, he found a hunk of lye soap and started to lather his body. The soap burned a little, but he didn't care.

As he brought the soap over his hairy chest, a small hand reached up to grab his wrist.

Raider's black eyes peered down at brown eyes and white teeth. He smiled at her. "Hello, Little Desert Flower."

She laughed. "I came to help you."

He did not protest. She took the soap from his fingers and picked up where he had left off. Raider had to stoop down so she could wash his neck and shoulders. Her soapy hands massaged the sore, tight muscles that rippled beneath his wet skin.

She kissed his cheek. "You are a brave man."

Raider stood up. "Maybe. Then again, maybe I'm just a lunatic. A crazy man who doesn't know any better. Hey . . . ow!"

Her fingers had slipped down to the swelling member between his thighs. Raider fought to find his breath. Little Desert Flower's seductive brown eyes rolled up to meet his gaze.

Raider touched her cheek. "What's on your mind, little woman?"

She giggled and released her grip on him.

Raider grabbed her shoulder. "Maybe we oughta go upstairs."

"No," she said playfully.

The big man frowned. "No?"

She lifted the bucket. "Wash first."

Raider had to kneel so she could pour the cool, refreshing water over his body. When the soap had been rinsed from his massive frame, Little Desert Flower reached between his legs again, giving his cock a playful tug. Raider reached for her, but she eluded his grip and ran quickly into the house.

"Damn you, teasin' little heifer."

He pulled on his pants and followed her. She led him upstairs to the same cornshuck mattress they had shared before. Her flour-sack dress hit the planked floor. She shook her hair, affecting the same vanity that Raider had seen in women from San Francisco to New Orleans.

His lips curled in a devious smile. "We gonna play games?" His fingers cupped the taut buds of her breasts.

"Give me a kiss, little punkin."

But she didn't want to kiss him. Instead, she fell back on the mattress, spreading her brown thighs. Raider dropped his pants and fell quickly between her legs, guiding the blunt end of his shaft to her wet crevice. She grabbed the tip of his cock and held him there, not letting him enter.

"What's wrong?" he queried.

"Slow," she whispered. "Not too fast. Slow."

Raider obliged her, slipping the length of his manhood inside her with a long, deliberate thrust. A low moan escaped from between her thick lips. She wrapped her legs around his waist, imprisoning him inside her.

"That slow enough for you," he whispered.

She replied with upward thrusts of her hips, bucking him off the floor like an angry bronc. Raider could do little more than hang on, wondering where such a small body got so much power. He finally collapsed on top of her, releasing deep inside her.

He rolled off, leaning back, relaxing for the first time since he had left Arizona in search of the Comanchero gang.

"More," she entreated.

"Honey, let me rest."

But she wouldn't. Her hands brought him back to life, and they repeated the process a second time. After the climax, Raider was adamant. He had to get some sleep. The sun was gone, night was upon them. He would service her again in the morning. His last request was that she go check on Doc.

The big man slept dreamlessly until a hand shook him.

"Let me sleep a little more, honey."

"It ain't honey. It's me, Hall."

Raider rolled over and looked up at the gun seller, whose face was illuminated by the first rays of the sun. "What the hell do you want?"

"Men outside," Hall replied. "Six of 'em. They got torches and guns."

"Shit." Raider jumped to his feet. "Maybe Tal had some stragglers we don't know about." He edged to the window, peering out at the riders.

A lean, red-haired man held a torch overhead. He

looked up at the second-story window. Was his face familiar? The voice sure as hell was.

"Raider!" the man called. "Raider, you in there?"

The big man whooped like an Apache warrior. "Son of
a bitch. Avery, is that you? P. W. Avery?"

"It's me, Raider." He waved the torch. "Mr. Pinkerton
sent us to find you. Ever'body's worried that you done
been kilt."

"Closer'n you'll ever know. Hang tight. I'll be down in
a second."

Raider started to pull on his pants.

Hall looked out the window. "Friends, eh?"

"Boys from the agency, just like me and Doc. Come on,
they'll be glad to meet you. You can tell 'em how you
kicked ole Tal's half-breed ass."

Raider hurried down the stairs to meet his compadres.
They all shook hands, laughing, glad to hear the trouble
was over. P. W. Avery looked around, his brow wrinkled.

"Don't see Doc Weatherbee," Avery said.

Raider frowned. "It ain't good, P.W. He's hurtin'. Ain't
never seen him like this before."

Avery rubbed his chin. "Anything we can do?"

Raider thought about it. "Just one thing."

"And what might that be?"

"Just get us to Carson City."

Avery tipped back his felt hat. "Hell, that's all?"

"Get us to Carson City safe-like and then tell me it's
easy."

Avery laughed. "Doggone it, Raider, it's good to see
you alive."

The big man from Arkansas just had to agree with that
opinion.

CHAPTER 7

The dispatch arrived at the Chicago office of the Pinkerton
Agency two weeks after the telegram from Carson City.
Wagner eagerly opened the envelope, expecting to find one
of Doc's carefully penned reports, detailing the encounter
and ultimate defeat of the Comanchero gang. Instead,
Allan Pinkerton's right-hand man discovered a tale written
in an unfamiliar hand. The syntax, however, was all too
familiar.

Dear Mr. Wagner,
    I am telling this to a good man named Cleveland
Hall, who is writing it all down for me 'cause I ain't
much on writing.
    Doc Weatherbee was took prisoner by them Co-
mancheros when we was chasing them in Arizona.
They took him north and I went after them. They
went all the way to Nevada where I did find them.
Mr. Hall who is writing this helped me rescue Doc
and kill every single one of them Comancheros.

How we done it ain't so important but we did it and that's all that counts.

P. W. Avery and the others sent by the agency came to find me. But they came too late, but it wasn't their fault. They helped me take Doc to Carson City where we are now. Everybody looked at us when we come into town. Doc was on an Indian rig 'cause he wasn't strong enough to ride a horse. I reckon the town thought we was outlaws, but we wasn't.

I took Doc to a real doctor, and the sawbones said he was good-like only he will have to rest some 'cause he is weak. Them Comanchero [the word *bastards* had been crossed out] was mighty rough on him. He's lower than a coyote's dinner. I put him at the hotel, where he is sleeping it off. They say he has been eating real good and takes drink and smokes his cigars. He don't say much which isn't like him but it ain't much to fret about.

I am doing this report 'cause I asked Doc and he did not want to have anything to do with it. He claims he ain't able to remember the first thing about none of what happened. His mule was killed and his wagon was burnt up so that nothing is left of it. This was a hard blow for him and I can't remember nothing worse ever happening to him.

I am much obliged if you could see fit to send Doc's back pay so he can buy himself some new clothes and such. That stuff always meant a whole lot to Doc and he would be better for it if he was to have it right now. I meant to give him some of my pay, but I spent a lot of it as I had debts to pay. I owed much to Mr. Hall and gave him what I borrowed. The rest of my pay had to be spent on Doc's hotel and my room at the boardinghouse.

P. W. Avery and the others have since moved on to other cases. I hope you will send us a new case as soon as you can. Doc is getting strong-like, but his spirits ain't no better as far as I can tell. Other times when he has been like this, only not so bad, a new case has made him feel better. He naturally wants to work on something to solve. Maybe if he had another case, he would stop being so stubborn and sad-like. He should start acting like his ownself real soon.

But don't fret none, Mr. Wagner, 'cause I have known Doc a long time and he will get better. Maybe if you send his back pay to the Sundowner Hotel, Carson City, Nevada, he will go about getting new clothes and a new wagon. All of his things is lost, and that is enough to make him ornery. Thank you, sir, and don't hold it agin me 'cause I can't write and stuff like Doc.

Wagner lowered the brown page and let it fall on his desk. He removed his spectacles and wiped the lenses. The report was the most intricate communiqué Raider had ever sent. Doc Weatherbee usually penned the accounts of their cases, and his prose was so polished it was usually suitable for publication. At least Raider had chosen someone else to do the actual writing. Raider's penmanship was something akin to random turkey tracks.

Wagner put on his glasses again and read the report a second time, trying to interpret the message between the lines. The most alarming thing was that Doc Weatherbee had refused to write the report in the first place. True, he was recovering from a brutal encounter. For Raider to say the Comancheros had been "mighty rough" was an understatement of tragic proportions. Nor should the loss of Doc's mule and his wagon be underestimated. The fact that Doc was "sleeping it off" left little doubt in Wagner's mind that the man from Boston been dealt a blow that required a great deal of recovery time.

Still, if Doc was eating and drinking, he had bounced back enough to decide if he was ready for another case. Raider seemed to think his partner was set to go into action once again. "Lower than a coyote's dinner." Wagner had to smile. Sometimes Raider could be very amusing.

The request for back pay had come on Doc's behalf, with no mention of Raider's need for money. Back pay had been sent to *both* of them. Where had Doc's money gone? Why did he need more? Perhaps he had used his money at the hotel, although Doc was usually the frugal one. Raider spent his pay on women, whiskey, and gambling, almost certainly in that order.

"He don't say much . . ."

That declaration stood out more than anything else. Doc was always quick with his wit. His sharp tongue could slice to ribbons anyone of lesser intelligence, although his quips and barbs were usually reserved for Raider's thick-skulled gruntings. Weatherbee's silence could be taken for something more serious, unless of course, Raider was exaggerating.

The final alarm was Raider's call to be assigned to another case. True, Raider was a tireless worker once he started out on an assignment. However, getting him into the saddle, especially after a rough encounter like the one with the Comancheros, could be difficult. Doc often had to track him down, searching the whorehouses and casinos in the seedier sections of whatever town they happened to be in.

Wagner shook his head, befuddled at the sudden shift in their partnership. He feared the syndrome he had seen before, the loss of interest by an agent after years of grueling time in the saddle. Doc's refusal to write the report and his claim to have no memory of the events did not sit well with Wagner. He picked up the report and headed straight for Allan Pinkerton's office.

Pinkerton read the communiqué and rubbed his chin.

Wagner nodded at his superior. "Do you see why I wanted you to read this report, sir?"

Pinkerton leaned back and sighed. "Weatherbee's a fine lad, Wagner. He's never let us down."

"He seems to be inordinately distressed at the recent turn of events."

"Perhaps," Pinkerton replied. "But look at the record. He and Raider have been on one case after another without a break. This time in Carson City has done him some good. He needed the rest."

Wagner shrugged. "I can't argue there. Still, there's a note of alarm in Raider's tone. He's worried about his partner. And what about Doc's refusal to convey the facts to us? Leaving Raider to write the report? That isn't like Doc Weatherbee."

Pinkerton refused to give up his optimism. "Well, now, maybe it's time Raider started pullin' some of his weight on the paperwork. And maybe Doc is tellin' the truth. After what he's been through, maybe he doesn't remember any of the facts."

Wagner sighed. "I'm still at a loss for what to do."

Pinkerton picked up an envelope from his desk and handed it to Wagner. "This came earlier today, marked personal for me."

Wagner took out the letter and read it carefully. "Hmm, the police chief of San Francisco, eh."

"A most heinous murder," Pinkerton rejoined. "And they don't have any proof to convict their main suspect in the case."

Wagner eyed the large man behind the wooden desk. "Are you suggesting we send Doc and Raider?"

Pinkerton looked at Raider's letter again. "Maybe the big galoot is right. Perhaps Doc needs to be involved in a case, get his mind off whatever it is that's eating him. Besides, being in a civilized place like San Francisco for a while always perks Doc up. Good food. Good manners. That sort of thing."

Wagner wasn't so sure. "I'd like to see him before we send him out on another assignment. Make a personal assessment of the situation."

Pinkerton shook his head. "There isn't any time for that, Wagner. Even with the railroad, it would take you forever to get to Carson City. By that time, the police chief in San Francisco would be out of patience with us. No, I'm sayin' we send Doc and Raider. If Mr. Weatherbee does not want to go, he can tell us himself."

"You're right as usual, sir. It's just that . . ."

"Go ahead, say it."

Wagner emptied his lungs. "I don't know, sir. I just can't shake this feeling I have."

Pinkerton laughed. "William, you've had these premonitions before. And Raider always proved you wrong, didn't he?"

"It's not about Raider, sir. I'm worried about Doc Weatherbee. Remember Johnson? A good man, just like Doc. Then he was taken prisoner by those Mexican pirates. He was rescued—"

"By Doc and Raider, if you'll remember," Pinkerton interjected, his finger raised to the sky.

Wagner nodded. "Yes, by Doc and Raider. Only Johnson was never the same after that. He became listless, uninterested."

"Aye," Pinkerton replied, "but you can hardly argue with the fate that befell him. He's married now, running that business in Denver, married with a gaggle of tow-headed youngsters given to him by that wife of his."

Wagner tried not to lose patience. "The point is, sir, that we lost him. His spirit was never the same."

Pinkerton eye's narrowed. He stared down his prominent nose at his second-in-command. "William, we're going to lose them all sooner or later. The agency will eventually lose you and me. No man lives forever or stays in the same place all his life. Now, I suggest you inform Doc and Raider that they should catch the next train for San Francisco. Is that understood?"

Wagner smiled officially and nodded. "Yes, sir. I'll see to it immediately."

Wagner got up and started for the door.

Pinkerton's booming voice stopped him. "William!"

"Yes, sir?"

Pinkerton grinned. "You're a good man, William. I'm pleased that you show such concern for our men. I wouldn't have it any other way."

"Thank you, sir."

Wagner employed the first messenger he found to take the directive to the telegraph office. He did not expect a reply for several days, as Raider usually took his time getting back to the home office. Something else to be concerned about. However, the messenger returned that afternoon with a telegram from Carson City. It was short but to the point: "On our way to San Francisco. Thanks. Raider."

Wagner should have been elated at the promptness of the big man's reply, but he was unable to shake the feeling of dread that had settled over him.

CHAPTER 8

The night train chugged out of Carson City right on time. Ordinarily, Raider hated train riding—the cinders from the smokestack, the stench of the day coach, the rocking motion that always left him nauseous. But on this particular trip, fortunate circumstance had provided accommodations that made the journey almost bearable.

A rich gentleman, some English lord, was traveling on the line with his private car. Given the Pinkerton Agency's relationship to the rail company, having provided security over the years, Doc and Raider were able to engage a fancy compartment for their comfort. The car was in the rear of the train, reducing to a minimum the unpleasantries that came with riding the public coach that was so close to the engine. It was the only time Raider could remember when he had stepped onto a train without a sense of dread and loathing. He wished his partner felt the same way.

Raider sat on the soft compartment seat, peering out into the dark night of the plain. There was plenty of room for his long legs to stretch their entire length without the cramps that usually set in after less than an hour of train

riding. He grinned and tipped back his Stetson. "Hell,
Doc, we're like a couple of country lawyers who done
made good and are headin' for the big city. Sure was nice
of the agency to swing this fancy getup. Don't you think
so?"

When his partner did not offer a reply, Raider turned to
regard him. The man from Boston was reaching into the
pocket of his new suitcoat, searching for his bottle of
brandy. Raider thought Doc was drinking too much. Not
like him at all. In fact, nothing about him was the same.

Oh, the flasharity was still there. Doc was all gussied
up in his dandified uniform: the curly-brim pearl-gray
derby fancy tricot long suit, five-button Melton overgaiters, silk shirt and vest—the works. He had been able
to find it all in Carson City. But it wasn't right. Gone was
Doc's trying disposition, the quick-witted mouth, the disapproving stare that he always gave Raider when the big
man put his foot between his teeth. The man from Boston
was sullen, distant, sad, detached. A man who had lost
something and didn't seem capable of getting it back. Not
even the promise of a new case had brought him around.

Raider tried his best to be positive. "Well, old buddy,
looks like we're on the trail again. Wonder what we're
gonna dig up this time?"

No response from the gentleman Pinkerton, except the
rise and fall of the brandy bottle.

"Agency didn't give me much to go on," Raider contin-
ued. "Just s'posed to meet up with some police captain in
San Francisco. Name of McCurley. You ever hear of him,
Doc?"

Doc shook his head, wiping the brandy from his lips
with the back of his hand and then taking another long
swallow.

"Yeah," Raider said, "them police need us again. Hell,
it'll be just like always. We'll mop up and they'll get the
credit."

Doc chortled dejectedly. "Once more into the breach,
eh. So fair and foul a day I have not seen."

Raider squinted at his partner. "Who the hell are you
talkin' like now? That some of that poetry stuff?"

Doc just turned and looked out the window.

Raider shook his head, sighing impatiently. "I give up,

Doc." He raised his hands. "You win. I never thought I'd see the day when you'd shut up tighter than a badger with lockjaw, but I reckon it finally happened. I oughta be praisin' the Lord, but I just can't sit here and watch you like this. It's kinda scary."

Stern blue eyes leveled on the big man from Arkansas. "You know nothing, you ignorant brute."

"Come again?"

Doc's lips were curled in a sneer. "You couldn't possibly know what goes through a man's mind when he's being tortured and humiliated. You think things that you never considered. You're reduced to the level of an animal."

Raider ignored the hateful tone, glad that Doc was finally starting to talk. "Go on, boy, get it off your chest. I'm listenin'."

Doc took another drink before he continued. "We're no better than Tal and his band of savages. We're just as homeless, just as nomadic. We're licensed murderers, separated only by a thread of decency that's missing in the men we pursue."

Raider wasn't sure he agreed with that assessment, but he had resigned himself to listening—a potentially disastrous fate if Doc got cranked up. But he had to endure it. He owed it to Doc after all they had been through together.

The man from Boston shook his head. "Raider, have I ever told you why I became a Pinkerton agent?"

"No. *But I reckon you're about to.*

Doc's tone was maudlin as he began his tale. "You've never known my real name. I was born John Alton Weatherbee. My ancestors came over from England on the voyages that followed directly after the *Mayflower.* They were industrious men and women. My great-great-grandfather founded a bank that still operates today. My father was the head of the bank until he died. My mother, God rest her soul, was well thought of in the highest social circles. And I daresay a finer woman never walked this earth."

Raider nodded appreciatively, trying to maintain his concentration. Sometimes Doc could ramble and would lose him on a story. He hoped his partner didn't become long-winded, although he knew better from experience.

"My early life could not have been better," Doc continued. "I was one of three brothers, the middle boy. I was by far the most rambunctious of the Weatherbee clan. Always getting into mischief, sometimes putting the blame off on my elder brother Peter or my younger brother Aaron."

Raider's brow fretted. "*You* were the hellion of them all?"

Doc nodded, half smiling. "Hard to believe, isn't it? Oh, I never got into any real trouble. And by the time I was enrolled in Harvard, I was ready to settle down to my studies. I excelled in all areas of academia, and I was particularly good at mathematics and physical science."

Raider tried to be encouraging. "I always wondered why you was so good at making potions and figuring things. Hell, you're the best I ever seen."

Doc ignored the compliment. "Naturally, upon my graduation, my father approached me with his expectations. He wanted me to take a position at the bank, find a good wife, settle down, and raise a family. My elder brother, Peter, was already the second-in-command in the business. He was expected to take over after my father retired. Aaron and I were to assume subordinate positions under my elder brother."

A pull from the brandy bottle. He offered it to Raider, who knocked back a swallow. The big man found himself taken in by his partner's story. It was a side of Doc that Raider could not even have guessed at, so far was it from his own Arkansas beginnings.

"So what happened?" Raider asked, handing the bottle back to Doc.

Doc sighed. "I was young, headstrong. I resisted my place in the family hierarchy. I wasn't one to assume my role in the pecking order. After graduation, I informed my father that I wanted to sign on with a cargo ship. I had plans to sail to adventurous ports unknown, seeking my fortunes in the most exotic climes of the world. My father had different ideas. He told me that if I left the family business, I would be disowned."

"Tough shit, huh?"

Doc glared at him. "Precisely. However, I did not take my father's ultimatum lightly. My family meant a great deal to me. I was considering my plight when disaster befell us. My elder brother contracted an infectious disease and died in less than a month. My father came to me, telling me that I was now the next in line for the top position at the bank. He pleaded with me not to go."

Raider watched him as he paused. Were there tears in his eyes? Could the hurt from so long ago still be with him? What the hell had those Comancheros done to Doc?

"Don't stop now," the big man entreated.

"My back was up," Doc replied. "I tied everything to my freedom—my manhood was at stake. I waited awhile after the funeral and then informed my father that I was going to sea. My brother Aaron could be successor to the family fortune. I suppose I wanted to escape, to get away from the memory of my dead brother. I loved him very much. To stay would have been to remind myself of him every day for the rest of my life."

"So you hitched up with a cargo ship?"

Doc nodded. "For a while, I was able to suppress my grief. The freedom of the sea was glorious. Then, while I was in Brazil, I received word that my mother had fallen victim to the same disease that had taken my brother. There was also a message from my father. He told me that I was never to come home again. Three years later, I read of his death in an old newspaper. Aaron had just graduated from Harvard and was ready to take over the bank. I wrote to my brother, but he never replied. I had been disowned by the last member of my family."

Raider exhaled. "Damn, and I thought *I* had a rough life."

Doc looked up. "Did you?"

The big man shrugged. "Some. My old man beat me till I was big enough to whip him. Never knew my momma. No brothers or sisters. But at least I learned to ride and shoot. My uncle taught me. I started driftin' west when I was a pup. Lucky enough that I was tall, so most took me for a man and I had to prove it a lot. Reckon that's where I learned to fight."

"Drifting west," Doc said pensively. 'Yes, I know the feeling. I started west after I had tired of the sea. What else was left for me? At least the western territories presented a challenge." He laughed sadly. "Who knows what I would have become if I hadn't met Allan Pinkerton?"

"How'd you hook up with the old man?"

Doc turned to the window, peering out into the darkness. "A friend of mine was murdered in Chicago. As it stood, he was also an acquaintance of Mr. Pinkerton. We worked together to find the killer. Pinkerton was impressed by my intelligence, if you'll pardon the immodesty. He also liked the fact that I had scientific training and schooling. He offered me a job and then proceeded to indoctrinate me in the form and method of detection. I took to it naturally, enjoying a challenge the way I do."

Raider smiled. "And you're the best, Doc. Even if Pinkerton did stick you with me."

"He needed a pair of troubleshooters. And never degrade yourself, Raider. You're a good detective. I daresay you would do well without me."

Raider frowned. "Now, you can hush up that talk right now. You're startin' to sound like a widow-lady with a bunch of regrets under her shawl."

"No regrets," Doc said. "Not about my position as a detective. But I must admit I have grown somewhat weary of living without roots. I wouldn't mind it at all if I had some gentler connection to the world. I fear that true happiness has passed me by. It would be nice to go home once in a while, to be with people I care about and people who care about me."

Raider, who was on the verge of impatience with Doc's self-pitying tone, pointed a finger at his partner. "You're startin' to feel sorry for yourself, Doc. Now, I know what it's like to have them sorrowful thoughts, but it ain't nothin' that men like you and me can do anything about. You savvy? Yeah, we're lonely and we ain't got no home. But that goes along with the job."

Doc peered fretfully at the big man. "Are you telling me that you never long for the hearth? For a wife to lay down beside you. For something more concrete than . . ."

Raider leaned back, shaking his head. "Doc, I know you've been through a rough one. You lost your mule and your wagon."

"All of it gone!" Doc cried. "My tools, my telegraph. All of my apothecary devices and inventions. I feel naked. The Comancheros took it all from me, along with whatever dignity and strength I had left."

"You got to put it behind you."

"That's easy for you to say! I had journals in that wagon detailing every move we've made since we became partners. Now it's gone, as if none of it happened. I have nothing! Do you hear me? Nothing!"

Raider tried to find some sympathy inside him. "I know, Doc, I know. You're feelin' beat right now. But it ain't like you to hang on like an old snappin' turtle. You got to stop feelin' sorry for yourself."

Doc lowered his head. "I hate everything at this moment. You, the agency, this train. I hate it all."

Raider felt something snap inside him. Heard himself saying coldly, "Well, old buddy, if you don't like the way things is goin', you can always hang it up. Just quit. That might ease your mind."

Doc lifted the brandy and drained the rest of the bottle.

Raider got up, reaching for the door of the compartment.

"Where are you going?" Doc asked.

"Anywhere to get the hell away from you!"

"That's right, what the hell do you know anyway!"

"Nothin', Doc. Not a goddamn thing!"

He went out and slammed the door behind him.

Raider felt bad about arguing with Doc, but he realized that it had been necessary. Sometimes a man needed to feel sorry for himself, but it wasn't something that should last forever. Raider had hoped to jar Doc out of his melancholy mood by a man-to-man confrontation. Hell, it just wasn't right to mope around like a spinster-lady who's been left at the altar. If their partnership was going to survive, Doc simply had to by-God snap out of it.

The big man from Arkansas stood between the cars, gazing out at the plain, taking deep breaths, trying to relax. The fight with Doc had rattled him more than it should have. He had a bad feeling inside. He wished like hell that things would get back to normal. He didn't know how much longer he could stand Doc in his present humor. He was damned tempted just to shoot him and throw him off the train!

The air rushed by him as the train moved on toward San Francisco. Raider was considering what involvement in a case might do for his partner when the door behind him swung open. In a reflexive gesture, Raider drew his Colt and thumbed back the hammer.

A man stared down the bore of the .45, smiling weakly. His voice came out in a polished British accent. "I say there, old boy, no need for that sort of thing. I mean you no harm. I heard you pass by my compartment, and I was just wondering if you might be free for the remainder of the evening."

Raider holstered the Peacemaker, shaking his head, embarrassed by his quick gun hand. "Sorry. I been a little edgy here lately."

The man's smiled broadened. "Well, I don't suppose you can be too careful in these parts. I say, are you one of those Pinkerton chaps who's traveling with us on this train?"

Raider nodded. "Guilty as charged."

The gentleman gave a snort of approval. "Oh well, I don't suppose you'd be interested in a friendly game of poker." He started to close the door. "Good night, old chap. Sorry to have put the devil's scare into you."

Raider caught the door while it was half open. "Whoa, there. Did you say poker?"

"Quite," the gentleman replied. "Nothing brutal, you understand. Simply a small-stakes affair. You see, there are four of us, good lads all, and we find that we're in need of a fifth player, you know, just to make things more interesting, as it were."

Raider extended his hand. "They call me Raider."

The gentleman returned the handshake. "Strang's the name. Sir Lionel Strang of London, England."

Raider tipped back his Stetson. "You wouldn't be the gent who owns this car, would you?"

"One and the same," Strang replied. "Do come along. I hope you're as anxious to play as the others."

Raider grinned, thinking that a good game of cards might just be what he needed to take his mind off his troubles with Doc. He started after Strang, who was making his way to a compartment just down from Raider's. As he followed the Englishman, Raider wondered what a rich man like Strang considered small stakes.

"I say," Sir Lionel called back, "do you think your associate might be game for a hand or two?"

"Naw," Raider replied. "I doubt it. He's got other things on his mind."

Strang sniffed a little—an aristocratic affectation. "Oh. Pity."

They turned into the compartment, which was elaborately decorated in deep green colors. Huddled around a small, round table were three other gentlemen who Sir Lionel quickly introduced. "The gentleman in the leather hat is called Slim, for obvious reasons. This fellow in the dark suit is known as Hudson, and the chap in the black Stetson is—"

"—Cleveland Hall," Raider said. "Hell, boy, I never thought I'd lay eyes on you again."

Hall laughed. "Same here. I didn't see you get on the train. How's your partner doin'?"

Raider shrugged. "He's alive."

Sir Lionel clapped his hands together. "Gentlemen, we are all hail and well met. Shall we continue with our gaming?"

Raider reached into his pocket and took out his money. He had about a hundred dollars on him, most of it from an advance on his wages. Wagner had come through with the request for more money right before they left Carson City. Raider wondered what Wagner would think if he knew the big man was going to risk their traveling money on a few hands of chance.

In a poker game, as in most other human endeavors, the strong parties emerged to challenge one another. On this particular night, Raider and Sir Lionel squared off early as adversaries. The other three players stayed in the hands as long as they could, occasionally winning a pot or two. But Raider and the Englishman were clearly the better players, and so it happened that they seesawed back and forth, taking one another's chips only to give them back.

Cleveland Hall, a man studied in the ways of confrontation, kept his eyes on both of them, waiting for the telltale signs of trouble—a doleful stare, a hand slammed down a bit too hard, the squinty-eyed glint of a loser. But both gentlemen (Raider was on his best behavior) retained their poise despite some good-natured ribbing.

"Two pair," Sir Lionel would say. "Aces over."

Raider eased his cards onto the felt tablecloth. "Three little deuces, Strang. Them aces ain't much good."

Hall braced himself for the feared reaction.

But Sir Lionel only clapped his hands together and replied, "Well played, cowboy. But I'll get you next time."

The others laughed nervously, awaiting the unpleasantness that sometimes accompanied winning and losing.

On the next hand, Raider grinned like a possum eating peach rinds. "Got me a baby straight, Strang. Ace-two-three-four-five."

His hand went out toward the pile of money.

Strang laughed out loud, reaching over to stop the big man. "Sorry, old boy. Heart flush, king high."

Raider's face slacked.

Hall shifted nervously.

Strang frowned. "Something wrong, old man?"

Raider laughed finally. "Nothin' that lady luck and a good dose of salts couldn't cure. Nice flush, Sir Lionel."

Strang dragged the chips to his side of the table.

Hall wiped his forehead. "If I didn't know better, I'd say you boys was a couple of sharpies."

Strang peered over the table at Raider. He was a handsome man, or at least the ladies might think so. Black, curly hair slicked with pomade, thin black mustache, clear brown eyes, straight nose, and a firm jaw. His roundish face might have been fat on a smaller man, but with his wide shoulders and strong arms, Strang appeared only to be stout and healthy. His taste in clothes rivaled Doc's for fanciness and flasharity.

"You ain't a sharpie, are you, Sir Lionel?" Raider asked.

Strang grinned. "Well, now, that remains to be seen. You seem to be doing well over there. You have at least twice as much money as you started with. You've been winning all night."

Raider knew it was true. He had close to two hundred and fifty dollars in front of him. Strang wasn't needling him about it, just making a point that Raider was ready to pick up on.

Raider leaned back, grinning. "You wouldn't be suggestin' that we raise the stakes, would you?"

Strang nodded politely. "Only if it is agreeable to all involved."

The others were not obliging.

Strang shrugged. "As you like it." He picked up the deck, as it was his turn to deal.

"Now hold on," Raider said. "Ain't no need for these boys to risk it all, Sir Lionel. You and me could fight it out head to head, table stakes, winner take all."

Cleveland Hall hesitated. "Raider, that ain't such a good idea, if you know what I mean."

Raider shook his head. "No, I don't know what you mean. Seein's how me and Strang here are both grown men, and seein's how we both are agreeable to a little bump in the wager . . ."

A weird, almost wicked smile crept across Strang's thin lips. "You know, Mr. Raider, I do believe that I am beginning to like you."

"We'll see how you feel after I take all your money, old boy!"

Strang shuffled the deck. "Five-card draw?"

"Fine by me."

The other three watched as the cards hit the table. Hall was wiping his brow with a handkerchief. He was damned near as jumpy as he was when they dynamited the Comancheros. It seemed like a bad idea for both of them to get into it. Hall knew Raider could be damned mean when he wanted to be. And Sir Lionel sure as hell wasn't a sissified English dandy. Hall was fairly certain he had seen a Wells Fargo pocket revolver in the inside pocket of Strang's coat. Sore losers and guns could be a bad combination.

Raider picked up his cards and grinned. "Open for ten dollars."

"See your ten and raise you twenty," Sir Lionel replied.

Raider saw the raise and bumped back with twenty of his own. Sir Lionel then raised fifty. Raider saw the raise but did not raise back.

"Draw," Sir Lionel said.

Raider tossed away two cards and drew two new ones.

Sir Lionel drew three.

Hall expected several hands to pass before the main challenge, but he was wrong. When Sir Lionel saw his new hand, he pushed his entire pile of money into the center of he table. Raider spread his cards, rubbed his chin, and considered the bet.

"How much you shovelin' in there, Strang?"

Sir Lionel shrugged. "Oh, I don't know. There must be several hundred. If it's too rich for you . . ."

Raider pushed his winnings in to match Strang's challenge. "Call, Strang. What you got?"

Sir Lionel grinned. "An incredible hand, really. Full house, aces over kings. Pretty, isn't it?"

The others exhaled, looking down at the pat hand offered by the smiling Englishman.

"Looks like he cooked your bacon," said the man called Slim.

Hudson shook his head. "Glad I stayed out of that action."

Sir Lionel reached for the pot. "Don't worry if you were a few dollars short, old boy. Cleaning you out is plenty."

Raider grabbed the Englishman's wrist. "Nice hand, I must admit. But it don't beat four nines . . . old boy!"

Strang's brown eyes bulged from their sockets. "Incredible. How did you . . . Unbelievable."

Hall feared the worst. He waited for the accusations of cheating. His hand closed around the derringer in his coat pocket.

Raider shrugged, his black eyes fixed on Sir Lionel's face. "You dealt 'em to me, Strang. Three on the deal, one on the draw."

"*I* dealt them, but . . ."

Hall watched his hands carefully, as did Raider.

"I win," the big man said.

Strang's body seemed to go limp. "Yes, I suppose you did."

"Any problem?" Raider asked.

Strang shook his head, frowning. "No." His eyes lifted to the big man's face. "No problem, old boy." His voice seemed to rise a little. He smiled weakly. "Four nines. Damn it all." Then he chortled. "Four bloody nines."

"My lucky number," Raider offered.

The chortle turned into a hearty laugh. "Four bloody nines. Hall, Slim, Hudson. Did you see that? Four of them." The laugh was definitely good-natured.

The others laughed with him.

"Four incredible nines!" Strang shouted. "Well played, old boy. Damn well played!"

Raider nodded, still unsure of his host's demeanor. He pulled the money over the table. There was a small fortune in front of him.

"Four nines!" Strang insisted. "That calls for a drink! Raider, name your poison."

"Whatever you got, Sir Lionel. For me and the others."

Raider shoved the money into his pockets. It wasn't polite to count it in front of the man who lost it. He kept a close watch as Sir Lionel got up to find the bottle and five glasses. The others were watching as well. The tension had not eased as yet.

"Good Irish whiskey!" Sir Lionel exclaimed. "We'll toast this fine gentleman called Raider. Until tonight, I thought I was the best gambler west of the Mississippi, but now the honor belongs to the gentleman with the black eyes."

The Englishman poured five glasses full of whiskey and passed them around. Several gulps of the smooth liquor helped to diminish the uncertainty that had fallen over them at the end of the game. As they refilled their glasses and became increasingly drunken, Sir Lionel led them in a round of English drinking songs that they all sang in spite of the fact that they didn't know the melodies or the words.

The poker game was officially over. Raider had won. And Sir Lionel Strang had turned out to be a gentleman, a gracious host, and a damned good sport.

CHAPTER 9

The following evening, an hour after sunset, the train pulled into San Francisco. Doc had always declared that San Francisco was the only true city west of the Mississippi, a claim that Raider could not refute. The big man stood on the rail platform, taking in the spectacle of the gas lamps and busy streets, a bit put off by the city smell, but still enthralled by the bustle of the city by the bay. A man could have a damned good time in a place like San Francisco, even if he wasn't a city slicker at heart.

Doc stepped up next to his partner, straightening his cuffs. "If you're through gawking, Raider, I suggest we pay a visit to the local constabulary."

Raider started to protest. His experience with city police told him that Captain Charles McCurley would not be in his office during the evening hours. However, the rough-hewn Pinkerton decided not to go against the grain. Doc was starting to show vague signs of recovery. Granted, the man from Boston was not his usual self, but there was now a note of professionalism in his voice, something that had been absent before.

Raider wondered if Doc had forgotten about their disagreement on the train. They had fought before, but they had always patched it up later. Raider wasn't much for grudges. A grudge could eat at a man, tear him up inside, keep him off his toes. People in dangerous lines of work had no business holding grudges against one another. Anything less than total cooperation could get them both killed.

Doc glared at him. "Are you coming or not?"

Raider shrugged. "Whatever you say, old boy."

Doc did not smile at the "old boy."

They started for the street, looking for a carriage to hire.

Doc glanced up and down the avenue, to no avail. "Damn, nothing to be found. I suppose we could walk. I have the address."

Raider just frowned, thinking the night could be a long one if his partner decided to be difficult.

"Here, here!" Doc exclaimed finally. He raised his hand, flagging the phaeton coach that turned a gaslit corner.

The driver, a young man in a top hat, reined back on the harness-bred, screeching to a halt.

Doc held up a silver dollar. "Sir, we need transportation to the police building. I have the address right here."

The lad tipped back his hat. "No need for that. I know where it is. I've bailed out my brother-in-law more than once."

Doc reached for the shiny handle of the coach door. "Then take us there at once. We have urgent business."

The driver shook his head. "Stop her right there, mister. Can't take you nowhere. I'm already engaged, as they say."

Doc raised an eyebrow. "I beg your pardon."

The driver took off his hat and removed a piece of paper from inside the sweat band. "Like I told you, I'm hired. S'posed to pick up a man named . . . now where is it? Ah yes, I'm hired out to a man name of Raider."

The big man's face tightened into a half-smile. "What the hell?"

Doc looked at his partner. "Are you playing games, Raider?"

Raider glared at the driver. "What you know about this, boy?"

"I was hired by some English fellow name of Strang," the driver replied. "He said to tell you that he ad*mired* your poker skills and that I was to take you wherever you wanted to go."

Raider laughed. "Sir Lionel don't fool around none."

"One of your less reputable friends?" Doc said sarcastically.

Raider decided to have fun with it. "Hell, no, Doc, he's a bona fide English sir. Related to them kings and queens and stuff. Plays a pretty good hand of poker, too. You know, some of them high mucky-muck types is just like me. They ain't got a thing against havin' a few laughs."

He opened the door and bowed mockingly. "Step on up, Doc. This ride's on me. Go on, it's paid for."

Doc straightened himself and climbed into the carriage. He stared out the window as they rolled through the busy streets. Raider just leaned back with a sly grin on his face. He was going to break Doc's melancholy if he had to get him in a wrestling hold and strangle it out of him.

"Police station," the driver called, reining back. "I'll wait here for you until you're finished."

Raider tipped his hat. "Dang me if it ain't a pleasure to be associatin' with a higher class of people."

Doc's face was as dry as the bleached skull of a buffalo that had wandered into the desert and died. "If you're through with your posturing, I believe that we should see to our duty."

"I might just see to a fist upside your head," the big man muttered.

"I beg your pardon?"

"Let's go, Doc. We got business, remember?"

Naturally, as Raider had figured, Captain McCurley was not in his office and was not expected to return until the morning. Doc left a note and informed the desk sergeant that they would be in right after breakfast. With that, the Pinkerton duo reboarded the carriage, bound for the Freemont Hotel, Doc's favorite establishment in San Francisco.

Raider peered out the window, wondering if a certain little gaming house was still in operation on the waterfront.

He could already hear the turning of the wheel and the bone-clicking rattle of the dice. And, after he seriously reduced the wad of money he had won from Sir Lionel, he would use the rest to procure the services of a willing young lady.

Doc had other ideas. "I see that look in your eye, Raider. And I'll have you know that I won't stand for any impropriety while we are dealing with the police captain. Our reputation as Pinkerton agents should not be sullied by any of your—"

Raider leveled a finger at him. "I've had about enough of your grousin', Weatherbee. If you want somebody else to work with you on this thing, you get on the wire and tell the home office about it. Otherwise we stop this fancy wagon and I kick your ass right here. Now, you're a smart boy. What'll it be, Doc? Just name it."

Doc did not say a word. He turned his head away, peering out at the city. Raider felt rotten about talking to him that way, but the big man was starting to lose patience.

"Look here, Doc," he said. "You know as well as I do that both of us have got to get along if we're gonna have any chance of solvin' a case. Now if you keep actin' like a bitty hen, we could both get hurt. Savvy?"

Doc nodded. "Yes, I agree. But if you're up to your usual mischief, our image could be tarnished in the eyes of the local police chief."

"Like I said before, if you don't want to work with me anymore, you can contact the big man in Chicago and request someone else."

The carriage stopped in front of the Freemont. "Hotel," the driver called. "All out, gents."

Doc checked in and went straight to his room without another word to his partner. Raider signed the register and climbed the stairs to the second floor. He was beginning not to care what Doc did or said. There was only so far you could go with a stubborn streak. After that, you just had to ignore it.

The big man admitted to himself that he liked the comforts the hotel had to offer. A hot bath, a shave, a soft bed. A couple of well-placed silver dollars produced a clean set of clothes and a shine on his boots. He stood at the window, gazing down on the avenue. There was a large clock in the window of the clock shop across the street. It was only nine in the evening, leaving plenty of time for a nocturnal frolic.

He called for the bellman again and ordered a steak dinner with home fries and a loaf of warm bread. After he ate, he uncorked a bottle of good whiskey that had come along with the dinner. He was feeling like a country squire when the light rapping sounded on his door.

It was probably Doc, come to apologize, he thought.

Raider let him knock again. Make him sweat it out. The way he had been acting, he deserved a little rough treatment in return.

The knocking grew harder. "Sir?"

That didn't sound like Doc.

Raider opened the door to a freckle-faced, red-haired messenger who handed him a neatly folded piece of paper. He gave the lad two bits and closed the door. Who the hell would be sending him a note? Maybe Doc didn't have the guts to come and apologize in person.

He unfolded the untimely dispatch.

"Greetings," it started. "Welcome to the fairest city this side of London. Request your presence tonight on the waterfront. That is, if you aren't afraid to face me again over the poker table. Give me a chance to recoup some of my losses. Gaming house located on the docks, behind the Hearty Grog Tavern near the fish house. Other diversions open to those so inclined. Come along if you're free. Strang."

Raider shook his head. Sir Lionel was certainly persistent. He frowned a little. What did the Englishman have in mind? Was he the type to lure somebody into a dark waterfront alley and club him over the head? The gaming house checked out. It was the same one Raider had been to before. He remembered the smell of fish and the aroma of salt air.

He decided to chance it. Strang hadn't seemed like a bad egg. And if he wanted to coldcock Raider to regain his lost money, there were better ways to do it than issuing a formal invitation.

Raider dressed, slipping his hunting knife into the boot-sheath. He dropped his derringer into his back pocket and then strapped his Colt to his right leg, using leather thongs to keep it in place. Nobody carried guns in San Francisco anymore, so he didn't want to stand out. It didn't matter, as long as his Peacemaker was close by.

As he pulled down his Stetson, he wondered what to tell Doc. Even if they had been at each other's throats, Raider should still inform him where he would be, just in case something happened. He decided to leave Sir Lionel's note in an envelope at the front desk. The message would be given to Doc if Raider did not make it back.

As he pushed into the street, the big man felt a stirring in his gut, the pleasant exhilaration of going on the prowl in a dark, unknown section of town. "Other diversions," conjured up images of large-chested women in skimpy clothes, lounging in gaslight, ready to do a man's bidding without all the words and entanglements that came with proper ladies.

"He's back!"

Raider looked up to see the carriage waiting in front of him. "You still here, boy?"

"S'posed to wait for you until you leave San Francisco," the driver replied. "That Limey done paid me for a whole week."

"He wants to win back his money pretty bad."

"What?"

Raider waved him off. "Nothin'. You know how to get to the Hearty Grog Tavern?"

The driver smiled and nodded. "Sure do."

Raider climbed into the coach and settled back in the seat. The Englishman had certainly thought of everything. Raider figured it was time to find out what Sir Lionel really wanted from him.

The carriage slid to a halt in a dark alleyway. Raider eased open the door and stepped out into the night. His nose told him he was near the fish house. He peered toward the black shambles of a building that sat in front of him. There were no lights in the Hearty Grog. If not for the lamps on the coach, Raider would not have been able to see the weathered tavern sign.

The driver's tone was decidedly nervous. "Ain't nobody here, cowboy. Maybe we ought to just leave."

Raider reached down, lifted his pants leg, and unstrapped the Colt .45 from his calf. "You hang tight. I'm gonna see if anybody is expectin' me." He started into a side alley, the Peacemaker preceding him.

The driver did not have the big man's courage. He shook the reins and guided the carriage away from the waterfront, leaving Raider to his own devices. The harnesses rattled in the stillness of the cool evening, growing softer as the driver hurried to a safer place.

"Chicken shit," Raider muttered under his breath.

Keeping his back to the wall of the planked building, he continued down the alley toward a diamond-shaped window of light. Did he hear the muffled murmur of voices? The light was emanating from a thick door at the end of the alleyway. Raider wanted to get close enough to have a look through the window, but he never made it.

Twin hammers clicked on a scattergun somewhere in the shadows. "Far enough, citizen. Put down that hog-leg and tell me what you're doin' here."

Raider fell back into a crease of darkness, listening to determine the direction of the gunman. He considered firing a round into the shadows but decided against it. If the man wanted him dead, he wouldn't have bothered to ask him why he was there.

"I mean it, citizen," the voice forewarned. "You better tell me who you are in a hurry. Don't want no police nosin' around here. Understand?"

"Ain't no police," Raider replied cautiously. "I'm lookin' for a friend. He invited me down here tonight."

"That so? Who's your buddy? Has he got a name?"

Raider was about to answer when the door with the diamond window swung open. A smoky cloud poured out of the door into the alley. The head of a man emerged, and he looked out into the shadows.

"Here, here," the man said. "Homer, what are you doing with that shotgun?"

"Intruder, Sir Lionel. Came here said he was lookin' for somebody."

Sir Lionel Strang squinted, peering toward Raider. "I say, who's there?"

Raider stayed back, wondering if his poker buddy was friend or foe. "Just me, Sir Lionel. Come on down here like you asked."

"Bravo!" the Englishman replied. "Do come out of there, and hurry. We have a whole table full of blighters who are dying to lose their money."

Raider slipped the Colt into his boot and started toward the door. Sir Lionel ushered him into the gaming house as though they were long-lost friends. The casino was full of ladies and gentlemen who were trying their hands at the various games of chance—blackjack, faro, roulette, dice, the wheel of fortune. Sir Lionel obviously had something else in mind. He directed Raider toward a red curtain at the back of the parlor.

"Now look here," he said confidentially, "just follow my lead, Raider. We won't exactly cheat, but we should avoid the kind of direct confrontation that marked our first encounter. If we play it right, we could both end up with a great deal more than we started out with."

Raider shrugged, following him through the curtain.

The poker players were seated around a large table. Raider was the seventh man. He sat down and immediately purchased two hundred dollars' worth of chips. High stakes. The Englishman liked his wagering to be big. The other players eyed the big man, but they quickly turned their attention back to the cards.

As Sir Lionel had intimated, he and Raider did not exactly cheat. They did, however, play together, helping each other along. If Raider had a good hand, he would bet heavily, prompting Sir Lionel to raise him enough times to keep the others in the game. Raider returned the favor, calling a bluff until he had the rest of the table convinced they should stay in. Raider would then fold on the next card, leaving Sir Lionel to bang heads with his challengers.

The scheme worked, so by the end of the night, Raider and Sir Lionel had cleaned out the others, who had no idea what had transpired. Indeed, even if they had been angry, there was no way to prove that the Englishman and the cowboy were in cahoots. Raider felt sort of bad about the deal until he counted his chips. Seven hundred dollars for a night of idle fun.

"Dang me, I oughta retire," he said to Sir Lionel when they were alone.

"Good show, Raider. I'll tender a libation for us."

While his back was turned, Raider reached for his Colt

again. He lifted it onto the table, setting it in front of him. As Sir Lionel wheeled around, his eyes grew wider. He spilled some of the whiskey he had poured.

"I say, old boy, you seem to have grown an extra hand." He smiled. "I do hope you're not upset about our little ruse. Those men had it coming. If you knew who they were, you'd be shocked. Why, I daresay they list themselves among the most prominent men in San Francisco."

Raider shook his head. "No, that ain't it. I can't say I'm proud of what we done, but it ain't exactly wrong."

Sir Lionel frowned. "Then what?"

"You," Raider replied. "How come you're doin' all this for me? You ain't one of them funny kind, are you? Up to no good?"

Sir Lionel laughed nervously. "Of course not, old boy. I shan't apologize for taking a liking to you. On the train, you impressed me with your gambling skills. As for the carriage, well, it was rather like a joke. You didn't have to honor my invitation, you know."

Raider still was not convinced. "Don't seem right somehow. A dandified Englishman like you wantin' to be friends with a man like me. I ain't got much learnin' or refinin'. Just ask my partner, if you don't believe me."

Sir Lionel sat down on the opposite side of the table and pushed a glass of whiskey toward Raider. "Well, to tell the truth, the aristocracy bores the hell out of me. And, I rather envy you."

"Envy me?"

"Yes," Strang replied. "Envy. You seem the type who finds adventure everywhere you go. I, on the other hand, must manufacture it. Do you know I've never even seen a wild Indian. Only those who are drunk in the small towns east of here. I've never seen a gunfight, let alone participated in one."

Raider shook his head, smiling. "Well, it ain't all it's cracked up to be. Some think it's excitin' to have a man shootin' at you, but it's really damned scary. Especially when you get hit."

Sir Lionel leaned forward. "You've been shot?" he asked eagerly.

Raider nodded. "Shot with gun and arrow, cut with knives, kicked by horses, bit by Injuns. You name it. If there's a way to be hurt, I been hurt that way, probably more than once."

Sir Lionel clapped his hands together. "How utterly delicious!"

Raider dropped the Colt in his boot again and then stood up. "Look here, Strang. I had me a good time tonight. I don't reckon I feel right about keepin' all this money. Here, I'll cut me out a couple of hundred and you take the rest."

"Old boy, I couldn't do that."

"Take it," Raider insisted. "I ain't much for carryin' big rolls of scrip. I'm sure you can find a use for it."

The Englishman raised his finger in the air. "Very well, but I think I know where we can spend it judiciously. Tell me, Raider, are you perhaps interested in some female companionship for the remainder of the evening?"

Raider grinned. He was still wary but a little more resigned to trusting his host. "You know somethin', Sir Lionel. I believe I'm startin' to like you."

"Well," the Englishman replied, "let's see how you feel after a night at Madam Wu's Paramour Emporium!"

That sounded just fine to the big Pinkerton.

The brothel was located several doors down from the gaming house. They had to go through two armed guards and then climb three sets of stairs to the top floor of an old warehouse. When Raider entered the dimly lit parlor, he realized he had come up in the world. Madam Wu's was by far the most ostentatious whorehouse he had ever seen.

Lavender walls were draped with thin silk cloth that fluttered in the breeze and reflected soft light from Chinese lanterns. Sprawled about on thick pillow were girls clad in the same kind of silk that hung from the walls. Raider had never seen such variety in women for hire—black, white, Oriental, Spanish, blondes, redheads, brunettes. They were all lounging with potential customers, which led the big man to believe he might have to wait his turn.

"Splendid, isn't it?" Sir Lionel said.

Raider nodded. "Yeah, but all the chippies seem to be taken."

"Fret not," Sir Lionel replied. "Ah, here comes Her

Highness. Be polite with Madam Wu. She has no tolerance for ruffians."

A slender Chinese woman came toward them with her gossamer robe flowing to both sides. Her face had been painted with thick cosmetics, no doubt to hide her true age. In spite of the fact that she was not a young woman, Madam Wu still exuded a fervid sexuality that had not diminished with the years. Raider wondered if she was going to be his choice for the night.

Madam Wu extended her hand to Sir Lionel, who touched his lips to her dainty fingers.

"Have you come for the private show?" she asked the Englishman.

Sir Lionel nodded. "Yes. I've brought a friend with me. I hope you don't mind."

Madam Wu gave Raider an up-and-down look. "He seems to be healthy and strong. It will cost you extra, of course."

Sir Lionel handed her all of the cash that Raider had given him. "Here's triple the going rate. My friend and I want the best."

Madam Wu thumbed through the scrip, counting it quickly. "This should see you through the night. Do you have a preference for the women?"

"Only the most beautiful girls you have," Strang replied.

Raider was scanning the room, quite sure that he detected the smell of opium in the air. "You want us to choose some of these?" he asked.

Madam Wu laughed graciously. "No, not at all. These girls are for the customers with very little money to spend. In fact, many of our guests never achieve the privileged status afforded to your companion."

In such a fancy damned place, Raider was wondering what she meant by "very little money."

"Come along," she said. "I'll ready the show for you."

As they followed her through the parlor, Raider leaned over toward Sir Lionel. "What the hell is this show thing?"

Sir Lionel smiled. "Raider, have you ever heard of the Garden of Earthly Delights?"

"Can't say that I have."

"Well, after tonight, you will not only be able to boast that you have been there, you will be able to describe in detail the taste of the most delicious forbidden fruit."

Raider frowned a little. "Does that mean we're gonna get some pussy?"

"More than you could ever imagine."

They were greeted at a narrow doorway by a Chinese girl who immediately asked them for their guns.

Raider was reluctant to give up his Colt and his derringer. "How do I know I'm gonna get 'em back?"

"Trust her," Sir Lionel replied.

The Englishman promptly surrendered the Wells Fargo pocket revolver from inside his coat. Raider had to go along, handing over both his firearms. He decided not to tell them about the knife in his boot.

When they were disarmed, the girl led them to a pair of plush chairs that faced a small proscenium. A green velvet curtain had been drawn across the narrow stage. The show, Raider thought. He took his place beside Sir Lionel, who had already eased into one of the chairs.

The Chinese girl clapped her hands and the curtain opened.

Madam Wu's voice prompted the action on the platform. "Come to me, says Sappho. I will love you, since we have no man. We will love and enjoy each other until our men return."

Raider wasn't sure about Sappho, but he knew what was happening onstage. Two sinfully beautiful women were lounging side by side on a large divan. Their bodies were covered only by transparent wisps of blue silk. One was a slender blond-haired woman with largish breasts, the other an Oriental girl with the blackest hair he had ever seen. They began to touch each other, slowly caressing the tender lines of their sweet bodies.

"Lovely, eh?" Sir Lionel offered.

Raider was not able to reply. He watched as the blonde kissed the dark neck of the Chinese girl. The blonde's pink lips slid down her chest, suckling on the pert mounds of her nipples. A delicate moan escaped from the thin lips of the Eastern beauty.

"Watch what they do next," Sir Lionel said.

Raider would not have been able to take his eyes off

them if he had been shot in the back by a Gatling gun.

They writhed and twisted until their faces were between each other's legs. The soft curves of their buttocks shifted up and down as their tongues brought pleasure; real or imagined, Raider could not be sure. Did it matter? He wanted to be onstage with them. The hardness was swelling inside his trousers.

Sir Lionel leaned over toward him. "Which one do you want, old boy?"

"Both of them," the big man replied. "Now!"

Sir Lionel clapped his hands together. "Done! Madam Wu, will you accommodate my friend here?"

"Anything you say, Sir Lionel."

The girls onstage stopped their activity. Madam Wu took Raider's hand and led him to an ornate bedroom behind the proscenium. In less time than it took to play a hand of blackjack, Raider was lying in bed with two of the most beautiful women he had ever seen.

CHAPTER 10

Raider opened his black eyes to the dull, diffused purple light of city daybreak. He suffered a momentary dissociation from his surroundings. The unfamiliar feeling caused him to sit up in bed. He rubbed his face, clearing the sleep from his eyes. Where the hell was he?

Something warm rubbed against his thigh. He felt the shifting of another body next to him. He peered down at the firm buttocks of the Chinese girl, whose backside had jutted out from under the covers. Raider remembered that he was at Madam Wu's. In a single rush of memory, he replayed the sinful night in bed with the two women, a night that would surely guarantee the big man a seat in Hell on Judgment Day.

The blonde rolled over, pressing her breasts against his side. Raider felt the sudden urge that started in his crotch and spread to the rest of his body. He touched the China-girl's ass, stroking the firm cheeks and the crack between them. Her hand came up reflexively, grabbing the stiffening member that throbbed between her fingers.

Her mouth followed her hand. She went up and down,

her eyes half closed. She wasn't even awake yet.

The blonde was stirring, though. She looked up to see Raider's erect shaft between the other's lips. She put her hand on the Chinagirl's face and pushed her away.

"My turn," she moaned. "Get off."

The Chinagirl reluctantly gave up her ministrations.

The blonde's hand began to work on him. She rolled out from under the covers and straddled his midsection. Raider looked up the half-sag of her huge bosom. The nipples were pink and erect.

"Got to get that big thing inside me," she whispered.

The Chinagirl was indignant. "Save some for me."

Raider grinned. "Is this mornin' gonna cost me extra?"

The blonde smiled haughtily, guiding the head of his prick to her wet crevice. In one sinking motion, she took Raider's length inside her. Her face contorted in an expression of agonistic pleasure. She began to bounce violently, riding him like a prize bull.

Raider felt the tightness of her vagina as she climaxed over and over. His own discharge was beginning to rise, swelling toward the summit of his cock. The blonde sensed his release, and jumped off before he came.

His eyes narrowed. "What the hell?"

"All yours, Wan Chur," the blonde said.

The Chinagirl looked and smiled. "I want it from behind."

She got on all fours, wagging her backside at him. Raider quickly positioned himself behind her, guiding his prick all the way into her. She grunted and started to rock backward, meeting his thrusts with equal ardor. They both came, collapsing into the soft sheets of the feather mattress.

Raider grabbed both of the girls, pulling them close to him. They laughed and kissed, touching, stroking, enjoying the aftermath of their loveplay. Raider was all set to go again when he heard the ruckus down the hall.

The big man sat up, listening.

"What is it?" the blonde asked.

"Shh."

A woman screamed. Then a man was shouting. Bumping and thudding as bodies slammed against walls.

Raider jumped up and grabbed his pants. He buttoned

the top button and reached for the knife in his boot. The girls begged him not to leave them.

"Stay put. You'll be safer that way," he warned them.

He opened the door and stepped out into the corridor.

The cracking of knuckles on bone resounded through the still air. A black figure tumbled from one of the doors, and landed against the wall. The man quickly regained his feet, and pointed something toward the room he had fallen from.

Raider gripped the blade of his knife and hurled it toward the shadow of the assassin. A loud scream from the attacker. He was holding his arm where the blade had gone in. Sir Lionel bounded into the hall and slammed a hard left into the wounded man's face.

The assassin dropped toward the floor, executing a sweeping move with his legs. Sir Lionel fell to the carpet, landing on his back. Bouncing to his feet, the intruder went straight for the window at the end of the hall and hurled himself through the glass.

Raider ran for the casement, figuring the three-story fall would break the intruder's neck. He stuck his head through the broken window, expecting to see a body at the bottom of the alley. But the assassin had been smarter than that.

"Son of a bitch," the big man cried. "He rolled out onto the gable and down to the lower porch roof. That was quick."

Sir Lionel was standing beside him. "Ruddy little bastard tried to kill me in my sleep."

"Guns," Raider said. "Now!"

When they had their weapons, they hurried downstairs and ran into the alley. The day was still and quiet. Raider listened for anything moving in the alleyway. Nothing.

"He couldn't have gotten that far," Raider said softly. "Not with a knife in his arm."

Sir Lionel held up his pocket revolver. "Let's find the wog and shoot him dead." He started down the alley.

Raider stopped him. "Is there another entrance to this alley, Strang?"

Sir Lionel nodded his head. "Yes. From the street on the other side of these buildings."

Raider gestured behind him. "Then you go and come around from that end."

"But I—"

"He's wounded," Raider urged. "Nothin' more danger-ous'n a wounded critter, be it bear, lion, or man. Get me?"

Sir Lionel nodded reluctantly. "All right."

"Never hurts to play it safe, Strang. Get goin'."

When Sir Lionel was on his way, Raider thumbed the hammer of his Colt and started down the alley. His eyes turned instinctively upward. When a wounded mountain cat came after you, it came from above, pouncing with all its weight. Raider's foot hit something on the ground. He looked down to find his hunting knife in the dirt. It was stained with the attacker's blood.

A *whoosh* of air above him. His eyes turned up to see a black shape flying from a low roof. Raider twisted the knife blade toward the vaulting figure. The man's chest landed on the point of the steel, splitting the breastbone with a sickening crack.

Raider pushed the twitching weight off him. The man died with a violent shiver. Raider reached down to lift the black cloth that covered his face. The man was Chinese. Why the hell had he been trying to kill Sir Lionel?

Shouts from the end of the alley raised his head. Two gunshots. A man fell from an overhanging roof, thudding to the ground. Sir Lionel came around the corner to stand over the body.

"Drag him on down here," Raider called.

Sir Lionel pulled the corpse behind him, dropping it beside the man Raider had killed. "Chinamen," he said. "This one was waiting up there near the street."

"Accomplice," Raider replied. "He was helpin' this other one. If he didn't make it back, the cover man was goin' to come after you."

Sir Lionel shuddered. "My God, why did they want to kill me?"

Raider squinted at the Englishman. "Maybe you can tell *me*."

Sir Lionel was agape. "I have no idea."

Raider reached down and grabbed the wrist of the man he had killed. "One black glove," he said. "And there's a little ax in his belt. You know what that means, Sir Lionel?"

Strang shook his head. "No, I don't."

"Tong," Raider replied. *"Black Hand.* It's a secret Chinese society. They operate up and down this coast, mainly in San Francisco. You musta done somethin' to get 'em riled."

"No," Strang insisted. "I've never had any dealings with anyone like that. It's unthinkable."

Raider scowled at the Englishman. "Look here, boy, it's time to get the wash off the line. You tell me what's really goin' on here, Sir Lionel."

"I assure you I don't know!" Strang replied. "I was lying in bed when this dirty little sod climbs through the window. Luckily the girl I was with had awakened me seconds earlier. I believe she heard him coming."

Raider exhaled impatiently. "These boys don't give up. Strang. If they want you dead once, you can bet they want you dead twice. It ain't none of my business, but you better be ready for another bushwhackin'."

Strang looked at Raider. "Here, here, old boy, I'll hire you to stand guard over me. Your agency provides that sort of thing, don't they?"

Raider nodded. "Yeah, but I'm on a case right now. Hell, I got to get movin' right away. Me and Doc are due at the police station this morning. You want me to tell them about these two?"

Strang's face blanched white. His face slacked into a frown. "No, that won't be necessary. I'll take care of this."

Raider shrugged. "Ain't no trouble to tell—"

"No police!" Strang insisted. "They stay away from the waterfront, and that's the way it should be. Madam Wu doesn't want them poking around down here. And, quite frankly, neither do I."

"Got somethin' to hide, Sir Lionel?"

"No, of course not! It's just that, well, I value my pleasures. If the police start nosing around here, soon or later some citizens' committee will tell them to close down the gaming house and Madam Wu's."

Raider nodded. "Yeah, I see what you mean."

"I'll have these bodies removed immediately."

As he turned away, Raider grabbed his arm. "Strang, if you're in somethin' you can't get out of, you better come clean. Tell me what you're hidin' and maybe I can help you."

"I'm hiding nothing, Raider! Now, if you'll excuse me . . ."

He hurried back down the alley. Raider gave it up. He went back to find his clothes. It wasn't none of his affair. He had other business to take care of.

After he was dressed, he headed back to the Freemont, only to find that Doc had already left. Raider glanced at the clock on the wall. It was eight o'clock. If he went straight to the police station, he could still be on time. Of course, Doc would probably be mad anyway because Raider hadn't spent the night in his hotel room.

The big man arrived at the precinct in time to see the man from Boston pushing through the front door. Good. He wasn't late. Doc couldn't say a thing to him.

Raider burst into the station just as Doc was sitting down at the captain's desk. Raider pushed past the desk sergeant and went straight to the captain's office. He eased down next to Doc, grinning.

Doc glared at him. "Where were you?"

"Don't start," Raider said. "I'm here, ain't I?"

"Gentlemen! Glad to finally make your acquaintance."

They both glanced up to regard Captain Charles McCurley, San Francisco Police Department. He extended a huge bear paw for a hearty handshake. He was a big, round man, completely bald, with a red moustache, clad in an official blue uniform. As he eased back in his leather chair, he regarded Doc and Raider with clear, piercing blue eyes.

His voice was deep and as clear as his gaze. "Gentlemen, you got anything that proves you are who you say?"

Doc quickly produced their credentials. McCurley nodded over them and then handed them back. "Can't be too careful," he offered. "Not when you're dealing with murder."

For the first time since they had left Carson City, Doc Weatherbee's face broke into a broad smile. "Suppose you tell us all about it," he said pleasantly.

Raider relaxed in his chair. At last they were back on a case. He wore a half-smile until the captain got deep into the facts. Then the big Pinkerton was not so sure he liked what he heard.

• • •

Captain McCurley leaned back, his hands steepled together. He was a man who wore the marks of his authority on a worried face. A man not used to failure. Raider knew that it hurt the captain to bring in outside help to clean up his dirty business. Pinks weren't always welcomed, even though they would probably finish what the police had started.

"Theodore Huntley was murdered three weeks ago, gentlemen." McCurley paused, watching both of them for reaction. "Never heard of him, eh?"

Doc shook his head. "No, in fact, the only Huntley of prominence that I have heard of would be the late William Huntley."

McCurley grimaced, nodding politely. "Theodore Huntley was William's son. Tell me, Mr. Weatherbee, what do you know about the senior Huntley?"

Doc thought about it for a minute. Raider was glad to see him involved again. At least he was using his head for something besides misery.

Doc offered what information he could recall. "William Huntley was a sailor in his youth. He knew the particulars of the sea when it came to transporting cargo to faraway ports, and he was able to return with imports not readily found on the mainland of North America. This talent enabled him to build one clipper ship into a company that operated up and down the Pacific Coast, from the tip of South America to Alaska. I believe at one time his business extended even to the South Seas."

McCurley nodded approvingly. "You Pinks are as good as they say you are. Yes, Huntley built up the company, but young Theodore wasn't one to keep a watchful eye on the business after his father passed on. Teddy, as they called him, went back east to live the life of a gentleman. He was the toast of Boston society, but he didn't know a thing about ships or their cargo."

Raider squinted at the good captain. "Where'd they find the body?"

"Floatin' face down in the bay," McCurley replied. "At first we thought he just drowned. But two of my men took a look at him and they found a couple of bullet holes in him. Shot in the back."

Doc put a fist under his chin. "You say Theodore Huntley had been in Boston?"

"Correct, for the past two years."

"What was he doing in San Francisco?"

McCurley put his hands on his stomach. "As far as we
know, he had come back west to sell a half interest in the
company. Like I told you, he hadn't been too keen on business, and the shipping firm wasn't doin' so well. A lot of
the ships were outdated. They were still using sailing vessels while most ever'body else had gone to steam. A lot of
the company's cargo routes had collapsed. Huntley Shipping was still operative, but it hasn't shown much of a
profit."

"I see," Doc said. "And who's running the operation, or
rather who was running it before Theodore was killed?"

"Man name of Judd Gilmore," McCurley replied.

Doc shifted impatiently in his seat. "I see. And did you
question Mr. Gilmore about his feelings about the sale of
the company?"

McCurley nodded. "Yes, we did. He was all for it. According to Gilmore, the new investor was supposed to provide the capital for revamping the old ships, making them
into steamers. He was also going to purchase three new
steam vessels from an English shipbuilder, as well as acting with Gilmore as co-manager of the firm. Unfortunately,
the death of young Teddy put an end to the deal."

"And why is that?" Doc asked.

"The new investor is the prime suspect in the murder,"
McCurley replied. "His name is Strang, Sir Lionel Strang.
We'd have brought him in long ago if we had any concrete
evidence."

Raider sat up in his chair. "Strang!"

McCurley regarded the rugged cowboy. "You know
him?"

"Well, yeah," Raider said hesitantly. "Met him on the
train from Carson City. Played poker with him." Raider
did not add details of the previous night, nor did he express
his feelings about Sir Lionel: the Englishman had not
struck him as a murderer.

Doc picked up his lead. "You believe that Strang had
something to gain by killing Theodore Huntley."

McCurley rubbed his chin. "That's where things start to

go sour. After Huntley was found dead, Strang insisted that he hadn't killed him. He also held to the claim that the papers giving him half interest in the shipping company had already been signed. But no documents were ever found to support Strang's claim."

"Wouldn't he have copies of the papers himself?" Raider asked.

"Says they were stolen from his office here in San Francisco," McCurley replied. "So far nothin' like that has turned up."

Raider shook his head. "I don't get it. If them papers was already signed, why would Strang want Huntley dead?"

"We believe that Theodore Huntley had backed out of the deal at the last minute," McCurley replied. "Then Strang either killed him or had him killed so he could deal directly with Judd Gilmore . . . only Gilmore decided not to deal with a suspicious man like Strang. Gilmore also insists that that deal was never completed. Strang even went as far as to lie and say that Gilmore was one of the witnesses when the papers were signed."

Raider slapped his knee. It was time to speak up. "Dang me, it may make sense to you, but I can't see Sir Lionel killin' anyone in cold blood. Hell, he lost a lot of money to me, and he took it like a sport."

McCurley frowned like a man who wasn't used to being challenged. "Are you tellin' me you're gonna give him a break because he's a good poker player?"

Raider scowled, looking away. He remembered Sir Lionel's expression when he had mentioned the police. Maybe there was something to the captain's claim. Although Raider had a different feeling in his gut: Strang wouldn't kill anybody to get what he wanted.

"Strang's a rounder," McCurley went on. "He's mixed up in some of the goin's-on at the waterfront. Frequents a place called Madam Wu's. Gambles a lot. He owns a rail line that comes into San Francisco. Had his trouble with the customs officials a time or two. Hell, they haven't been able to nail him on anything either."

Doc wasn't ready to stop his line of inquiry. "Tell me, Captain, if a transaction had taken place, Strang buying half the shipping company, as it were, wouldn't there be some kind of bank records, you know, a check possibly, a record of funds being transferred between accounts?"

McCurley nodded. "Good thinking. We thought the same. Sir Lionel did withdraw a sizable amount of cash from his local account, but it never turned up at Huntley's bank. More proof that the Englishman is lying."

Raider had to stick up for his new friend. "Facts, McCurley. Anybody see Strang kill Huntley? Or did the Englishman come up with any kind of alibi?"

McCurley sighed defeatedly. "No to both questions. Sir Lionel wouldn't tell us where he was the night Huntley was killed. He challenged us to prove that he had anything to do with Huntley's death."

"Why would Huntley have reason to back out of his deal with Strang?" Doc asked. "If he needed the money, why would he renege?"

"To keep his power," McCurley replied. "And, according to Gilmore, they could have gotten a bank loan to provide the same capital that Strang was going to supply. Huntley had second thoughts. Decided he didn't want to let the business out of the family."

"Speaking of family," Doc said, "are there any heirs to the shipping company besides Theodore?"

"One sister," McCurley replied. "Only we haven't been able to find her. She was back east going to school in Boston. I reckon she had been living with her brother until he was killed. We sent word to her, but she never showed up. The Boston police haven't been able to find her. Some think she's in Europe, but there's no way to tell for sure."

Doc sat up in his chair, a half-smile on his lips. "Interesting. And you say Strang is the only one with a motive for killing Theodore Huntley?"

"As far as we know, Weatherbee. We been rackin' our brains tryin' to pin him on this. He's as slippery as a rock cod. Just seems to escape us and comes up smellin' like a rose every time."

Raider offered what he thought was an obvious point. "Maybe he didn't do it. Maybe y'all are missin' somethin' that's right in front of your eyes."

Doc shot him a disapproving stare. "Raider, just because Strang shares your taste for debauchery, it doesn't mean that he's innocent. Unless you know something you're not sharing with us."

Raider scowled back at his partner. "Maybe we can talk about this later, Doc."

McCurley also shot him an accusing look. "If you're hidin' somethin', you better get it out now."

"I ain't hidin' nothin'," the big man replied. "I'm like you, Captain. I ain't got no proof of nothin'."

McCurley threw up his hands, abdicating any responsibility in the matter. "Well, gentlemen, regardless of the facts, I'm handing the case over to you. It's up to you to settle the matter once and for all. Keep me posted, and let me know if you need any assistance."

As McCurley rose from his chair, Doc and Raider stood up to shake his hand. Doc bowed politely and hurried to usher Raider out of the police station. The big man came along without any trouble, even though his ire had been raised by their refusal to believe his assessment of Sir Lionel's character.

When they were on the wooden sidewalk, Doc turned immediately to his partner. "Raider, first of all, I think apologies are in order. I have been acting like a cad and a bounder for the past weeks. I only hope you can forgive my unprofessional attitude."

Raider was taken aback by the suddenness of his partner's turnaround. "Well, hell, Doc, I reckon there wasn't much you could do about it. I mean, you did have reason to be lower than a sidewinder's belly."

"Good," replied the man from Boston. "Now that we've settled our differences, suppose you tell me about Madam Wu's and the gambling house."

Raider's eyes narrowed. "What are you talking about?"

Doc reached into his pocket for an Old Virginia cheroot. "Come, come. You can't fool me. You were out all night. You left in Sir Lionel's carriage, I saw you from my window. Logic tells me that you didn't attend a prayer meeting, so you must've enjoyed the more carnal treats offered by the waterfront."

Raider frowned like a thief caught red-handed with the evidence. "You're so damned smart!"

"Convince me that I'm wrong," Doc offered.

Raider laughed cynically. "All right."

"All right, what?"

"All right, I'll come clean," the big man replied. "But only if you buy me breakfast."

Doc torched the end of his cigar. "Well," he said dryly, "at least things are back to normal."

Raider downed a huge breakfast: five eggs, a steak, potatoes (no grits available), biscuits, jelly, ham, and several cups of coffee. Doc also enjoyed a filling repast, about half of what his partner had consumed. When they were finished eating, Raider glanced at the man from Boston. The look in Doc's eyes told the big man that he had better tell the truth.

"All right," he said resignedly, "I was with Strang last night."

"And?"

Raider belched heartily. "We went to the gaming house and played poker. After that we were at Madam Wu's. I tell you, I ain't never seen a bunch of chippies with any better—"

"Spare me," Doc said, interrupting. "I'm more eager to know why you are so quick to defend Strang. Is it because he shares your taste for the lower things in life?"

Raider ignored the uppity tone of Doc's question. "He ain't a cheater, Doc. He's shrewd. You might even call him a schemer. But he don't cheat, and he ain't a poor loser. Hell, if that boy had backed out of the shipping deal, I don't think Sir Lionel would be the kind to kill him for it. He would have found somethin' more . . . how would you say it?"

"Subtle?" Doc offered.

"Yeah, that's it."

Doc stirred his coffee, staring into the cup. "Raider, this seems to be one of your hunches. And, while I have known your intuition to be accurate in the past, I daresay the facts point in a different direction."

"There's more," the big man replied.

Doc looked up. "Well?"

Raider drew a napkin across his mustache. "This morning, somebody tried to kill Sir Lionel."

Doc did not seem shocked or surprised. "Any idea who?"

"Tong," Raider replied. "Black Hand. There were two of 'em. Tried to bushwhack him while he was sleepin'. That's why I can't believe Sir Lionel killed that boy Huntley. I mean, somebody wants Strang out of the way, just like Huntley. It could be that the same person tried to kill both of them."

Doc served up a patronizing smirk. "You can't see it, can you?"

Raider frowned. "See what?"

Doc gestured toward the street. "The carriage, the good times on the waterfront. Even the poker game."

"What are you gettin' at?"

"Just this," Doc replied. "Sir Lionel does not seem to be a man without resources. I contend that he found out we were on the case. He wanted to get close to one of us, to try to influence our view of him and the crime of which he is suspected. He saw that I was not inclined to any of his pastimes, so naturally he chose you. I daresay he has succeeded in his scheme. You're quite ready to pick up the banner in his defense."

Raider lowered his eyes. "Yeah, I see what you mean. Hell, he did act right scared when I mentioned the police. But I don't see how he could have staged that attempt on his life. That boy was really tryin' to kill him. And I don't think he could hire two Chinamen to be killed. No man would give up his life to help another man prove he was innocent."

Doc shrugged. "All right, suppose the attempt on his life wasn't staged. Surely a man like Sir Lionel would have more than one enemy. Perhaps he crossed the Tong in one of his transactions."

"I thought of that," the big man grunted.

"If Strang is involved in Huntley's murder, we'll catch him," Doc offered. "He may be keen, but I doubt if he's covered all his tracks."

Raider felt an aching in his gut. "What do we do now?"

"I suggest," Doc replied, "that we go to see Sir Lionel Strang."

Raider had to agree that it seemed like the thing to do.

CHAPTER 11

Strang's address, as given by Captain McCurley, was a new townhouse a few blocks away from the Freemont Hotel. Doc and Raider had a definite plan in mind. Raider would enter first, leaving Doc to hang back and gauge Sir Lionel's reaction to their arrival. As Doc had never met the man, he wanted a clear first impression of the Englishman.

The smell of redwood and cedar filled the stairwell as they climbed the stairs to Sir Lionel's second-floor offices. The ground floor had been rented to an attorney's firm, leading Doc to remark that Strang was a judicious businessman, extracting every possible dollar from his investments. Raider eased up to the door marked *Strang & Associates, Ltd.* As he lifted his hand to knock, he felt rather like he was betraying a good friend.

Sir Lionel's deep voice bade them enter. The Englishman was sitting behind a huge redwood desk that was covered with papers. He smiled and rose to his feet when he saw Raider. The big man stepped in with his Stetson in his hands.

"Good show, Raider," Strang said. "Glad to see you,

old man. I didn't know if you'd be back after that ugly business this morning."

Raider lowered his eyes, looking at the shine on his boots. "I ain't exactly here on a friendly visit, Sir Lionel."

Strang's sophisticated brow tensed and wrinkled. "Oh?" He sat back down behind the desk. "Then why have you come?"

Raider glanced up, thinking it was best to look Strang straight in the eye when he said it. "Theodore Huntley," the big man said blankly. "You knew him?"

Strang nodded dolefully. "So it was you they brought in to stay on my back about this thing. I suppose I should have made the connection earlier. It makes sense that they would hire a Pinkerton. God knows their own force is entirely inept."

"You mean you didn't know I was on this case until now?" Raider asked.

Strang chortled derisively. "Why should I? I don't go digging around in people's private affairs." A note of anger crept into his voice. "That's *your* job, isn't it?"

Doc pushed in, sliding past Raider. "If you didn't know Raider had been hired to look into the Huntley case, Strang, then why did you work so hard to ingratiate yourself with him?"

Strang threw out his hands. "Ah, splendid. You've brought your partner along. Why don't both of you have a seat? I'll have my secretary bring us some tea. Or would you prefer coffee?"

"Coffee's fine with me," Raider said.

"We didn't come here to socialize," Doc replied. "Now, it you'll just answer my question, Strang. Why did you—"

"I have no friends out here," Strang said quickly. "Raider seemed like a good chap. He may not be long on social amenities, but he does have a certain flair and exuberance for life."

Raider frowned. "Thanks, Sir Lionel. I think."

Sir Lionel nodded. "Your partner here could use some of your élan, Raider. For someone who presents himself as a gentleman, he certainly is short on manners."

"Weatherbee's the name. Doc Weatherbee."

Sir Lionel did not accept Doc's offered handshake. Instead, the Englishman leaned back, slumping in his chair.

"Well, gentlemen, I suppose I'm sunk now that the mighty Pinkertons have me in their grip. I hate to lose a friend, Raider, but don't worry. I know you're only doing your job. I suppose you'll be able to do something the San Francisco police have been incapable of."

"And what might that be?" Doc asked.

"Finding me guilty of a crime I never committed."

Raider shook his head. "That ain't how it is, Sir Lionel. Me and Doc are here to get to the truth. If you're innocent, there's no way anybody'll be able to nail you. Just one thing, though, you got to shoot straight with us."

Strang sat up. "How? Tell me what to do and I'll be more than happy to oblige you."

Doc sat down in one of the chairs opposite Strang's desk. "You can start by telling us the truth about your dealings with Theodore Huntley."

Strang thought about it for a moment. At last he gestured toward the other empty seat, urging Raider to sit down. The big man eased into the chair, his black eyes focused on his unfortunate friend.

"Why did you want to purchase a half interest in Huntley Shipping?" Doc asked.

Strang sighed, leaning back again. "Have you ever had a dream, Weatherbee?"

Doc just sat there, staring blankly at Sir Lionel.

"I had a dream until Theodore Huntley died," Strang continued. "Since I came to this great country, I watched the railroads grow. I saw the great spike driven to connect the two oceans. Naturally, I realized that my future lay in the West. The first time I saw the Pacific Ocean, I wondered what it would be like to stretch the connection of the trade lines all the way to the South Seas, the Orient, China, even the Japans. Sure, some have already done it, but I envisioned a steady line of logistics, ending in the East at the source of the transcontinental railroad. Can you imagine that? Goods from the Orient winding up in New York, Providence, Boston?"

Raider had a puzzled expression on his rugged face. "Sir Lionel, if you was so hot to make these things happen, why'd you go try to buy a broken-down shippin' outfit like Huntley?"

Strang gestured impatiently. "Don't you see? I had to

buy into a company that was on its last legs. I approached several major shipping firms, but no one wanted to take a chance on a speculator like me. Hell, my entire career has been built on speculation. Several times I've almost lost my shirt."

Doc Weatherbee decided to resume the lead. "Sir Lionel, you told the police you had signed the papers for the transaction between you and Theodore Huntley."

"Correct," Strang replied. "I made the mistake of allowing Huntley's people to be the witnesses at the contract signing. I'm new in San Francisco and haven't any legal counsel. Of course, I thought I was safe, having copies of the papers myself, until they were stolen."

"Your office was broken into?" Doc asked.

Sir Lionel nodded. "The door was kicked open and my entire office was turned upside down. The papers were in my desk, locked of course, but that did not deter the thief."

Doc glanced back toward the door. "I see you've had the damage repaired."

"Would you like the name of the locksmith?" Sir Lionel challenged.

"No need," Doc replied. "Things can be manufactured to fit any appearance, don't you believe so, Sir Lionel?"

Strang laughed. "Ah, Weatherbee, I had no reason to want Theodore Huntley out of the way. In fact, young Teddy was delighted to have new capital in his floundering company. He had gone through the trust fund his father had left him. With the money I gave him, he was going to head back to Boston and live quite comfortably for the next ten years or so. For the rest of his life, if our merger was successful."

"What of Huntley's sister?" Doc asked.

"I know nothing of her," Strang replied, "except that her name is Rebecca. Theodore mentioned her once or twice. I believe she's abroad, in Europe."

Raider glared at his partner. "Ask him about the money?"

Strang frowned. "Money?"

Doc straightened himself in the chair. "Yes, according to the police, you withdrew a large sum of money from your bank, and you claimed to have paid Huntley for your interest in the shipping firm."

Strang groaned and shook his head. "Damn me, they saw me coming. Me, the big gambler and businessman. Me, from the streets of London. Young Teddy insisted on cash. He wanted to leave immediately for Boston, get back to the life he so adored."

"Understandable," Doc rejoined. "I'm from Boston myself. Sometimes I would give anything just to be there for a day or two."

Strang regarded the gentleman Pinkerton. "Is that so? Well, perhaps you should go there now. Would you like free passage on the train? I can arrange that for you."

Doc sniffed condescendingly. "Sir Lionel, any lack of cooperation on your part certainly indicates incrimination in the matters at hand."

"I'm bloody well tired of everyone pointing the finger at me!" Strang cried. "I've done nothing but deal fairly with Huntley and with the police. Why would I want him dead? It's a certainty that Judd Gilmore doesn't want to sell to me. Why doesn't anyone ask Gilmore where my money went? He should know. He was there when I delivered it."

Doc's eyes narrowed. "Strang, do you really want us to believe that you were foolish enough to deliver cash, without witnesses on your behalf, to the office of Huntley Shipping?"

"I don't care if you believe it or not," Strang replied. "I was eager to get on with my business. I wanted to get things rolling, as it were. I had planned to order three new steamers from a shipbuilder in Liverpool. And two shipyards on this coast were prepared to begin revamping the entire Huntley fleet."

"Did you finance this whole operation with proceeds from your railroad?" Doc asked.

Strang looked away. "You're on dangerous ground now, Weatherbee."

"Answer him," Raider entreated.

"All right." Strang smiled. "Yes, I make money on my rail line. But I don't make enough to buy Huntley Shipping. Raider, you were with me. The gaming house, Madam Wu's. I have an interest in both of them. And a few other shady enterprises where I pay the right people to look the other way."

"Admirable," Doc said sarcastically.

Strang's expression became hostile. "Things have a way of moving on their own, Weatherbee. Anytime the law sees fit to close me down, they can come in with their papers. Until then, the city fathers have a way of lining their own purses with gold, if you know what I mean."

Doc only grinned. *"Sir* Lionel Strang. Tell me, for what were you knighted?"

"For meritorious service to the Royal Family."

Doc kept his gaze level. "There are ways to confirm that."

Strang sighed defeatedly. "I was never knighted, Weatherbee. Does that make you happy? The 'sir' is my own invention. I wanted to impress you Yanks, and so far it's worked."

"I'll do my best to keep your secret," Doc offered.

"I'm sure you bloody well will!"

Doc had other things on his mind. "Let's turn our attention to the events of this morning. The attack on you by members of the Tong."

Strang's face paled at the mention of the attempt on his life. "Weatherbee, I swear to Saint Joseph that I never had any dealings with the Tong."

"Not even with your involvement in Madam Wu's?"

"She pays them something," Strang replied. "And I give her some tribute from the gaming house. But she's always taken care of that."

"Maybe she wants you out of the way," Raider offered. "Or maybe the Tong wants to move in and take over everything. Could be that Madam Wu is shortin' them on their cut."

Doc waved both of them off. "We are not here to protect Sir Lionel from his enemies. In fact, we are here to determine his guilt or innocence. Peripheral activities are not our concern."

Strang stood up, hands on hips. "You just want to hang me, is that it?"

Doc smiled. *"If* you killed Theodore Huntley."

"I swear I didn't."

The man from Boston shrugged his shoulders. "I wish I could believe you, Strang, but there are too many loose ends that need to be knotted. We must continue our investigation with or without your help."

Sir Lionel's expression of dismay eased into a look of curiosity. "You probably think I'm going to resist you every step of the way."

"That had crossed my mind," Doc replied.

"Well, you're wrong," Strang insisted. "In fact, I'm going to do everything I can to help prove my innocence. Penelope!"

He called twice more before the tall, slender young lady entered the office. Raider thought she was attractive, even with the thick wool dress and the wire-rimmed glasses. Brown hair, blue eyes, thin, aristocratic neck. Prominent forehead, strong chin, straight nose. The clothes hid her body, but the big man could guess as to the curves hidden there.

"This is my new personal secretary, Penelope Bloodsworth. I hired her recently to take care of my correspondence, but now I'm assigning her to help you two gentlemen."

Penelope nodded, her face blank and unreadable. "Good day, sirs," she said in a delightful English accent. "Your names, please?"

"This is Raider," Strang said, "and the gentleman in the tricot suit is Doc Weatherbee."

"Raider? Is that what they call you?" she asked in her blank tone.

The big man nodded. "Yes'm."

He knew she was too proper for him. Best not to get any ideas. Especially with Doc on the warpath.

Penelope turned her brown eyes on the man from Boston. "Doc Weatherbee. Should I call you Doc or Mr. Weatherbee?"

No reply from the gentleman Pinkerton.

Raider glanced at his partner, who had turned as white as a ghost. Sweat beaded his forehead. His eyes were focused on the young woman, but he seemed to be looking straight through her. His lips trembled, as if to speak, but not a single sound came out of his mouth.

Raider smiled at Miss Bloodsworth. "Call him Doc. Don't worry, he's just a little agitated right now."

Penelope glared defiantly at the man from Boston, taking his silence as an insult. Raider saw the tension between them. He regarded Penelope. Yeah, she was the type.

Proper, refined-looking, stiff as a board. One look and Doc was petrified.

Doc shook his head, seeming to come out of it. "Um . . . I applaud your efforts to help us, Sir Lionel, but you must understand that this in no way lessens the suspicions directed at yourself."

Sir Lionel stepped out from behind the desk. "I'm trembling in my boots, Weatherbee. Now, if you will excuse me, Penelope will assist you further. If you need me, I'll be in my rooms above. Good day, gentlemen."

Sir Lionel left them with Penelope.

Doc gazed at her once again, the sweat gathering on his brow.

Penelope glared back at the Boston-bred detective. "This investigation is a sham," she offered immediately. "My employer did not kill that man, I can assure you."

Doc mopped his forehead before he challenged the lovely Miss Bloodsworth. "'The mind of man doth tend to and seek after truth,'" he said grandly. "Sir Walter Raleigh said that."

Penelope grimaced. "No, I believe it was Sir Philip Sidney."

Doc was taken aback. Raider had to smile. Nobody ever challenged Doc on anything, much less his quotes.

Doc stammered his words. "But . . . well . . . it could . . . I mean . . ."

"Look it up," she rejoined.

Her blue eyes were devastating. Raider almost found himself melting. The effect on Doc was much worse. Maybe he hadn't recovered from the fight with the Comancheros. Something was weak inside him. Maybe his heart.

"I hope you intend to look elsewhere for the killer of Theodore Huntley," Miss Bloodsworth offered. "I assure you, Sir Lionel did not kill anyone. Do you hear me, Mr. Weatherbee?"

Doc nodded absently, but then with a forced air of bravado, he replied, "If you know so much about literature, Miss Bloodsworth, perhaps you are familiar with this quotation: 'They also serve who only stand and wait.'"

"Milton, isn't it?" she said with a haughty smile.

"Very good," Doc continued. "You should take the sentiment at face value. Wait, while we attend to the investigation. *We'll* name your role in the proceedings, but in the meantime, you should keep your nose out of our business."

Raider was enjoying the verbal fencing. Doc seemed to be getting the worst of it. Penelope's face never wavered. What the hell would she look like with that hair down around her shoulders?

"To paraphrase Shakespeare, Mr. Weatherbee, my name is not frailty. Just because I am a woman, don't think that you can stop me from speaking my mind. I'll say what I please. Is that understood?"

When Doc just sat there, Raider said it was understood completely.

Penelope thrust her nose into the air and sat down behind the desk.

Raider looked back and forth between her and Doc. It was a rocky damned beginning. But Penelope was the type. She could get to Doc. As far as Raider could see, the man from Boston didn't have a chance.

Doc straightened himself, summoning every bit of his sense of propriety. "Miss Bloodsworth, if you'll please excuse us, I'd like to speak to my partner alone."

Penelope's full mouth formed a perfect pout. "I see that you're going to dismiss me as if I were nothing."

"Sir Lionel instructed you to assist us," Doc said.

"Yes, but I—"

"Then please assist us by kindly leaving the room."

She blushed, her fair white skin turning a horrid shade of pink. For an instant, she turned to regard Raider, who was sympathetic but thought it best not to rile Doc. He nodded, prompting Miss Bloodsworth to storm out of the office, leaving a hostile cloud of emotion behind her.

Raider grinned slyly. "You two was made for each other."

"I beg your pardon!" Doc protested. "I can't stand that horrid woman. The nerve of her. You'd think she was a man. Such impudence."

"Yeah, I liked her too."

Doc shook off his partner's implication. "Enough. I'd like to hear your observations concerning Sir Lionel. Try to keep them as unbiased as possible."

Raider tipped back his Stetson and slumped in the wooden chair. "I don't know, Doc. He seemed to be glad to see me, but he wasn't really shocked that we were on the case. 'Course, he did say that he hadn't knowed until now that we had been hired by the police."

"He was obviously lying," Doc replied. "He was ready to offer you more compensation when you walked in here."

Raider leaned forward a little. "All right, but you pushed him hard. You made him come clean about some of his shadier businesses. He told you the truth. He didn't have to do that."

Doc reached for a cigar in his pocket. "Yes, you're right. Only he was all too quick to confess. He probably figured we would find out about his nefarious activities sooner or later, so he really had nothing to lose by telling us everything."

Raider frowned at his partner. "All right, Mr. Smarty-pants, maybe he did reckon we'd catch on. But you're missin' somethin' that jumps out at me like a Comanche warrior leapin' off a rock."

"I'm listening."

"Okay," Raider continued, "say he did have somethin' to do with Huntley's killin'. Now that other boy at the shippin' place won't deal with him."

"Gilmore?"

"Yeah, that's the one. So Gilmore won't come around. What's to stop Sir Lionel from puttin' the whammy on him, huh? Just get him out of the way like the other one. If he wants all this stuff so bad, what would stop him from usin' force again?"

Doc puffed on his cigar, staring at the ceiling. "Exposure," he replied. "Now that he's in the public eye, namely the eye of the police, Strang can't risk trying another deadly maneuver. If something were to happen to Gilmore, Strang would draw more attention to himself."

"Hell," Raider offered, "if this company is in such bad shape, why didn't Gilmore sell out to him anyway?"

"Family loyalty, perhaps. He might be a man of integrity. He might just be scared of Strang."

Raider shook his head dejectedly. "I just don't think he has much to hide, otherwise he wouldn't be so straight with us."

"Sometimes," Doc replied, "the best place to hide something is in plain sight. You're also forgetting that *Sir*

Lionel has a bogus title. He invented his knighthood to further enhance his image and credibility. A man who hides behind a name may be guilty of past crimes that are far worse than you and I can imagine."

The veins bulged in Raider's neck as he grew madder. "What about that secretary, huh? And this office?"

"The office allows him to keep an eye on us," Doc replied confidently. "And the girl . . . well, you should be able to figure that out yourself."

Raider's eyes narrowed. "What are you talkin' about?"

"Another offering," Doc replied. "A distraction, the way he took you to the casino and to Madam Wu's. No doubt he hopes that one of us will fall head over heels for Miss Bloodsworth. Or even better, that we will fight over her."

"Yeah, well, maybe he was right about one thing. You sure turned a whole circle when she came in."

Doc glared at the big man. "How dare you!"

"Don't be too quick to groan, Doc. You're gonna make me think I'm right."

They locked eyes, Raider with his coyote smile and Doc with his refined expression of indignity. A fight might have ensued, but all fisticuffs were postponed by the entrance of Miss Penelope Bloodsworth. Doc turned toward her, expecting the same hateful look that had marked her recent exit. Instead, he saw the soft, glowing face of a frightened woman.

Penelope did not regard Doc, but rather focused her brown eyes on the Arkansas cowboy. "Mr. Raider, might I possibly talk to you alone for a few moments? Please?"

Raider stood up. "Well, I don't know."

Penelope slid next to him, peering into his eyes with her doleful face upturned. "You seem to understand Sir Lionel better than your partner. If I could have few moments of your time, I might convince you to—"

Doc stepped between them, pushing Miss Bloodsworth back toward Sir Lionel's desk. "Do you really think that tactic is going to work, Miss Bloodsworth? Separating us? Well, it won't, you hear me! If you have anything to say, hold forth to both of us."

She turned away, fighting with herself. What did she have to tell them? Doc moved closer to her, spinning her around. She would not look at him.

"Tell us the truth, Miss Bloodsworth. Did Sir Lionel hire you to distract us? To come between us?"

"You wouldn't believe a thing I told you!" she cried.

Doc tried to pull her close to him, a gesture of comfort. Penelope only shrugged away, turning toward the desk, crying. Doc seemed helpless in the wake of her tears. Raider knew the feeling. When they started to cry, it was all over.

Raider reached into his pocket and took out a ten-dollar bill. "Here, Doc, take this money. You and the little lady there have dinner on me."

"Where are you going?" Doc asked.

"To take a nap," Raider replied. "I'll meet you back at the hotel in a couple of hours."

Doc grabbed his arm. "You aren't going to leave me alone with her, are you?"

Raider winked. "Hell, I reckon y'all deserve each other."

Penelope turned around, raging at him. "You're just as impudent as your partner. But wait." All the air seemed to go out of her. "Don't go. I mean, I'll help you. Both of you. I don't mean to be difficult, but these have been trying times for Sir Lionel."

Raider squinted at her. "I thought you only been working for Sir Lionel a little while."

She lowered her brown eyes. "Well, yes, only a few weeks, but it grates on you. I mean, the police have been here and. . . . I'm just bloody well tired of it!"

Raider started for the door. "Well, you two work it out. Send for me if you both decide to start actin' grown-up."

He slammed the door behind him.

Doc and Penelope turned to one another at the same time. Penelope averted her eyes, showing a cold shoulder to Doc. There was an awkward moment where neither of them knew what to do.

Doc's voice was hesitant. "Miss Bloodsworth, did you mean what you just said? About helping us, I mean?"

She spun quickly toward him, her eyes suddenly hopeful. There was a new strength in her voice, summoned from inner reserves. "Yes," she replied. "I do want to help. But I know Sir Lionel, I don't think he—"

"Shh, let me worry about those things. If Sir Lionel is innocent, I will find out sooner or later."

Her lower lip bulged somewhat. "But you don't believe he is innocent, do you?"

Doc sighed deeply. "Dear girl, what I think or don't think makes no difference. If we work in the right direction, the facts will ultimately present themselves."

"I'm telling you, Sir Lionel did not kill Teddy Huntley!"

He frowned at her. "Teddy, eh? Did you know him?"

She shook her head. "I've only heard his name before."

Doc stared into her brown irises. "Miss Bloodsworth, you've exhibited an extraordinary amount of passion and interest regarding this case."

Turning away, she moved toward the window. "Why, I don't know what you mean, Mr. Weatherbee."

"Well," he said, slipping up behind her. "If you don't know the deceased, then it must mean that you feel closer to someone else." He spun her toward him, holding her shoulders. "It's Sir Lionel, isn't it? You're in love with him!"

"Preposterous!" she cried. "I never! You insolent blackguard!" Her hand came up, delivering a stinging slap.

Doc winced. He released his grip on her and gingerly lifted his hand to his cheek. "You protest too much, milady." He smiled broadly, thinking he had bested her.

Penelope straightened herself stoically. "If you won't be needing me any more today, I'll excuse myself. I have much business to clear up for Sir Lionel."

"I'd wager that you do," he replied coldly.

She glared at him. Her words were slow, calculated. "I sense that you are a good man, Mr. Weatherbee. But you insist on being stubborn. I agree with you that the truth will indeed present itself, but it will not necessarily be what you had in mind. Remember what I have told you. It may haunt your dreams someday."

"If you don't leave at this moment, I shall!"

She darted from the office.

Doc was livid. He tried not to think of her. He lit his cigar and sat down at Sir Lionel's desk. He wanted to go over some of Strang's private papers. Better that Penelope was not there.

Doc thought he heard laughter from the third floor. His

eyes narrowed as he leaned back in Strang's chair. He tried to go back to the papers, but he found that he could not sit still. He found that he had an urge to move, to ask questions, to inquire about the dealings of a certain Englishman.

He got up and headed for the stairs, pausing only once to look up toward Sir Lionel's quarters. He could not see Penelope laughing with Strang, but the unmistakable tone of her voice resounded in the stairwell. With weak legs and one hand firmly on the banister, Doc descended toward the street below.

CHAPTER 12

When Raider left Sir Lionel Strang's office, he had no intention of going back to the hotel for a nap. The way the big man had it figured, he had to handle a few things by himself. Doc wasn't up to snuff yet; he still hadn't recovered one hundred percent. Doc's trouble with the woman was proof of that. Usually, the gentleman Pinkerton had the ladies in the palm of his hand, wooing and cooing with all his refined charms. But Penelope Bloodsworth had thrown Doc for a fall, causing him to lose his composure. It wasn't like Doc, and it wasn't professional.

As he hurried toward the waterfront, Raider had to worry. If he couldn't count on Doc to be rational and helpful, then he had to take up the slack by himself. He considered wiring the agency, to get another man to help him. But after all their years as partners, Raider could not betray Doc in any way. To cut him out of the case would be the same as sticking a knife in his back, something Raider had wanted to do many times during their arguments. He'd just have to tough it out alone if necessary. Maybe Doc would come round eventually. It would sure make things easier.

For the first time in his career as a Pinkerton, Raider considered the drawbacks of working by himself. The big man had never been good at communicating with strangers, especially when delicate questions had to be asked. Doc always handled the interrogations smoothly, with Raider contributing some well-timed force in the tougher instances. Raider figured if he was going to be asking the questions, he had better try to be a little more subdued. He wondered if he had the patience to pull it off.

A stiff breeze blew in from the bay, chilling the late morning air. Raider never got used to the San Francisco weather. How the hell could it be so cold on a midsummer day? The waterfront was even colder.

A few inquiries led him to the offices of Huntley Shipping. One name had been popping up along with the others, and that was Judd Gilmore, the de facto head of the shipping firm. Captain McCurley had seemed reasonably convinced of Gilmore's innocence in the matters at hand, but Raider knew from experience that every stone had to be turned over. The rock you left undisturbed always held the rattlesnake underneath it.

Raider stopped in front of a warehouse where a faded, paint-peeling sign declared HUNTLEY SHIPPING, SAN FRANCISCO AND THE WORLD—a mighty claim for a company that was supposed to be going under. The big man started to search for an entrance, stopping only when he heard the loud voices from the edge of the docks. Two men were quarreling in different languages, English and Chinese. Raider eased down behind a pile of crates to get within earshot of the altercation.

The Chinaman seemed to be getting the best of the argument. He was jumping up and down, ranting at a ratty-looking sailor. The disagreement seemed to be over a long, rectangular crate.

"I told you we got to make room below!" the sailor cried.

Raider peered over the crates, watching as the Chinaman railed on in a jumble of foreign words. The big man caught sight of the ship they were loading, an old clipper named *China Princess II*. He ducked back down behind the crates. Why did the name of the clipper seem so familiar to him?

The argument did not abate. Raider slid around the side of the crates, watching the two men as they began to shove one another. While they fought, two more Chinese workers came out of the warehouse toting another elongated crate on their shoulders. As they approached the scene of the fight, the sailor pushed the Chinese man toward the men who were carrying the crate. The Chinaman crashed into the bearers, forcing them to drop their burden. The crate shattered as it hit the dock.

Raider saw what looked like carved pieces of wood that had fallen out of the crate. The box had Chinese writing all over it, as though the wood was being shipped out to the Orient. As the men picked up the spilled cargo, Raider realized that the contents of the crate was not wood at all, but rather firearms. The carved wood belonged to the butts and stocks of old Army rifles, single-shot breechloaders.

Forgetting about their differences, the Chinaman and the sailor helped the two dockworkers carry the rifles aboard the clipper. Somebody didn't want the rifles to be seen. But why? It wasn't illegal to ship firearms, unless the guns were stolen. Hell, what did it matter to Raider anyway? The clipper didn't necessarily belong to Huntley Shipping, even if the guns were coming out of the Huntley warehouse. Best to take it up with Judd Gilmore, Raider thought. He might have a few answers if pressed for the truth.

Slipping away from the crates, Raider headed for the warehouse again. A gruff voice stopped him. He turned to see the sailor who had been arguing with the Chinese man. The rough-looking old salt ambled slowly toward the big cowboy. He was weathered, Raider thought, but he had a toughness about him. It might be an interesting fight.

"You got business around this waterfront?" the sailor asked.

Raider saw the long scar from ear to chin. The man had been in a few knife fights. Best to keep an eye on his hands, anticipating the flash of polished steel.

"Lookin' for a man named Judd Gilmore," Raider replied.

The sailor frowned, his scar sagging a little. "Ain't nobody around here by that name. Better move on, mate."

Raider gestured toward the faded sign. "Huntley Shipping," he said.

"So?"

"Man name of Gilmore's mindin' the store now that the Huntley boy got hisself murdered."

The sailor began to inch around, circling the big Pinkerton. "I'm tellin' you to push off, mate."

The three Chinese men had come around to watch them toeing up. Raider moved with the sailor, keeping his arms loose. He wanted to avoid fisticuffs if at all possible. Not that he was afraid of the salty dog, he just didn't feel much like fighting.

"Whoa there, Jack Tar," he said, smiling. "Ain't nobody wants to get hurt here. You savvy?"

"Yer yellow!" the sailor replied with a hearty laugh. "And I'm gonna open you a new pooper." The knife came out of his sleeve, a long, curve-bladed dagger, probably from China or the Japans. "Yer gonna learn not to be stickin' yer head in the wrong hole, mate."

He swung hard with the dagger, barely missing Raider's belly. The big man sprang backward, wondering if he would have to pull the derringer from his back pocket. After watching the sailor's awkward movements, he decided the pistol wouldn't be necessary. He'd try to disarm the salty dog without the help of a bullet.

The sailor began to huff and puff. Raider just kept moving, avoiding the dagger. He felt his back come up against the crates at the edge of the wharf. The sailor charged full force, driving the blade toward Raider's torso. At the last possible instant, Raider moved easily to one side, causing the dagger to lodge and then break in the hardwood of the cargo crates.

He grabbed the salt's arm and brought a knee up into his groin. When he buckled, the Chinese men cheered, clapping their hands. The sailor groaned from the deepest pit of his stomach.

"You ready to quit?" Raider asked.

He just kept moaning, lurching toward the warehouse. Raider started to move for the door, keeping his eyes on the sailor, who lay bent over a pile of rope. The Chinese men cried out when the salt sprang from the rope with a hook in his hand. He started after the big man again.

Raider had had enough. He reached for his derringer, bringing it up quickly. The sailor hesitated, peering at the tiny bore of the weapon.

"Don't let it fool you," Raider warned. "It's big enough to kill you."

"Drop it, mister!"

The call had come from behind him. Raider turned to see a smallish man holding a shotgun on him. With his eyes diverted, the sailor seized the opportunity to charge Raider headlong with the hook. Again the Chinese men cried out, calling Raider's attention to the man in front of him.

The big man waited until the sailor was on him before he stuck out his leg. The sailor tripped and flew face first, thudding at the feet of the man with the shotgun. Raider wheeled with the derringer, facing down the twin barrels of the scattergun.

"Let's see who's ready to pull the trigger," Raider offered.

A wide-eyed stare from the short, balding gunman. He had a long, broad nose, a few black hairs at the temple and in back, was clean-shaven, and wore a dark suit and tie. His reaction indicated that he had never been in a gunfight before. Too much hesitation. Raider could have killed him in a heartbeat.

Raider forced a brave smile. "What say we drop the iron?"

"Who are you?" the shotgun man asked. "What do you want?"

"Name's Raider. Been hired by the police to look after the death of one Theodore Huntley. Come down here to find a man named Gilmore, Judd Gilmore. He's supposed to be in charge now."

The double barrel dropped immediately. "Oh. That's different."

The sailor was up, hiding behind the scattergun. "I tried to tell him you wasn't here, Mr. Gilmore. I knowed you didn't want to be bothered."

The balding man, who was apparently Judd Gilmore, glared at the red-faced seaman. "Ulysses, you fool. This man represents the law. We want to cooperate to the fullest, do you understand?"

"Sorry," Ulysses replied, "I thought he was sent by Strang to spy on us."

Raider eased the gun into his back pocket. "Just payin' a friendly visit, Mr. Gilmore. Heard your name mentioned a couple of times, and I wanted to hear what you had to say."

Gilmore pushed Ulysses away from him. "Get back to work, you fool. And no more fighting with Lee Fong. I want that warehouse cleared before dark."

Ulysses slunk toward the clipper ship, breaking into a jog when he heard the Chinese men making fun of him.

Judd Gilmore shook his head and sighed. "Accept my apologies, mister?"

"Raider."

"Yes, of course." He gestured into the warehouse. "If you'll come along. I'll be happy to answer your questions."

Raider looked back toward the clipper. "That your boat?"

Gilmore squinted, taking a hasty glance before nodding his head.

"Floatin' guns," Raider said blankly. "How come?"

Gilmore wheeled around with a dazed expression on his white face. "It's a contract with the government," he said quickly. "We're disposing of old surplus for the Army, dumping them at sea."

Raider nodded, but then asked, "How come there's Chinese writin' all over them crates?"

"Instructions for the laborers," Gilmore replied. "Would you like to go aboard the ship and have a look?"

"No need. Let's talk in private."

Gilmore's office was at the back of the warehouse. The whole place was dark and dank and full of mysterious crates and bundles. More Chinese workers were busy stacking and sorting.

"Seems to be a lot of activity for a company that's sinkin'," Raider said as soon as he had sat down. "How is that?"

Gilmore, who was sweating now, wiped his brow with a handkerchief. "Don't let appearances deceive you, Mr.

Raider. I'm scrambling here to keep things afloat. One bad week and Huntley Shipping could fold. There'd be nothing left for young Rebecca. Tell me, has anyone heard from her? As the heir to all this, she's entitled to know what's going on. I'd like to think I'm preserving the family business for someone."

"How long you been here?"

"Fifteen years," Huntley replied. "I started with William himself. He was a brilliant man. When he died, well, I suppose you're aware of Theodore's lack of interest in his father's business."

"Yeah, I am," Raider replied, shifting in his chair. "What did you think about young Teddy?"

Gilmore shrugged. "He wasn't all bad. A little too much like a girl, but I always thought that was his upbringing. His father wanted him to be a gentleman, the same way he wanted Rebecca to be a lady. But Theodore was more like a . . . a Philistine. Are you familiar with the Bible?"

Raider said he was, acting like he knew a Philistine from a gopher hole. He reckoned it was something bad. Gilmore didn't think too highly of the departed son. Which led to the next question.

"Mr. Gilmore, why don't you sell half the company to Sir Lionel? If things are as bad as you say, then this daughter may lose everything. Why chance it when there's money to be made?"

Gilmore shook his head, scowling. "Strang is the lowest form of filth in this city! He's responsible for Theodore's murder, everyone is sure of it. Why, look at the way he lied about the papers being signed before Theodore was killed!"

Raider stared right into his eyes. "Strang claims you were one of the witnesses at the signin'."

"Balderdash!" Gilmore cried a little too loudly. "Another untruth! I was there that night. Teddy told him he wouldn't sell. But later that week, Sir Lionel talked him into a last-chance meeting. That was the night Teddy disappeared. Strang claims they never talked, but I was there when Teddy left to go see him."

"Would you sell if Sir Lionel is proven innocent?"

"I . . . why, I don't know . . . I . . . What kind of ridiculous question is that? You're bound to find proof of

Strang's guilt if you keep looking. I'm sure he was the one who killed Teddy."

Raider leaned back, pausing, a trick he had seen Doc perform more than once. After a few awkward moments, he said, "You got a lot of Chinese folks workin' for you, Gilmore."

Gilmore shrugged. "So?"

"Ever have any trouble with the Tong?"

The bald man's eyes narrowed. "Tong?"

"Come on, Judd, you tryin' to tell me you never heard of the Tong? The Black Hand?"

"Well, yes, I have," Gilmore replied hesitantly, "but I've never had any dealings with them. They've never approached me, and I've managed to stay out of their way."

"Couple of boys from the Tong tried to kill Strang last night," Raider offered. "Any ideas about that?"

Gilmore raised an accusing finger. "I'm not surprised. A man like Strang probably has his forks in too many fires. Trying to play both ends against the middle. They could have saved everyone a lot of trouble by doing away with that blackguard."

Raider stirred, starting to rise. "I reckon I heard about enough, Mr. Gilmore. Thank you for your time."

"Wait!"

Raider eased back into the chair.

"I'm sorry," Gilmore replied. "I didn't mean to be so petulant."

"That's okay." Raider didn't know what 'petulant' meant anyway.

"Please," Gilmore said in a desperate tone, "you must find Rebecca Huntley. I fear for her life."

"I'm doin' my best."

"Contact me immediately if you hear any news of her," Gilmore said. "She deserves the best. She's really a fine girl."

"You'll be the first one to know if we hear from her."

"Thank you. Thank you so much."

Raider took Gilmore's sweaty hand, shaking the weak grip. Gilmore showed him to the door, again entreating Raider to inform him of Rebecca Huntley's whereabouts if she showed up. Raider tipped his Stetson and started away, glancing back when he was sure Gilmore had receded into the warehouse.

Raider immediately doubled back, hiding under a canvas that covered a pile of crates. He waited most of the day, watching the comings and goings of Gilmore's men. They continued to load the elongated boxes into the clipper ship, following the last crate with cubical containers that bore the same Chinese writing.

The big man thought dark would never come, but he managed to wait it out. At dusk, the warehouse was closed and locked, and Gilmore and the Chinese men left for home. Raider slid out from under the canvas and headed straight for the *China Princess II*. It was an old bucket of boards, a testimony to Strang's claim that the Huntley fleet was indeed outdated.

Raider hesitated in the dark, peering toward the clipper's deck. No watchman above. He had to get below and look firsthand at the crates. Maybe Gilmore was telling the truth about disposing of the weapons for the Army, but Raider had to see for himself. He stole up the gangplank and headed for the forward hold.

It was dark below, but he managed to find his way between the cargo crates. He counted twenty-five crates of rifles and another twenty of the cube-shaped boxes. His eyes could not make out the writing on the crates. He fumbled in the dimness, searching until his hands found an old lamp with several sulphur matches stuck to the base. When the lamp was aglow, he turned back to the wooden crates.

Some of the writing bore out the claim that the rifles had come from the Army. The point of origin had been Fort Laramie, Wyoming, and the destination was marked Huntley Shipping, San Francisco. Nobody could deny that Gilmore was telling the truth about that.

Raider found the broken box and took out one of the rifles. He tried the lever and found the mechanism to be in working order. The rifle was oiled and ready for use. Why would anyone want to ditch a perfectly good weapon? Of course, the Army had gone to repeaters, which made the breechloaders obsolete. Maybe they had paid Gilmore to get rid of them.

He had to see what was inside the square boxes. Using a

metal pry bar, he loosened the top and reached in, finding smaller containers that were also marked with the Fort Laramie insignia. Raider opened the container to find shiny brass cartridges meant for the breechloaders. Gilmore was dumping perfectly good rifles and perfectly good ammunition. Or was he?

"Well, now, look who's back!"

Raider turned to see the ruddy-faced sailor with a grin that matched the scar on his face.

A knife blade gleamed in the lamplight. "Looks like I got you trespassing this time, mate. I . . . *ugh!*"

Raider had heaved the box of cartridges at him, catching the sailor squarely in the belly. When he bent over, Raider brought up a knee into his face, knocking him backward. Jack Tar hit his head and went out cold.

"Looks like I done caught you sleepin'," Raider mused.

It was time to get the hell out of the cargo ship. He stole up to the deck, moving in the shadows. Someone shouted in Chinese as he tiptoed toward the gangplank. He reached the side of the vessel, but the gangplank was no longer there. The clipper swung away from the dock, heading out into the bay.

Two men were now shouting in Chinese. Raider glanced over his shoulder to see them running straight for him. A gun exploded in the darkness. The slug whizzed by his head. He started to return fire, but two more men came behind the other.

"Ain't no place to be," he muttered to himself.

He took a deep breath and dived headfirst into the cold drink of the bay. Slugs tore through the water around him. Raider kicked deeper, swimming in an uncertain direction. The men above continued to fire at the swirlings on the surface.

Raider swam until he felt his lungs would explode. He came up quickly, sucking for air, expecting the rifle slugs to tear his head open. But there was no more shooting. He looked around, treading water, waiting for his eyes to focus. His wet Stetson floated up next to him. He grabbed the hat and kicked forward, running into the bulkhead of the wharf. The barnacles scraped him as he pulled himself onto the dock. He waited for more men to jump him, but no one came.

Raider trudged along the dock, wet and cold, his boots full of water. There was only one place to go, a place to dry out and maybe get some answers. He headed straight for Madam Wu's, intending to talk to the head lady herself. It was time to find out just what the hell was going on at the waterfront. And Madam Wu seemed like the logical person to ask.

The two men with shotguns stopped Raider as soon as he entered through the weathered door. "Far enough, boy. You just take it on out of here."

"Come to see Madam Wu," Raider replied.

"She ain't open for business." The barrel of the scattergun directed him toward the door. "You come back later."

"I'm a friend of Sir Lionel Strang," he offered. "We was here last night. You boys remember me, don't you?"

They said they had never seen him before in their lives.

Raider sighed and then sneezed. "Look here, boys, I'm wet and feelin' pretty mean right now. If you don't let me pass, I'm gonna come back here with every policeman I can find and we'll take this place apart, board by board, until that lady agrees to talk to me."

Four hammers clicked back on both scatterguns. "Out, cowboy. Or we cut you in two."

Raider started to turn toward the door. "I'll be back."

"Wait!"

A woman's voice resounded through the stairwell. Raider glanced up to see Madam Wu at the top of the stairs. She gave a grand gesture with her silkdraped arm.

"Let him enter. I will talk to him."

Raider clomped up the stairs, past the hateful stares of Madam Wu's men. The Oriental lady gave a polite bow as Raider approached her. He tipped his soggy hat.

"Sorry to bother you, Madam Wu. I just come to—"

"I know why you have come," she said coldly. "But first, you must get out of those wet clothes. Come in. I will have my girls attend you."

"Okay," he replied, "but only one girl at a time. That other thing liked to wore me out."

"As you wish."

She led him through the parlor, back to the same room where he had slept the night before.

The Chinese girl, Wan Chur, appeared to help him undress. Raider was careful to clean his Colt and the derringer, taking the time to douse them with oil brought by Wan Chur. When he was sure the guns were operative again, he reached for the robe that had been spread out on the bed.

Wan Chur slipped up beside him, rubbing her hands over his cold buttocks. "You should be warm," she said softly.

Raider gently pushed her away. "I got to talk to your boss lady first."

"Madam Wu will call you when she is ready," the girl replied. "We have time."

Raider felt the stiffening between his legs. "You sure you don't want to stab me while we're in bed?"

She reached around, taking his cock in her hand. "Why would I do that? Here, feel me." She guided his fingers to the wetness of her cunt. "I have no weapons there. You can find out for yourself when you enter me."

Raider pulled her close, pressing his lips to her soft mouth. Their tongues mingled, their hands began heated explorations. Wan Chur pushed him back on the bed, using her mouth on him. Raider allowed her a few minutes before he turned her over, putting her on her backside.

"No," she moaned. "From behind."

"We do it my way this time."

She spread her dark thighs, inviting him inside. Raider prodded her wet crevice until he entered with one quick thrust. Wan Chur shivered, a blank grin on her mouth.

"Shake the bed," she whispered. "Shake me."

Raider obliged her, driving his cock in and out until he achieved the desired effect for both of them. When he had climaxed, he rolled off her, reclining on the bed, feeling a lot warmer than he had upon entering the cathouse.

He sat up and reached for the robe again.

"No!" Wan Chur grabbed his hand, guiding it to her smallish breast. "Stay with me," she moaned. "Just for a little while. Hold me."

Raider shook his head. "I got to see your boss lady."

"I'm telling you, she'll call when she's ready. I'm supposed to keep you company until then."

"Nope. I'm ready now."

He started to get off the bed.

"Wan Chur is right." A female voice came from the shadows on the other side of the room. "Madam Wu isn't ready to receive you yet."

"You!"

The blonde from the night before stepped toward the bed. "Yes, I was watching just now. You know, Raider, you're about the best cocksman we've ever had in here. Sir Lionel is a close second, but nobody—"

"Spare me the soap," Raider replied. "What's goin' on here? Why are you two tryin' to keep me from seein' Madam Wu?"

The blonde laughed. "You wouldn't believe me if I told you."

"Try me."

"All right. Every day at this time, Madam Wu prays, or at least something close to it. She's what you call a Buddhist. Does a lot of funny things in front of an altar. It ain't that much different than real religion. I was brought up a Catholic, you know."

Raider laughed. "Yeah, I bet you go to Sunday meetin' ever' chance you get."

She eased down on the bed next to Raider. "She'll be finished in a little while. Until then, why don't you let me . . ." She reached for his crotch.

Raider pushed her hand away. "Ain't much left down there."

The blonde swung around, kneeling in front of him. "Let me try it. I can bring it back to life."

"Hey," Wan Chur protested. "He's mine."

The blonde scowled at her partner in bed. "Oh, shut up, Wan Chur, you spoiled little bitch. You've had your turn."

The Chinagirl got off the bed and stomped across the room. "Well, I'm going to watch, just like you did."

Raider sighed. "Ladies, why don't you leave me alone?"

The blonde lifted his cock toward her mouth. "I will go if I can't make you hard. . . . My God, what a big one."

She made him hard. Raider had to take her through the paces. They did it several ways, ending up in a canine posture. When Raider came, the blonde collapsed into the pillow, gasping for air. Raider flopped down on the sheets, lying back, trying to find his own breath. He felt sleepy, but he knew he had to stay awake. The water and the wet clothes had taken a lot out of him.

"One of you women think you can find me somethin' hot to drink?"

Wan Chur slid on the bed next to him. "How about tea and whiskey?"

Raider was about to say that tea and whiskey would be fine. But a woman screamed somewhere in the house. He sat up immediately. Suddenly his eyes were wide open. The last thing on his mind was a long nap.

CHAPTER 13

Raider leapt off the bed, grabbing the robe to cover his nakedness. He picked up the freshly oiled Colt and started through the dim shadows of the brothel. Again the woman cried out, but this time her voice was smaller than before. Raider hesitated, trying to determine which room she was in.

Wan Chur slid beside him, clutching a silk robe to her neck. "It's Madam Wu," the girl cried. "I know it."

"Where is she?"

"In the back, where she prays."

Wan Chur led the way, taking him through the house. The door to Madam Wu's chapel was locked. Raider opened it with a hard shoulder.

The assassin wheeled around when the door splintered. His face was covered with a black cloth that hid everything but his eyes. Raider lifted the Peacemaker, but the man was too fast. He moved toward the open window where he had entered. The fiery discharge from the Colt missed him by inches.

"Raider!" Wan Chur screamed and pointed to the left.

A second man ran out of the shadows, a weapon lifted over his head. Raider fanned the hammer of the .45, blasting two holes in the man's chest. He staggered forward and flopped onto the floor, his body twitching in a pool of his own blood.

Raider stepped over him and ran to the window. He heard the ruckus from the bushwhacker who was escaping into the alley. Raider fired the rest of his shots at the shadow that fled into the night.

Wan Chur cried out frantically, calling him back into the room. "She's hurt. Raider, she's hurt."

The big man peered toward the red and gold altar where Madam Wu lay slumped over incense and candles. "Easy there, Wan Chur. Let me have a look at her."

Raider put down the Colt to attend the wounded lady. He rolled her over to see the polished hatchet protruding from the middle of her chest. Blood poured from the wound, staining the Chinese woman's flimsy silk garment. Her eyes flickered open. Raider looked down into her blank death stare.

"Hold still, woman," he said in a soft voice. "We're gonna get you to a doctor."

"No," she whispered. "I am dead."

Raider lifted her head. "You ain't no such thing."

Her thin lips moved for the last time, proving him wrong. "The White Dragon," she moaned. "Whi . . . Dra . . ."

Then she was gone.

Wan Chur hovered over the body, shrieking like a madwoman.

The blonde appeared at the door, followed by several of the other women who worked in the house. "Is she . . . Oh my God!"

Raider waved them back. "Nothin' we can do for her. Y'all clear out of here. Not you, blondie. You stay."

The golden-haired girl moved in to comfort Wan Chur. She cradled the Chinagirl in her arms, muffling her sobs in her bosom. She peered over Wan Chur's shoulder, tears in her eyes.

Raider turned back to the body. He grabbed the hatchet handle and yanked the shiny blade from Madam Wu's chest. The weapon clearly belonged to a member of the

Tong. He held it up for the blond girl.

"Don't show me that," she cried, looking away.

Raider went to the body of the man he had killed and found a hatchet that was identical to the one that had murdered Madam Wu. "Tong," he said to the blonde. "They wanted her dead. You got any notion why?"

She shook her head.

Raider lifted the black cloth from the dead man's face. "Yep, he's a Chinaman. There was two of them the last time they tried this."

He glared at the two girls who held each other tightly. "Y'all must know somethin'. Why'd she have to tell me about that white dragon?"

Wan Chur glanced up, wiping her eyes. "She never said anything about it before. I never heard her say anything."

"That's right," the blonde seconded.

Raider held up the hatchet again. "The Tong done split her open, and you tell me she didn't have nothin' to do with them?"

"She paid the Tong every week!" Wan Chur cried.

The blonde pushed her away. "Shut up, Wan Chur. That ain't none of his business."

"This killin' is my business," Raider replied. "Go on, Wan Chur."

"The Tong knew about this place," the girl insisted. "But they left her alone. She didn't pay much, a few hundred dollars a week. That was all they wanted."

"What about this white dragon?" he asked.

Wan Chur shook her head. "I don't know."

Raider exhaled. "Damn me, if she was payin' the Tong, why would they kill her? Unless . . ."

Wan Chur's eyes were wide. "What?"

"Maybe she was gonna tell me somethin'," Raider replied. "And I reckon she did with this white dragon stuff."

He turned his black eyes on the blonde. "You sure the white dragon don't mean anything to you, honey?"

She shook her head. "I'm a white girl. Madan Wu never let me in on any secrets. But I can tell you one thing, mister. If you go askin' for trouble with the Tong, they're gonna give it to you."

Raider gestured toward the body of the dead man. "Looks like they already tried."

He stepped back to the body of Madam Wu. The blood had started to dry on her chest. If she hadn't wanted to pray, she might still be alive. His head was spinning as he tried to sort it all out.

"Reckon I better get the police captain," he said finally.

The blonde stepped in to stop him as he went for the door. "No coppers," she said. "We'll take care of it."

"But they should—"

"No," Wan Chur replied. "She's right. This is our problem. We'll take care of it. If you see Strang, you can tell him. But don't tell the police. They'll just hurt us if you do."

Raider shook his head. "Goddamn bodies pilin' up like a tornado's been through here, and you two don't want me to tell anybody."

"They don't want to know," the blonde replied. "They'd just as soon stay out of our business."

"All right," he said. "I won't tell the police. But you can bet your ass on one thing."

The blonde's eyes shifted nervously. "What?"

"I'm gonna tell Strang," the big man replied. "And he's gonna give me a few answers!"

"Madam Wu is dead."

Strang looked up from the papers on his desk. "What!"

Raider dropped the bloody hatchet in front of the Englishman. "Tong. Opened her up this evenin'. I was there to ask her some questions. They got to her before I could finish what I started."

Sir Lionel got up, pacing nervously about his office. Raider watched him. He didn't seem surprised, only scared.

Raider, whose clothes were still damp, sat down in the chair opposite the desk. "Sir Lionel, I think it's high time you told me about your connections to the Tong."

The Englishman turned to look at him. "*My* connections! I have no connections at all."

"The girls told me that Madam Wu was payin' money to the Tong ever' week. Then they up and kill her. Either she missed a payment or—"

"I know nothing of that!" Strang cried. "Nothing, do you hear me! Madam Wu took care of everything. I know nothing of her dealings with the Tong. I told you that before."

Raider eyed the Englishman. "You wouldn't be the white dragon, would you, Strang?"

Sir Lionel flinched. "Where did you hear that name?"

"From Madam Wu. It was the last thing from her mouth before she died. Sound familiar?"

Strang sighed and sat down behind his desk. "Yes, it sounds all too familiar. But it isn't me, I tell you. No one knows the identity of the White Dragon. He—or she—has strong ties to the Black Hand."

"A white man?" Raider asked.

"Yes, or a woman. I told you, no one knows. It could be the name of an organization. Or it could be one person."

"What's this White Dragon got on the Tong?"

Strang lifted the hatchet. "I don't know, Raider. I really don't. Usually the Tong refuses to deal with anyone outside their organization. But the White Dragon is in league with the Black Hand."

Raider's eyes narrowed. "How come you didn't tell me all of this before? You seem to know a whole bunch about it."

"I didn't think it mattered," Strang replied. "After all, you are looking for Theodore Huntley's killer."

Raider nodded. "True. But it looks like I uncovered a whole lot more. You think this White Dragon had anything to do with killin' Huntley?"

"Why should they?" Strang replied. "Huntley never dealt with them. He knew nothing of the Tong, either. He only came to San Francisco to deal with me. Why would the Chinese want him dead?"

"Lots of Chinamen workin' for Judd Gilmore," Raider offered. "You know anything about that?"

"It's not uncommon to have Oriental workers in a waterfront business. Practically every shipping company in San Francisco has some Chinese on the payroll."

Raider stood up, pointing a finger at Strang. "Look here, Sir Lionel, the barn dance is over. You and me had a few chuckles, but it's time for you to come clean. You better tell me everything you know about the Tong and about this White Dragon. And you better tell me now, otherwise there ain't gonna be a thing I can do for you when they tie the noose around your neck."

Sir Lionel jumped to his feet, glaring back at the big man. "I am telling you the truth, by God! How can I prove it to you?"

"Good question. How can you?"

Strang snorted and then stormed out of the office.

Raider wondered if he had been wrong about the Englishman. Maybe Doc had been onto something with his suspicions. Maybe Strang was trying to lead Raider off the path when he offered him girls and gambling. It was time to find the man from Boston and talk it over.

"Raider?"

He turned toward the sweet voice that had come from the shadows. Penelope Bloodsworth eased into the office. Her brown hair was down, touching her white shoulders. She looked up at him with those soft eyes. Her full lips were trembling as she spoke to him.

"Raider, you're wrong about Sir Lionel."

The big man frowned. "You readin' my mind?"

She put her hands on his arms. "I'm telling you, Sir Lionel has done nothing. I've been working with him for nearly a month. I know all about his enterprises."

"Did you know about Madam Wu's?"

She nodded sorrowfully. "Yes. Oh, I admit that he's a bit of a rogue. A scoundrel even. But he hasn't killed anyone. Of that I can assure you."

"I wish I could believe you, honey. But things ain't lookin' so good for your boss man. Madam Wu was killed tonight."

"No!"

He nodded, peering down into her wide eyes. "I'm afraid so. And you know as well as I do that she was one of your boss's business partners."

Penelope buried her pretty face in Raider's chest, hugging him. "No! It can't be."

"Seems like doin' business with your boss is dangerous."

She looked up again. "No, Raider. He didn't have anything to do with her death. He was here all evening. He never went out."

"Things like that can be ordered," he replied, carefully

studying her face. "Maybe it was ordered by the White Dragon."

Her face was blank, no recognition of the name. "Who?"

"I ain't sure," he replied. "Madam Wu said it right before she died. The White Dragon. Ever hear it before?"

"No, I . . ." She began to sob.

Raider pulled her close to him, stroking her brown hair. "Don't fret, honey. I'm gonna get to the bottom of this."

Her arms wrapped around his waist. "Please," she entreated, "stay with me for a little while."

"I can't, sweetheart." He kissed her forehead. "I got to go find my partner."

"Don't bother," came the rejoinder from across the room. "Your partner is already here."

Doc Weatherbee sauntered into the office with an expression of satisfied anger on his countenance. "So," he said dramatically, "the moment I turn my back, you two can't wait to fly into each other's arms."

Raider gently pushed Penelope away from him. The Englishwoman straightened herself, affecting a tight-lipped glare of indifference. Raider felt guilty, even though he knew there was nothing to fret over. Doc had no claim to Penelope, even if he was acting to the contrary.

Doc pointed a finger at Raider. "I suppose I should have known you'd try somethin' like this." Then, to Penelope: "Miss Bloodsworth, I thought you had some breeding, but I can see now that your tastes run to the lowbrow side."

Raider grimaced, shaking his head. "Doc, it wasn't like that."

Penelope smiled wickedly. "Let him think what he will, Raider. I don't give a whit for his presumptuous attitude."

"Now y'all stop usin' them twenty-dollar words," Raider said. "Let's all simmer down and . . . Doc . . . you better not!"

But Doc did it anyway. He swung from the basement with a right hand that Raider saw coming a mile away. The big Pinkerton lurched to one side, avoiding the brunt of the blow. He decided not to give Doc another chance to hit him. When the man from Boston swung the left, Raider blocked it and then hammered a solid left hook to Doc's rib cage.

Weatherbee grunted and stumbled backward, slamming into the wall. He gasped for air, trying to find the breath Raider had knocked out of him. His face turned a dull shade of red that quickly changed to purple.

Penelope knelt beside Doc and touched his cheek. She glanced back at Raider with horror in her face. "Do something."

Raider shrugged. "He'll come out of it,"

Doc drew in a long, wheezing breath. His head shook as he filled his lungs. The normal color came back to his skin after a few minutes.

"Damn you, Raider!" he said immediately upon the return of his voice.

Raider tried not to laugh. "You had it comin', Doc."

Penelope was still gazing into Doc's blue eyes. "Mr. Weatherbee?" Both hands were caressing his face. "Are you quite all right?"

Doc scowled at her. "How could you let him hold you like that?"

"I'm afraid," she replied.

He pushed her hands away. "As well you should be. When you hear what I've got to say!"

Penelope stood abruptly, her body going rigid. "Nothing you have to say interests me!"

She started for the stairs.

"Penelope!" Doc scuffled to his feet. "Penelope, you come back here this instant!"

Raider flopped down in the chair behind Strang's desk. "You ain't gonna tell that one what to do, Doc."

The man from Boston turned back to his partner. "You never give it up, do you? Every woman has to be a target for you. You can't bear to let one pass you by without trying to—"

"Save it," the big man replied, waving a hand in the air. "The girls at Madam Wu's have been takin' care of me. I got no reason to go after your little lady there."

"*My* little lady!"

Raider grinned, "Well, she won't be yours for long if you don't stop all this childish nonsense. We got us a humdinger of a case here, Doc. There's a whole lot of shit fallin' down at the waterfront. If you're willin' to get your head out of your butt, I'll tell you all about it."

"Oh you will!" Doc replied huffily. "Well, go ahead and say your piece. Then I may just have a few surprises for you!"

Raider's eyes narrowed into a hostile squint. "You want to go at it again, Doc? You're startin' to make me mad."

Doc sat politely in a wooden chair, folding his hands over his lap. "I'm listening."

Raider nodded. "That's better. Now, I called on Judd Gilmore today."

"Oh, really?"

"Don't keep talkin' that snot-talk," Raider warned. "Just sit there with your flap closed and hear me out. Now, Gilmore seemed nervous to me, which could mean a lot of things. But there was somethin' else."

"And what might that be?"

Raider shot him another angry look. "One more time . . ."

"Go on, go on."

"Gilmore's men was loadin' rifles onto a clipper ship. Hell what was the name of that boat? Anyway, Gilmore said the rifles was supposed to be dumped for the Army. Only, I hopped on board myself and had a look-see. The rifles was in good workin' order and there was plenty of ammunition loaded with them. There was also a lot of Chinese men workin' for Gilmore."

Doc frowned. "Well what does that have to do with anything?"

"Just this. There's a connection somewhere in this thing between the Tong and somebody called the White Dragon."

"Preposterous!"

"Madam Wu was killed tonight," the big man continued. "The Tong went after her. Only she was supposed to be payin' them to stay off her back. Anyway, right after I pulled the hatchet out of her, the last words off her lips was 'White Dragon'. She was tryin' to tell me somethin', only they got to her before she could."

"Are you finished?" Doc asked patronizingly.

"Well, just to say this. I think this White Dragon is one

of the local outlaws. He's strong, too. Why else would the
Tong do business with him? I think Theodore Huntley
found out somethin' he wasn't supposed to know. He was
killed either by the Tong or by this White Dragon."

"Is that all?"

Raider nodded.

Doc stood up, ceremoniously dusting his suit. "Now I
shall refute your claims one by one. First, I paid a call on
Judd Gilmore myself. He told me the exact same story
about the rifles. Only, I bothered to wire the U.S. Army
post north of here and they confirmed the story. They're
paying Huntley Shipping to dump those guns at sea."

"They say anything about ammunition?"

"I didn't ask," Doc replied. "I didn't have to. Gilmore
strikes me as honest. I checked with a few of his colleagues
and clients. He has an unblemished reputation."

Raider grimaced, shaking his head. "That's one. What
about the Chinese all over the place down there?"

Doc shrugged. "San Francisco has a large Chinese section. It makes sense that they would seek work on the waterfront."

"And the Tong?"

Doc sighed impatiently. "Raider, you're stretching here.
The Tong, a murdered proprietor of a whorehouse, some
fictional character called the White Dragon. It sounds like
a fairy tale. And even if some of it is true, it has nothing to
do with the case we're assigned to. I'm sorry, your facts
just don't stand up in the face of real evidence."

Raider scowled at his pretentious partner. "Real evidence, huh? I suppose you've got a ton of real evidence."

Doc pulled a piece of paper out of his coat pocket. "Not
a ton, but enough. And all of it points toward Sir Lionel."

Raider wasn't sure he was going to like what came
next, but he figured he owed it to Doc to listen.

"Strang is a scalawag, Raider. He thinks nothing of
breaking the law when it suits him. The customs agency
has a list of violations as long as your arm. Mind you,
nothing he could be locked up for, but he has paid several
fines."

"He did pay them, then?" Raider queried.

"Yes, but that doesn't make him innocent. It makes him

guilty. The same holds true for his dealings in Nevada and Colorado. He was taken to court and sued for breach of contract in a land deal. He was found guilty and had to pay a substantial penalty."

"Paid again?"

Doc just smiled. "He fought a duel in Louisiana, and a warrant still exists there for his arrest. The other party didn't die, but he was wounded for life."

Raider chortled. "Who started the fight in the first place?"

Doc ignored him. "Strang is not from London, but from Liverpool. He started in the streets and worked his way to America. Since he's been here, he's been making money any way he can. In fact, he never even let on to the true extent of his empire."

"Keep goin'," Raider urged, his interest piqued.

"The rail and the shipping lines are small change when you look at his importing operation. He brings in goods on both coasts. That's why he wants Huntley Shipping, so he doesn't have to deal with the middleman. Though nothing has been proven as yet, Strang is under investigation for several things, including the proposition that he's an importer of opium and other contraband goods."

Raider leaned forward a little. "Anybody prove anything yet?"

"Damn it, man, will you stop defending him! Can't you see that Strang is involved in more than one heinous activity? Why, he may even be this White Dragon you've been harping about."

Raider nodded reluctantly. "Maybe he is. Hell, I don't know what to believe anymore."

"You can't deny the facts!"

Raider leaned back, his hands behind his head. "You're forgettin' somethin' too, Doc. All of this evidence don't point to Strang as the killer of Theodore Huntley. He may have a rotten core, but how can we prove he killed anybody?"

Doc began to pace back and forth. He had a plan. They would draw Strang out and force him to incriminate himself. If they backed him into a corner, he would crack sooner or later.

Raider disagreed. He felt it would be better just to pull out and hand the whole thing back over to the police. There were too many loose ends.

Doc frowned at the big man. "You've never been one to give up, Raider."

He shrugged defeatedly. "We ain't been workin' together on this one, Doc. We've been goin' in two different directions. Maybe we oughta get out. If the police still want Pinks on the case, they can get replacements."

"You refuse to believe me!"

"It ain't that, Doc. It's just that nothin' has come together on this case. And I think you're crazy to overlook this thing with the Tong. If you don't keep watch over your shoulder, you could wind up blown to bits."

"I still say we ought to flush out my plan. It could work if you'd cooperate. You're suspicious of Gilmore."

"I didn't say that," the big man protested. "I said there were some funny things goin' on down there. Hell, Gilmore may not be involved. He may be under pressure from this White Dragon, just like Madam Wu was."

Doc sat down again, looking at his partner. "You're quite right, Raider, we have been at cross purposes here. But we can remedy that in a hurry."

"Spill it."

"My plan," Doc replied. "If you'll just hear me out."

Raider knew about Doc's plans. He had seen them work for years. He said he was willing to listen. When Doc was finished, Raider said it sounded all right to him, as long as they were careful.

"Good," replied the man from Boston. "Now I've other business to attend to. I'm going to give Penelope a piece of my mind."

Raider stopped him. "Doc, leave her alone."

"What are you saying?"

"You better get yourself straight about her," Raider replied. "I mean, you seem to feel pretty strong about her, but when we finally get at the truth, she could be covered with mud. You savvy?"

Doc straightened indignantly. "Mind your own business. I'm going to find that girl and tell her exactly what I think of her."

"That won't be necessary!" Sir Lionel had come down

the stairs, with Penelope right behind him.

Doc glared at both of them. "Ill met by moonlight?"

Strang clicked his heels together and stood rigid. "Sir, I don't care a damn what you think of me. But I won't have you insulting this young lady's honor. Do you hear me?"

"Perhaps you'd like to fight a duel," Doc replied triumphantly. "Just as you did in New Orleans. A pity that you can't duel with the customs clerks. You'd be able to smuggle everything into this country."

"I paid my fines," Strang insisted. "And you shall pay as well by apologizing to Penelope. Is that clear?"

Doc turned away with a snort. "I'll do no such thing. It is she who owes me an apology. Although I shouldn't expect reparations from a woman whose lack of breeding fits her like a ragged coat."

Strang raised his fists. "Enough. If you don't take that back immediately, I shall have to thrash you soundly."

Raider jumped up between them. "Maybe we oughta take this outside."

"I'm agreeable!" Strang shouted.

"As am I," Doc replied.

But they never reached the stairs.

A hot ball of fire exploded through the window of Strang's office. Suddenly glass and wood were flying everywhere. The force knocked them all to the floor. When Raider lifted his head, he saw Penelope lying on the carpet bleeding from a gash in her arm. He moved to help her, but Doc beat him to the punch.

The man from Boston cried out for a tourniquet. Strang immediately offered his tie. They were all bleeding, but Penelope was the only one who had lost consciousness.

Doc bellowed for Strang to get his carriage. The Englishman obeyed without hesitation. Doc tended the wound, tightening and loosening the tourniquet as needed. He was muttering under his breath, pleading with her not to die.

Strang came back up the stairs, saying the coach was ready. He helped Doc carry Penelope down to the street. Before he followed them, Raider glanced back at the charred hole where the window used to be. He had no idea what had caused the explosion. And it wouldn't be until the next day that he finally figured it out.

CHAPTER 14

Penelope Bloodsworth opened her brown eyes and gazed blankly at the face of Doc Weatherbee.

Doc peered anxiously over his shoulder. "Doctor, she's awake. Come here immediately."

The old physician turned away from his other two patients and ambled slowly toward the bed where Penelope rested. "Good color," he said, "for someone who has lost so much blood. Let me look at that arm."

They had taken her to the residence of a doctor who lived a few blocks away from Strang's offices. Raider had summoned the surgeon from his dinner table, claiming a grievous emergency. The older man had shown great skill in sewing up the gash in Penelope's arm, stopping the flow of blood for good.

The physician nodded approvingly as he examined the fresh stitches. "You're a lucky young lady. This gentleman in the derby saved your life. Where did you learn to use a tourniquet, young man?"

Doc wouldn't take his eyes off Penelope. "How are you feeling, dear girl?"

Penelope smiled weakly. "After the way I've spoken to you, you saved my life, Doc. I shall be forever grateful."

Doc held her hand. "I'd gladly do it again."

She closed her eyes. "Thank you."

"I care a great deal for you, Penelope. I really do."

"I'm tired," she whispered. "So very, very tired. When I'm better, I'll tell you the truth. I promise."

"Sleep," Doc replied. "I'll be here when you wake up. I won't let anyone else hurt you."

Doc felt a hand on his shoulder. He looked back at Raider, whose wounds had been dabbed with a fiery tincture. The surgeon had spent several hours picking glass shards and wooden splinters from their skin, remarking as he worked how lucky they all had been.

Doc snorted impatiently. "What is it, Raider?"

"Funny," the big man replied, "her voice sounded different."

"She almost bled to death, you fool!"

The big man frowned. "Doc, you and me oughta be goin'. We got work to do."

Doc turned back toward Penelope. "I'm not leaving her."

"Doc . . ."

"No! Until she's better, I'm staying by her side. Both of you can just clear out of here."

Strang stepped up beside Raider. "Weatherbee, I want to hire you to find out who did this terrible thing to Penelope."

Doc went after the Englishman, seizing the lapels of Strang's coat. "You did this to her! It's your fault, Strang! And I intend to prove it."

Raider managed to get between them before the fight erupted again.

The old doctor glared at them with his disapproving eyes. "This is not the proper way for grown men to conduct themselves. I suggest you take your dispute elsewhere."

Strang backed off, straightening himself. "I shall be at my rooms if you feel inclined toward—"

"Easy, Sir Lionel," Raid said. "We're goin' with you."

"I'm staying here with Penelope," Doc insisted. "Both of you can go to the devil for all I care."

Strang looked as though he were ready to brawl again,

but Raider dissuaded him from throwing another punch.
"You wait outside, Sir Lionel. I'll be right with you."
When Strang had gone down the stairs, Raider turned back
to his partner. "You sure about stayin', Doc? We got work
to do."

"I won't leave her side, I tell you."

The doctor glanced helplessly at Raider. "This is highly
unusual, sir. I prefer to take care of my own patients."

Raider nodded. "Let him stay. He'll be all right. He
won't hurt her."

The doctor reluctantly agreed.

"I'm goin', Doc." Raider started toward the door.

The man from Boston wheeled around, pointing a finger
at the rough-hewn detective. "Don't do a thing without
me," he insisted. "As soon as Penelope is better, I'm going
to get to the bottom of this."

"Sure, Doc. Whatever you say."

Doc had it bad, Raider thought. Either he was going
crazy or it was the woman. Or maybe both. He left and met
Sir Lionel on the street. When they climbed into Strang's
carriage, Sir Lionel called for the driver to take them directly to his office.

Raider leaned back, sighing and shaking his head.

Sir Lionel gaped at him. "What now?"

The big man took a deep breath. "You ain't gonna like
this, Strang, but I got to go to the police."

Strang gazed disbelievingly at the tall Pinkerton.
"You're going to bring the coppers to my office?"

"Ain't got no choice," Raider replied. "Doc's about as
useful as a no-dick gopher in a pissin' contest. I need a
hand. McCurley and his men can cover a lot of ground.
This thing is growin'. No tellin' how many more'll be
killed if we don't get a handle on it."

Sir Lionel became sullen. "If you must. Although I
daresay that you no longer trust me."

"I don't trust anybody, no way, no how. You got that?"

"Well, I suppose you're going to have them stomping
all over my house tonight. A midnight intrusion, as it
were."

Raider shook his head. "No, tomorrow. But I'm stayin'
the night at your place to make sure nothin' gets lost. I'll
send word to McCurley first thing in the mornin'."

Strang gazed blankly out the window of the coach. "You'll pardon me if I'm not in attendance at your little soirée. I'm not exactly the favorite son of the San Francisco constabulary."

"Don't take none of this personal," Raider offered. "Hell, all this ruckus could end up savin' *your* life too."

"Pardon me if I don't care," Strang replied. "From now on, I'm not helping anyone in this case. Least of all you!"

"Suit yourself."

Raider pulled down the limp brim of his Stetson. He was too tired to argue. He didn't much care if Strang helped or not. All he wanted was to get some sleep so that he would be fresh for the investigation the next morning.

Bright rays of white sunlight spilled through the hole in the wall of Sir Lionel's office. Raider stood next to Captain McCurley, examining the damage that had almost killed them all. It still seemed like a vague nightmare, as if it never happened.

"Impressive," McCurley said. "You're all lucky you were on the way out. If you had been standin' flush with the windows, you'd've had the life scorched clean out of you."

Raider took off his Stetson and wiped his forehead with the back of his arm. "Is it hot in here?"

The captain laughed heartily. "That was only the Devil's fires lickin' at your behind. You came close to meetin' him, Raider."

A shiver ran back and forth over his shoulders, the familiar tingling that occurred on those numerous occasions when Raider had barely escaped death.

"What do you think it was?" McCurley asked.

Raider shrugged. "I was hoping you'd tell *me*."

McCurley turned with a puzzled look in his eyes, stroking his bushy mustache. "You're the Pinkerton. Big man with the answers. Go ahead and tell me."

Raider sighed, fixing his gaze on the charred casement. "Well, it wasn't dynamite. That close, even a small stick would've taken us all to our graves. And there wasn't much of an explosion, it was more like a giant ball of fire."

McCurley nodded. "Impressive. I believe you're right. No dynamite. Then what?"

Raider touched the casement and then looked outside, on the brick wall of Strang's townhouse. Powder burns were all over, just like a muzzle flash. He came back in, inspecting the wall on the other side of the room. The same powder had scorched the walls opposite the window. "We're damned lucky this place didn't burn down."

McCurley leaned over the sill and gazed out into the street. "Pretty inept way of tryin' to kill somebody."

Raider glanced down at the broken glass and sharp wedges of broken wood. "Not if you was tryin' to get somebody with the richochet."

"Wouldn't it make more sense to shoot through the window with a rifle?"

The big man shook his head. "You start shootin', you get one, maybe two before we hit the floor. Blow out the window, you got a chance to git ever'body. Even if you don't, all our heads are so scrambled that we can't go lookin' to see who done it. Not till now."

"Who do you think they were after?"

"Hard to say. Probably all of us." He told the captain about the Tong's attempt on Sir Lionel's life. "And there's plenty of reason to want me and Doc dead. I been pokin' around on the waterfront. Ever hear of somebody called the White Dragon?"

McCurley flinched at the name. "You've been workin' hard, Mr. Raider."

"Then you know him?"

"Officially, the White Dragon doesn't exist," the captain replied. "But I have heard of him—at least we think it's one man."

"The Tong and the White Dragon are in cahoots," Raider said.

"Are you sure?"

"No, but I got a hunch about it. I also got a hunch that if we don't get this thing cleared up fast, you're gonna have more bodies floatin' in that bay than you can count in a week."

McCurley turned away, gazing out the window. "I hope you're wrong, cowboy. But I fear you're right as the rain. Hello? What's this?"

Raider looked out of the charred casement, toward a rooftop across the street. One of McCurley's men, a blue-coated constable, was waving at them. He pointed down toward the roof when he got their attention.

"He's found somethin'."

Raider tipped his hat to the waving patrolman. "Good work, McCurley. Maybe this is what we're lookin' for."

They hurried across the street, to the roof of a law office. The constable had discovered a charred, triangular structure with a V-shaped trough nailed to the top. Burnt powder covered the trough as well as most of the roof behind the structure.

Raider took off his Stetson. "Damn me if I know what this is."

McCurley eyed him dubiously. "Come on, Raider. Any child of ten years can tell you what happened here."

"Clue me in, Captain. I'm ready for some answers."

McCurley laughed. "Ya never been to Chinatown on Chinese New Year?"

"Beggin' your pardon, Captain, but this ain't no firecracker."

"No, it was a rocket."

Raider's eyes widened. He looked down the V-shaped trough and saw that it was aligned with the window of Sir Lionel's office. His head snapped up. That was it, all right. He had seen the same kind of rockets before, only smaller. Sometimes they were used for fireworks. This one had been intended as a murder weapon.

"They missed," Raider said, sweat pouring from his forehead on the cool morning. "Just barely, but they missed."

"You're undoubtedly right about the Chinese involvement in this, Raider. They're experts with these rockets. Any one of a hundred men could've made the one they shot at you."

Raider stared at the demolished window across the street. "Well, I guess I'm in this thing until the end. I can't speak for my partner..."

"You don't have to speak for me."

They turned to see Doc Weatherbee strolling over the rooftop.

"Weatherbee," the police captain said. "Glad to see you. How did you happen to find us?"

"Your men were polite enough to show the way," Doc

replied, smiling. "And I *am* a detective, after all."

Raider wanted to ask about the girl, but he refrained, not wanting to set off a fistfight in front of McCurley. Besides, the smile on Doc's face and his chipper spirits told him all he needed to know. Penelope was probably well and resting in the doctor's office.

McCurley gestured toward the launching device. "Seems you were attacked by a Chinese rocket."

Doc sniffed condescendingly. "I could have told you that by looking at the office window."

Raider looked away, frowning. "Yeah, I bet you could."

Doc shook hands with McCurley. "I'm glad you're here, Captain. I have a few things to discuss with you. I don't know if Raider told you or not, but I have a plan to draw out some of the players in this little drama."

"Hardly little," McCurley rejoined. He looked at Raider. "What do you say, cowboy?"

Raider shrugged. "Hear him out. Some of it makes sense. And with the way things is goin', it seems like our best chance."

McCurley gestured toward the roof door. "Then let's go back to Strang's office and hash it out."

"No," Doc replied firmly.

McCurley looked puzzled. "You want to talk right here on the roof?"

"I won't tell you my plan until we reach our ultimate destination," Doc insisted. "If you gentlemen will accompany me."

Raider grunted. "Where we goin' now?"

Doc wore a complacent smirk on his tight mouth. "To the offices of Judd Gilmore."

Finally, the big man thought, they were getting somewhere.

"You want me to do what?" Judd Gilmore cried, his eyes wide with disbelief.

Doc puffed on his Old Virginia cheroot, looking terribly self-satisfied. "I want you to deal with Strang," he said. "I want you to accept his offer to buy half of Huntley Shipping."

Captain McCurley shifted uncomfortably in his seat. "You can't be serious, Weatherbee."

"I am and I am not," Doc replied cryptically.

Raider just stared at the wall, wondering if Doc had lost his mind. Would the plan work, or would Doc simply make fool of himself? It was that damned woman. She had gotten into his head and spoiled him for everything else.

"Deal with Strang," Doc reiterated. "It's the best thing. It's the only thing."

Gilmore steeled himself against the idea. "I'd sooner give this business to the Devil himself. No, I won't sell half of Huntley Shipping to anyone, let alone the man who killed Theodore Huntley."

"That ain't been proved yet," Raider reminded him.

A billow of foul smoke floated over Doc's derby. "You won't be selling anything to Strang, not really."

Gilmore shook his head. "I don't understand."

"Tell him you're interested," Doc continued. "Meet with him to discuss a potential deal. Take your time, draw him out. I only want you to deal with him, not sell to him. You don't have to sign any papers. If things get that far, you can always pull out."

Gilmore leaned back in his chair, eyes narrowed, stroking his chin. "It sounds risky," he said dubiously. "Strang is an unpredictable sort. My life could easily be endangered. I'm not sure I'm ready to take that chance."

Doc threw out his hands. "We'll be protecting you all the way. Raider and myself, along with the entire San Francisco Police Department. What more could you want?"

McCurley concurred. "The risk is small, Judd. We won't be far away."

Gilmore sighed. "I don't know, gentlemen. I'm not the adventurous kind."

Doc frowned disappointedly. "Then I'm afraid we're lost if you refuse to help us, Mr. Gilmore."

McCurley raised a bushy eyebrow. "What are you gettin' at, Weatherbee?"

Doc shrugged. "The only way we can keep Strang in town is to get Mr. Gilmore here to deal with him."

"You think he's gonna run?" Raider asked.

"He's starting to feel the heat under his collar," Doc replied. "We're after him, the police are on his trail, the Tong have it in for him, and, of course, there's this White

Dragon that you keep harping about."

All the blood rushed out of Gilmore's face. "The White Dragon?"

Raider glared at the man behind the desk. "Ever hear of him, Judd?"

Gilmore shook his head. "No . . . I mean, well, yes, I have heard of him. But rumors about him, nothing else. I tend to believe he doesn't exist."

"What about helpin' us?" Raider challenged. "You believe in that, Judd? Or maybe you're hidin' somethin' like ever'body else in this loco town."

Sweat popped out on Gilmore's rutted forehead. "This is all so sudden. I don't know."

Doc glared at Gilmore. "You do want us to find Theodore Huntley's killer, don't you?"

"Of course," Gilmore replied indignantly. "Teddy was like a son to me."

McCurley gestured with his thick fingers. "It would look better if you helped us, Judd."

"I'm afraid," Gilmore confessed.

"And you have a right to be," Doc replied. "But it's as we said before, you'll have complete protection from us."

Gilmore stood up, facing the wall behind him. "But what if nothing happens," he offered. "Then I back out of the deal and Strang comes after me."

"We'll be waitin' for him," Raider replied. "And he won't get you."

Gilmore turned around to meet their expectant stares. "You're all going to get me killed."

"Will you help us or not?" Doc asked.

Gilmore nodded. "I'll help you. But I won't be held accountable if anything goes wrong. I'll play my part the way you asked me, but I won't be involved in any violent undertaking."

Raider smiled. "Leave that to us, Judd. We'll be right on top of it, won't we, Doc?"

"Gentlemen," McCurley said before Doc could redress his partner. "If we play our hand correctly, no one but the murderer of Theodore Huntley will get hurt. Isn't that right, Weatherbee?"

Doc was still glaring at Raider. "Correct. No unnecessary gunplay. Is that understood, Raider?"

The big man nodded, even though he wasn't sure what constituted necessary or unnecessary use of firearms.

"Then it's set," McCurley chimed in. "When do you want to get moving?"

"As soon as possible," Doc replied. "How about this afternoon?"

Everyone but Gilmore agreed to the starting time. The de facto head of Huntley Shipping thought it was too early. But they finally convinced him, and Gilmore gave in. They set to work, planning the details, figuring the angles.

When they were finished, everyone but Judd Gilmore was smiling. Gilmore sat behind his desk with a doomed frown on his countenance. And nothing anyone could say would cheer him up.

When the meeting was over, Raider made excuses to slip out, saying he was going to get them some food and drink. No one seemed to care, although Doc warned him that he had better be back in time for the proposed meeting between Strang and Gilmore. Raider nodded and left the warehouse in a hurry.

He intended to go back to the hotel for the provisions, but he also wanted to make a stop along the way at a certain doctor's office.

Penelope Bloodsworth was exiting from the building as Raider approached. She headed straight for him, walking slowly as if she had not yet regained all her strength. When she saw Raider coming toward her, the young lady went pale, swooned, and fell toward the sidewalk. Raider managed to catch her in his arms before she hit the deck.

He carried her to a bench in front of an apothecary, easing her down in the shade. The chemist inside the shop saw her predicament and came out with a small vial of smelling salts. In a few seconds, her eyes were open and she was sitting straight.

Her brown eyes regarded the big man from Arkansas. "What happened?"

"You were walkin' down the street when you went out."

The chemist came back with a glass of water. Penelope thanked him and drank every drop. She smiled weakly at Raider, who sat next to her on the wooden bench. "I'm embarrassed," she said meekly.

Raider tipped back his Stetson. "You never shoulda left

that sawbones, honey. You're too weak."

She looked at the bandage on her arm. "It still hurts, but not that badly. More like a dull ache."

He shook his head. "Don't matter. They spilled some of your blood. It'll take a while before you feel better. Why don't you go back to the doctor?"

She leaned against the wall of the apothecary store. "I want to find your partner to thank him again. He really is a nice man."

Raider sighed. "Yeah, well, he's got it pretty bad for you."

She glared at him. "No!"

"I'm afraid so. I seen it before, only he's never been this far gone. I was hopin' you'd be honest and tell me what you feel toward him."

She frowned. "I don't know. I don't think I'm in love with him."

Raider groaned, shaking his head. "Damn it all, I knew it. Look, lady, he ain't hisself right now. He don't need . . . whatta you call it?"

"Rejection?"

"Yeah, I reckon that's it. Anyway, Doc don't need it."

She started to get to her feet. "In that case, I'd better get back to Sir Lionel. He'll probably need my help."

Raider grabbed her good arm, pulling her back onto the bench. "That ain't such a good idea either."

Penelope's eyes grew wide. Her nostrils flared, and her breath became erratic. "What are you going to do to Sir Lionel?"

Raider avoided her gaze. "Honey, I—"

"You're going after him, aren't you? Answer me!"

Raider nodded. "Yeah, we're goin' after him, but it ain't like you think. We're gonna try to smoke out ever'body and see which one runs away the fastest."

Penelope grabbed his shirt. "Strang is innocent, I tell you."

"I hope you're right."

"You don't believe me, do you?"

"I don't know what to believe anymore," Raider replied. "There's too many dead people in this thing."

Her face slacked into a frightened expression. "Dead people. Yes, I was almost one of them. Raider, promise me you won't let anything happen to Sir Lionel. Please."

"I'll try," he replied sadly. "But like it or not, you're gonna have to face the truth, Penelope. Even if it involves you."

She glanced sideways at him. "What do you mean by that?"

He took her hand, so as to lessen the blow. "Honey, when you was half out in the doctor's office, you said somethin' about tellin' Doc the truth when you was better. What was that all about?"

She pulled her hand away. "I don't know what you're talking about. I must have been in a fever."

"Yeah? Well, you didn't sound English when you were tellin' him. You sounded just like one of us."

She forced a laugh. "I suppose I've become American-ized, eh what? I was talking gibberish because I was in pain."

Raider didn't believe her, but he figured it wasn't worth pursuing. "Two things," he said. "First, I want you to go back to the doctor's office and stay there until tonight. One of us will come for you when it's over. If it's over by then."

She nodded reluctantly, saying the old physician had agreed to let her stay as long as she liked. "You said there were two things, Raider."

"My partner," the big man replied. "You could cut him pretty deep if you wanted to."

She glared indignantly at the big man. "Are you saying I should lead him on? I don't think that would be wise."

"That ain't what I'm sayin'. I'll just tell you what I told him. Y'all better get straight about all these fireworks goin' on. It ain't healthy for neither one of you. Savvy?"

Penelope nodded, her eyes cast downward.

"You got anything else to say to me, honey?"

"You're the detective," she said rudely. "Aren't you the one who's supposed to learn the truth?"

Raider glared right back at her. "Yeah, that's so. But if somebody gets killed because of somethin' you wouldn't tell us, you're gonna feel pretty bad. Unless you got a rock for a heart."

Penelope got up and stormed away from him. She wavered a bit at the door to the doctor's office, but she managed to enter without passing out again. Raider felt better that she had sought sanctuary, but he stayed on the bench for fifteen minutes, just to make sure she didn't leave again.

When he was satisfied that Penelope was safe, he headed straight for the hotel. The cook in the kitchen offered to make sandwiches for two dollars. Raider gave him five to throw in a bottle of whiskey. He told the cook to wrap it all up and put it in some sort of picnic basket. He'd be back for the refreshments as soon as he paid a visit to his room.

Upstairs, Raider found the real reason he had come back to the hotel. He unwrapped the Winchester '76 that the gun seller had given him. He filled the rifle with cartridges and then put the rest of the shells in his pockets. Raider wanted to be ready in case Doc's plan went haywire. He was agreeable that things should be settled peaceably if possible. But if that didn't work, the big man planned to settle it with a little old-fashioned Winchester music.

CHAPTER 15

At three o'clock, while Doc, Raider, and McCurley were eating their sandwiches, a messenger arrived at the Huntley Shipping warehouse and delivered a note to the office of Judd Gilmore. The nervous, sweating Gilmore fumbled with the envelope, staining the flap with moisture from his palms. His head twitched as he read the dispatch from Sir Lionel Strang.

Gilmore looked up at Doc and Raider. "He's agreed to come at four-thirty."

Doc nodded. "We have an hour and a half."

Raider looked at the police captain. "You gonna donate any men to the cause, McCurley?"

Doc waved off his partner. "We don't need them."

Raider studied McCurley's face, looking for approval. It hurt him that he no longer trusted Doc's judgment. He didn't want to feel that way, but he did.

McCurley thought about it for a moment. "Your partner's right, Raider. The three of us can handle it today. It's only the first meeting of many."

Raider slumped in his chair, pulling his brim down low.

"I reckon you're right. Hell, I'm beginnin' to wonder if this dark warehouse is such a good place for them to meet. We got to lay low back in the cargo stacks, a good two hundred feet from the door."

Doc gestured to the windows behind them. "We can see from there. Mr. Gilmore will just have to leave his curtains opened."

Gilmore stood up behind his desk. "Yes, that's it. I want you to be able to watch every move we make. I won't feel safe any other way."

"The fellow's makin' sense," McCurley said tentatively. "But I got to think Raider here has a point. We'll be back in the dark—"

"Where we can't be seen!" Doc interjected. "Don't worry, gentlemen. This meeting is nothing more than two business associates discussing a transaction. Mr. Gilmore, I want you to feel out Sir Lionel. Just get him to talk. Hint about his possible connection to the Tong. Drop the name of the White Dragon and see how he reacts. If you must, tell him you can't make a deal until you know the extent of all his operations. Do what you can to make him talk. You can report to us later."

Gilmore nodded, leaning back in his chair. He seemed calmer all of a sudden, as though he realized the danger was really less than he had expected. Raider took his change of temperament to be a good sign. He still felt like there was something more they should be doing to prepare for Strang's arrival.

"I guess there's nothin' left to do but wait," McCurley said tiredly.

Raider reached into the food basket and brought up a good bottle of Irish whiskey. "I'm gonna take the edge off."

Doc tried to grab the bottle out of his hand.

Raider pulled back, knocking his paw away. "That's a good way to lose an arm, Doc."

"Drinking on duty is prohibited by agency policy."

Raider grinned. "Hell, I ain't on duty till four-thirty." He took a long swig from the bottle.

The good captain licked his lips. "Might I be havin' a little taste of that mother courage, Mr. Raider?"

"Find a glass, Captain."

Doc glared disapprovingly at both of them. "That's all we need. Two drunks with guns in their hands."

Raider and McCurley only laughed good-naturedly.

Judd Gilmore put two glasses on his desktop. "I wouldn't mind a short one," he said with a weak smile. "If you have enough."

Raider poured a shot in each glass and then revisited the bottle one more time himself. That was all he needed. It took some of the pain out of waiting. And it helped him shrug off the indecisive chill that ran up and down his back, refusing to leave no matter which direction he stretched in.

"There he is!"

Doc ducked down behind the canvas-covered stack of crates. Raider and McCurley were also behind the stack, listening as Sir Lionel's footsteps resounded through the shadows of the warehouse. They could stick their heads up when Strang entered the office.

His rhythmic footfalls stopped, and a door swung open and closed.

Raider came up first, aiming Doc's telescope at the windows of Gilmore's small office. Doc also had a pair of opera glasses he had purchased earlier in the day. It was Raider, however, who had the best view with a shortened version of Doc's spyglass.

"Okay," he said, "they're talkin'. Hell, I can't see Gilmore, Doc. Can you?"

"No. Strang's in the way. Good God!"

Raider saw it too.

"What is it?" McCurley asked impatiently.

"Strang just pulled out a goddamn gun," Raider replied. "It's that pocket revolver he's always carryin'."

McCurley grabbed the opera glasses from Doc and looked for himself.

"Strang's turnin'," Raider continued. He dropped the glass. "Damn, Sir Lionel is pullin' the drapes. We better get in there!"

He started up, but Doc pulled him back down. "Wait. We could get Gilmore killed if we rushed in too quickly."

Raider levered the Winchester that had been leaning on the boxes next to him. "I'm goin'. . . . Shit!"

A pistol exploded inside the office. As Raider leapt over the canvas, a second, less noisy shot erupted in the muffled confines of the small chamber. Raider sprinted across the warehouse floor with Doc and McCurley right behind him. The door was locked, so the big man used his boot as a key.

The stench of burnt powder wafted in a gray billow, smelling like boiled eggs that had been in the sun too long. Raider waved through the cloud, almost tripping over the body that lay on the floor. Sir Lionel writhed in agony, clutching his forehead. Blood gushed between his fingers.

Judd Gilmore stood frozen behind his desk, holding a smoking .45. "He tried to shoot me," the little man cried. "He said he was going to kill me the same way he killed Teddy Huntley!"

Raider leaned over the Englishman, trying to pull his hand away from his head. "Hold on there, Sir Lionel. Hold on, boy."

But Sir Lionel was already gone. His eyes were rolled back in his head; his mouth was gaping open with sputum trickling out. In a few seconds he stopped moving altogether.

Raider stood up, turning to glare at Gilmore. "He's finished."

Gilmore dropped the .45 on his desk, backing away like it was a rattlesnake. "He pulled a gun on me!" he said blankly. "I had to defend myself."

"We saw it all," Raider replied. "Did you grab your pistol after he turned to draw the curtains?"

"Yes! That's it," Gilmore whined. "I was trembling, I tell you."

Doc squinted at the weapon on the desk. "You never told us you had a gun on you."

"I had a right to one!"

"You did," Doc said. "And a good thing you were loaded for bear. Don't you think so, Captain?"

McCurley reached for the pistol that had killed Strang. "I reckon we can close the books on this one."

Raider began to search around for something on the floor. "Where's Strang's pistol?"

Doc found it a few inches away from Sir Lionel's feet. It had been fired once. Doc spun the sylinders and then frowned. He threw the pistol to Raider, who also examined the pocket revolver.

"Only one bullet," the big man said.

He gave the weapon to Captain McCurley. "Well, don't that beat all. I reckon he planned to plug Gilmore with one shot."

Raider kept his eyes trained on the floor. He pointed to the spot where the pistol had been. "How'd his gun get down there by his shoes?"

"He must have dropped it that way when he fell," Doc offered.

Gilmore pointed to the wall behind him. "Strang shot at me. He almost hit me in the head."

Raider stepped around the desk and examined the hole in the wallpaper. "Lot of powder burn around this hole. I guess he was close to you. Doc, don't that look like a lot of powder burn to you?"

Doc gave the wallpaper a hasty look. "Well, it is rather thick." He went back and stood where Strang had been when he had fired the pocket revolver. "No, he was extremely close. That powder burn is normal at this range."

Raider smiled in a weird way. "Good. I want you to put that in our report. I want it clear."

McCurley frowned at the big man. "What are you gettin' at, cowboy?"

"Oh, I ain't gettin' at nothin', Cap. We just always take down these little details, don't we, Doc?"

Doc's smile was almost approving. "I'm pleased at your professionalism, Raider. It's refreshing."

Raider came around the desk. "Well, Doc, I'm just goddamn happy that you're pleased with my fuckin' professionalism." He reached up and, with a violent gesture that startled everyone, yanked down the curtains from Gilmore's office window.

Doc gaped at him. "Raider!"

The big man spread the cloth over the body of Sir Lionel.

Gilmore was wide-eyed but said, "Yes, I see."

Raider looked down at the bulk of his old gambling buddy. "I don't care if he was a outlaw, he was still a pretty good ole boy when you got down to havin' a good time. Maybe he wasn't a real gentleman, but he by God wanted to be, and he tried real hard to pull it off."

Doc tried not to look embarrassed for his partner.
"Noble sentiments, Raider. I commend you."

"Commend your ass, Doc. Sir Lionel is gettin' a decent
burial with a preacher and a headstone. His name is gonna
be in the paper. He's gonna have a funeral march and a few
words spoken at the church. Is that all right with you, Captain?"

McCurley threw out his hands. "Gentlemen, as far as
I'm concerned, the case is closed."

The funeral came off just as Raider had predicted. A
Methodist preacher was paid enough to hold a ceremony
and to say a few kind, watered-down words for Sir Lionel.
Raider was the only pallbearer who had not been hired.
Doc refused to carry the coffin, even though he did attend
the church service and the burial. Sir Lionel's gleaming
black coffin was pulled to the cemetery in a huge under-
taker's hearse that had been bedecked with flowers by Penelope Bloodsworth, the only other person in attendance at
the graveside ceremony.

A bright sun reflected off the coffin as it was lowered.
Raider manned the shovel to cover it up. He had to take off
his shirt about halfway through the operation. The good
Lord had given Sir Lionel a hot day for a send-off, evidence that the Englishman would probably spend his after-
life in a warm place below.

Penelope stood next to Raider during the burial, refusing to look at Doc. She held the big man's arm, staring
blankly through a black veil. When Raider went to work on
the grave, she lifted her veil and watched calmly.

Doc gazed painfully at her, pining because she would
not look at him. As Raider packed down the dirt, Doc
slipped closer to the Englishwoman. She felt him next to
her, but she still would not look at him. Doc twirled his
derby in his hands, his face sagging like a mooning hound
dog.

"Penelope . . ."

"I want to thank you for paying your respects," she said
quickly. "Even though Sir Lionel was not guilty of anything beyond his own careless dealings."

Doc grabbed her shoulders and spun her toward him.

"He tried to kill Judd Gilmore! What more proof do you want? I saw the gun in his hand."

"I don't know what you saw," she replied frantically. "but Sir Lionel could not kill anyone."

"I heard Sir Lionel shoot first!"

She shrugged away from him. "There are ways to deceive, Mr. Weatherbee."

"And I suppose you know them all!"

Her head lowered. "Touché," she said softly. "I . . . I want to tell you the truth, Doc. I haven't been fair to you. If I had told you earlier . . . but I was afraid. I . . ."

Doc turned with her to see the coach coming down the path toward the grave. When the carriage halted, Judd Gilmore got out. He started toward the granite headstone with SIR LIONEL STRANG chiseled in big letters.

Doc looked back at Penelope. "It's only Gilmore. Nice of him to come. I do think he really feels badly about killing Sir Lionel."

The brown-eyed woman pulled down her veil. "I'll send for you." She started away, walking between the headstones.

Doc took a few steps after her. "But you said you had something to tell me. Penelope, please."

"I'll send for you!" she called over her shoulder. "I cannot talk here. Wait at your hotel."

Doc was taken aback for a moment, but the fact that she was going to send for him greatly bolstered his spirits. Why the hell did she run away from Judd Gilmore? Given Penelope's spunky nature, he figured she would have a few harsh words for the man who had shot her employer.

Raider came up next to Doc, his body covered with dirt and sweat. "What happened? You lay the bad mouth on her?"

"No," Doc replied. "She's going to send for me. She said she's finally going to tell me the truth. I hope . . ." He turned to the big man. "Do you think she's involved in any of this? Criminally, I mean?"

Raider nodded toward Gilmore, who was almost on them. "Let's talk about it later. We got company."

"Gentlemen."

Gilmore held out his hands, smiling. "I wanted to come and thank you personally for expediting this matter as quickly as you have. By the way, I don't suppose either of you ever ran across Teddy's sister, Rebecca?"

"Nope," Raider replied. "Never did."

"Oh." He glanced toward the grave. "Well, I can tell you that I'm sleeping better at nights. It worried me a bit, but I realized I had no choice in the matter. I had to kill him."

Raider flicked the shovel, sending a clod of dirt to explode on Gilmore's white shirt.

"What the devil!" the little man shouted. "You did that on purpose."

Raider threw the shovel at Gilmore's feet and stomped away.

Doc tried to use his handkerchief to help Gilmore tidy up, but the dirt was wet and clung to the starched fabric. "Dreadfully sorry, Gilmore. My partner can be a bit testy at times."

"Get away from me," Gilmore snapped. "I shouldn't have come here. It was a waste of time."

Gilmore huffily made his way back to his carriage, leaving Doc alone at the graveside. But Doc didn't seem to notice the ill humors of those around him. He picked a carnation from the funeral wreath and slipped it into his lapel. He couldn't be sad when he was thinking about Penelope. She was going to send for him. He decided he had better get back to the hotel.

Doc paced back and forth in front of Raider, who was anchored in an easy chair with a bottle of whiskey in his lap. The big man had been in Doc's room for nearly an hour, watching his partner as he went through the kind of agony that could only be inflicted by love. It wasn't a pretty sight, but for some unknown reason, Raider felt like he had to help his partner through the thing with Penelope. Doc really had it bad.

"She's going to send for me," he kept saying. "It's only a matter of time. I know it."

"Sure, Doc."

How could it creep up on you like that? One minute a man was walking along just fine, doing his duty, not a care in the world. The next instant he saw *her* and it was all over. He had to be with her. He had to hear her telling him that he was worthy of her. Raider had felt like that once or twice in his whole life. He had come to the conclusion that love was fine, but it got in the way of everything else.

"She said she would send for me," Doc said nervously. "Do you think she will, Raider?"

The big man grimaced. "How the hell would I know? I ain't never been able to figure women. I enjoy 'em, but I can't tell you the first thing about a woman like Penelope."

Doc sat on the edge of the bed, wringing his hands, regarding his partner with a pathetic expression. "Raider, do you think she loves me?"

Raider shrugged. "You love her?"

Doc blushed.

"Come clean, Weatherbee."

"Yes!" he replied in a loud screech. "Yes, I love her. Are you satisfied? I love Penelope Bloodsworth. Do you want to shoot me for it?"

Raider handed him the bottle of whiskey. "Simmer down, Doc. Take a snort of this. I'm gonna be honest with you."

Doc took a long drink, as if Raider's honesty was the thing he feared most in the world.

Raider folded his hands over his chest. "Doc, while you was at the warehouse with the others, I called on Penelope at the doctor's office. I asked her how she felt about you."

Doc's face went white. "What did she say?"

Raider sighed, looking away. "I don't think she loves you, Doc. She likes you okay. But she said she wasn't sure about anything more than that."

Doc stood up and started pacing again.

"I wouldn't take it so hard," Raider offered.

"She'll send for me. She said she would."

"Don't count on it, Doc. She might not."

At that exact moment, a knock came on the door of Doc's room. Doc snatched open the door, glaring at the hotel clerk who had an envelope in his hand. After giving the lad two bits, Doc ripped open the message and read it with wide eyes.

When he had finished, he smirked triumphantly at his partner. "Not going to send for me, eh? Here, read this!"

In a precise, flowing hand, Penelope had asked Doc to "Meet me at the doctor's office immediately. Please come alone."

Raider wasn't sure it was wise to go alone. "Doc, wait."

But the door slammed as Doc hurried to his tryst.

Raider exhaled and picked up the bottle again. As he drank, he wondered what felt wrong inside him. The usual calm after a closed case had not overtaken him. He still felt antsy, nervous. Maybe because he saw a few things that didn't fit.

Captain McCurley had declared the case officially solved. He was even going to write a letter of commendation to the Pinkerton home office. That seemed to be enough for Doc. Raider decided to sit with the bottle, drinking until the sun was down. He figured to find a few nighttime diversions to get rid of the ants. Maybe then he'd feel like the whole thing was finally over.

The lights of San Francisco did not seem as bright to Raider as he wandered through the streets, heading for the waterfront. What was it that didn't fit in Strang's confrontation with Gilmore? They *saw* the gun in Strang's hands. They *saw* him pulling the curtains. Then two shots, a loud one and a small one. Gilmore had said that Strang fired first, but wouldn't the pocket revolver have made the lesser explosion? Maybe Strang's body had muffled the second shot. That would explain the difference in the noises from the guns.

The powder burns were thick on the wall behind Gilmore. How could Sir Lionel have missed at that range? He had shot straight enough at his duel in New Orleans. But they *saw* the damned gun in his hand!

Raider stopped under a street lamp. Damn it, it just wasn't Sir Lionel's style to pull such a tinhorn maneuver. Strang had been a gambler, somebody who enjoyed the game as much as he enjoyed winning or losing. He wouldn't blunder in with a gun, demanding results. Penelope had said it all along—Sir Lionel didn't have it in him to kill anyone.

He started walking again, thinking over and over that he had *seen* the pocket revolver in Sir Lionel's hand. A pistol with one bullet. Why would Sir Lionel only have one round in the cylinder? A die-hard killer would have come with a full load, probably even a bigger weapon. But they had *seen* the smaller gun in his hand when he turned to close the drapes.

What had Gilmore been doing in there? They couldn't see him. He had managed to fill his hand with the Colt while Sir Lionel's back was turned.

He shook his head. McCurley had pronounced the case closed.

What had they really seen?

As he walked, he tortured himself with the details. He missed Sir Lionel. He wondered about Doc and Penelope, if they were kissing to make up or if she would break his heart. Maybe it was best to forget everything, to spend some more money at the blackjack table.

But the gaming house was closed. No lights inside, no guard, big padlock on the front door. Closed because Sir Lionel was no longer there to administer his affairs. He had been a scoundrel. Maybe Strang really had come to the warehouse to kill Judd Gilmore. Maybe Sir Lionel had killed Teddy Huntley.

He wandered along the wharf until he came to Madam Wu's. Raider figured the cathouse would be closed like the casino, but to his surprise, when he opened the door, he was greeted by the two men with shotguns who had stood sentry while Madam Wu was still alive.

"Look who's back," one of them said.

Raider glared at the scatterguns. "We gonna have a hard time about this?"

They both raised their weapons to the ceiling. "Pass on, Pinkerton. Get it wet if you got the money. Ain't nobody here gonna give you a rough time."

Raider clumped up the stairs, pushing into the silk-draped parlor of the whorehouse. The Chinese lantern burned dully through the parlor, casting pastel shades on the men and women who languished in the warmth of the night. A smiling Chinese woman in a silk robe flowed toward Raider like a billowy pink fog.

She looked up and winked at the big man. "Hello, Raider. I'm glad you came tonight. I was hoping I'd see you again."

Raider gaped at his former paramour. "Wan Chur! I didn't recognize you with all that paint on your face."

"I'm big doin's, cowboy." She turned around for him so he could see the whole package. "I took over. Tonight, everything is free for you."

"No more trouble?" he asked.

"All trouble gone!" she replied. "Pick a girl."

Raider smiled. "Where's blondie?"

"Who?"

"You know, the girl that me and you . . ." He made a circling motion with his finger.

Wan Chur frowned, shaking her head. "You mean Goldie. She's not here anymore. She ran off with a rich man."

"Anybody I know?"

"I'm glad she's gone," Wan Chur replied.

"Goldie, huh? I never even asked her name. She wasn't a bad girl. She had a nice set of . . ."

Wan Chur started away. "Wait here. I'll see what I have."

Raider shook his head, thinking that no woman ever liked to hear you building up another woman. It just wasn't in their nature to listen to it. *Goldie.* He had liked her, and he wished she was still around.

Wan Chur came back toward him, waving until she got his attention. She led him through the corridor, to the same room where he had been on his two other visits to the brothel. A lanky Spanish woman was reclining on the bed, naked from the waist up. She wore only a loose slip on the bottom half of her body.

"She has a big chest," Wan Chur said.

Raider looked down at the new Madam Wu. "Why don't you stay with us? Or better yet, just me and you."

Wan Chur kissed his cheek. "Maybe later. I'm a working girl now. I have to keep my clients happy."

When Wan Chur was gone, the Spanish woman glared at Raider with her huge brown eyes. "You do not want me?"

Raider shrugged. "Yeah, I want you."

"I will do everything I can to show you I am the best," she said in a sultry voice. "Let me undress you."

So she did, gasping when she saw the length of Raider's penis. Tearing off the slip, she reclined on the bed, spreading her brown thighs. Raider fell between her legs, giving her what she wanted for the better part of the night. He never climaxed, however. He could not find a release.

"You don't like me!" she accused.

He sighed, lying next to her. "It ain't that, honey. I just got a lot on my mind."

The Spanish woman leapt off the bed. "I hate you. *Maricone!*"

Raider just lay there, listening to the early morning quiet of the cathouse. He was starting to close his eyes when the door opened again. A naked Wan Chur tiptoed toward the bed, snickering as she came.

"My girl says the dragon doesn't want to breathe his fire," she teased.

Raider sighed. "I hope she didn't take that personal. I had a good time with her. I'm just off my feed since Sir Lionel got killed."

Wan Chur slid next to him, gripping his turgid member. "I'll make the dragon spit. I have tricks and ways."

Wan Chur was true to her word, exacting a fiery release from Raider's prick within minutes of her arrival. She kept him going, in and out, different postures, various entries, techniques of forbidden love.

When they were finished, she was surprised to find Raider still tense and restless.

"What is it, cowboy? What are you carrying in your heart?"

Raider just shook his head, pulling her close to him. "I don't know, Wan Chur. None of it feels right. I've hammered it out in my skull a hundred different ways, and there's still a few rough places in the metal. I got a feelin' that somethin's gonna go wrong, but I don't have the slightest clue as to what it might be."

"You'll figure it out."

He tried to laugh. "Aw, it's just a stupid hunch. Nothin' to it. Not a damned thing."

But then, the next day, when Doc didn't come back, Raider knew his hunch had been right on target.

CHAPTER 16

On a bright summer day in Chicago, a messenger hurtled down Fifth Avenue toward the thick wooden doors of the Pinkerton National Detective Agency. The lad pushed through the entrance and looked about for William Wagner, for whom the message was intended. When he saw the bespectacled supervisor, he ran quickly to his desk, gulping for air as he tried to speak.

"Easy, son," Wagner replied graciously. "We wouldn't want you to pop a fitting, now would we."

"A telegram," the lad said between heaving gasps. "Come a few minutes ago. From California."

Wagner gestured with his hands. "Well, don't just stand there, boy, let me have it!"

The messenger blushed, averting his eyes. "It's collect, sir. My boss says I can't give it to you unless you sign."

"Collect, eh? How much are the charges?"

"Two dollars," the young man replied.

Wagner straightened in his chair. "Two dollars! This agency doesn't grow money on trees, young man."

The boy took in a deep breath. "It's from Raider."

Wagner signed without hesitation. He opened the message, which was quite lengthy for a wire. The lad hung close by, trying to see what was written on the paper. Wagner chased him away with an icy glare.

As the messenger ran out into the street, Wagner turned his attention to the tome sent by the big Pinkerton. Raider didn't mince words: "Doc Weatherbee has disappeared. I have looked for him but he ain't nowhere to be found. The last time I seen him, he was going to meet a woman named Penelope Bloodsworth. She was the secretary of Sir Lionel Strang, who was killed by a man named Gilmore. Strang was said to have killed Theodore Huntley, and the police have said it is so. I have other beliefs, but they aren't as important as finding Doc."

Wagner shook his head. Doc Weatherbee gone! How could something like that have happened? Damn it all, it had to be Raider's fault. He turned back to the rest of the dispatch.

"It ain't my fault that Doc is gone. I warned him not to see that woman alone. I believe she is the one who has helped make him disappear. But it don't do no good to ask her because she has also left without a trace. They were to meet in a doctor's office, and the old man said they did. Only they left there and he don't know where they went. I don't either."

"Shoddy!" Wagner exclaimed. "Uncalled for!"

There was still more from Raider. "I know this don't look good, but it couldn't be helped. Doc had his reasons for doing what he did. I think they were bad reasons, but nobody ever cares what I think anyway. He is in love with the woman who sent him along, which I hope is not to his grave. Doc has not been himself since the Comancheros got ahold of him. I have asked the police to help and they have said they would, but you know how that goes. It ain't really their problem. And they are happy to have closed the case that we was sent here to work on."

Wagner knew about that. He had received a wire from Captain McCurley, commending Doc and Raider on their good work. Now Raider was expressing doubts about the final verdict in the Huntley case. Did Doc's disappearance tie in with the murder of Theodore Huntley?

He read the last paragraph. "I had a hunch something

wasn't straight about all this. Now that Doc is gone, I believe I was right. I have searched everywhere in San Francisco and I don't think he is here. If he is still alive, he is someplace else. I aim to look for him. The agency can pay me or not. I will do it by my ownself if you ain't going to say it's all right. I'm going to wait until tomorrow for your reply. If I don't hear from you, you'll know that I am looking for Doc and that's where I will be until I find him."

Wagner felt a burning in his chest. It was just like Raider to come up with something of this nature. Although, of late, Doc had certainly been careless in his dealings. Perhaps the man from Boston had gone on a holiday with the woman, but that seemed unlikely. Doc would have informed the agency of any leave of absence on his part. He was a true professional, even if he did seem to be slipping recently. Wagner reread the telegram before he took it into Allan Pinkerton's office.

Pinkerton pored over the communiqué with his usual care, shaking his head when he had finished it. "This isn't like Weatherbee."

Wagner sighed. "I'm afraid I have to agree with you."

Pinkerton dropped the message on his desk. "Now Raider wants to look for him."

"He's *going* to look for him," Wagner replied. "He doesn't care if we give him permission or not."

"Blast it all!" Pinkerton railed. "We stand a chance of losing two agents instead of just one."

Wager eyed his boss. "Should we send someone else to work with Raider? We have some good agents in the field near San Francisco."

Pinkerton made a frustrated gesture toward Raider's telegram. "He's only going to wait until tomorrow before he starts looking. I doubt we could get a man to him even if we could spare one."

Wagner agreed. Raider was on his own. The only decision to make would be the agency's sanctioning of his investigation of Doc's disappearance. Their official okay might mean trouble if Raider killed anybody. Wagner conveyed that fear to Pinkerton.

The big Scotsman only laughed. "*If* he kills somebody. You mean *when* he kills somebody."

Wagner nodded. "Yes, it does seem inevitable."

Pinkerton slammed his hand on his desk, a display of his anger toward Doc Weatherbee. "Why did he have to go and get himself involved with a woman? He's smarter than that."

"Reason and love keep little company together," Wagner offered.

Pinkerton's eyes narrowed. "What did you say?"

"A man in love doesn't always think straight."

Pinkerton grunted. "I don't pay our agents to fall in love. I pay them to solve cases. Weatherbee is slipping, William. When he's found, I want to see him on the carpet in front of my desk!"

"Then you are going to send Raider to look for him?"

"Not in an official capacity," Pinkerton replied. "But I want you to give him permission to search for Doc. Wire him any back pay that he has coming to him and add fifty dollars to the total."

"Fifty dollars!"

Pinkerton stood up, stretching. "We can't turn our back on these men, William. I can't forget the service Doc has done for us. I just hope Raider finds him in the arms of that woman. Then if he turns up, I'll make him wish he was dead."

Wagner agreed it was the thing to do.

"Get to it, William."

Wagner went back to his desk, where he opened the ledger book that contained the paysheet for all of his agents. Raider had about twenty dollars coming to him, along with the fifty Pinkerton had authorized for a supplement. Wagner wrote the voucher for payment.

When he was finished, he started to hail one of the office boys to take the message and the voucher to the Western Union key operator. However, given the importance of the dispatch, Wagner decided to deliver the papers himself. He hurried along Fifth Avenue at such a pace that he had broken a sweat by the time he reached the telegraph office.

The key operator looked up when Wagner came in. "Well, now, it's the boss himself. You must have an important wire there. Wouldn't have anything to do with that long one that came in today?"

Wagner frowned. "I suppose I could tell you to mind

your own business, but that wouldn't be valid since you read all of the messages that come into this office."

The operator shrugged. "How could I write 'em down without readin' 'em?"

"Well," Wagner said, "this will be a short one. Do you have your pencil ready?"

"Right here."

Wagner cleared his throat. "Send seventy dollars along with this message to Raider, care of Western Union, San Francisco. 'Proceed with investigation. Keep me informed. Wagner.' Did you get it?"

"First time, every time!"

The operator immediately began to tap the key. Wagner waited until he was finished, watching him all the while. When the operator had completed the message, he looked up at Wagner.

"Somethin' the matter, boss?"

Wagner shook his head. "I'm sorry if I've been short with you. I just want to say that you've always done a good job for us."

"Do a good job for everyone, chief."

"Yes, I suppose you do. Good day."

Wagner came out of the office, pausing on the sidewalk to take in the beautiful day. He decided not to go back to the agency. He'd have an early lunch and then maybe take a walk by the lake. He would try to enjoy the afternoon. Something to take his mind off Doc's untimely disappearance. Anything to forget the fact that Raider was going after him.

But after lunch, a dark cloud came down from the north, ruining Wagner's walk by the lake and turning his mind back to the stormy problems at hand.

CHAPTER 17

When Raider could not find a trail to Doc Weatherbee and Penelope Bloodsworth, he figured the most logical place to look for answers was the warehouse of Huntley Shipping. His gut feeling about Judd Gilmore would not leave him, so he decided to stake out the warehouse to keep an eye on the workings of the shipping operation, which, according to Gilmore, was on the rocks. The big man chose a suitable rooftop and used Doc's telescope to watch the comings and goings on the waterfront.

The telescope was just one of the things Doc had left behind when he disappeared. His room had not been touched since he departed for his meeting with the brown-eyed Englishwoman. Penelope was the kind of woman to make a man lose his head. Raider wondered if she might make him lose his life.

After two solid days of watching, Raider began to grow frustrated and impatient. No one, not even Judd Gilmore, went through the locked doors of the warehouse. Maybe things had finally folded up, which meant that Gilmore had probably been telling the truth all along. But Raider decided to stick it out, and on the fourth day he struck pay dirt.

Early in the morning, a large box wagon rumbled over the wharf and stopped in front of the Huntley warehouse. A soldier in cavalry blue waited the better part of an hour before Judd Gilmore arrived with the keys to open the big doors. A swarm of Chinamen came out of nowhere, led by Ulysses, the sailor who had given Raider such a hard time. Actually, Raider thought, it had been the other way around.

The dockworkers labored all morning to unload box after box of Army rifles, the same kind of crates Raider had seen before. The only difference was that the new containers did not have Chinese writing on them. When the job was finished, Gilmore signed a sheet of paper and sent the soldier on his way. Raider put down his telescope, thinking that nothing wrong had transpired. After all, Doc himself had checked out the deal and had found that the Army had indeed paid Huntley Shipping to dump the obsolete weapons.

But something inside Raider told him to wait. He kept watch until late afternoon, when another wagon, a small buckboard, creaked to a halt in the same place the first vehicle had stopped. Again Gilmore came out to check the cargo, nodding appreciatively to the driver. His men proceeded to unload square crates marked CAUTION. LIVE AMMUNITION.

Raider slapped the telescope together. "Blackjack!"

Gilmore was getting the rifles from the Army, but he was buying the cartridges from a private dealer. Why would he buy shells for the guns if he was going to dump them? Raider considered informing the Army about the deal, but he decided that would not go very far toward finding Doc. If Gilmore fried, that still left Doc in the grease, wherever he was.

He waited until dark, figuring the men would load the firearms onto another ship. But no vessel docked in front of the warehouse. They'd do it in the morning, the big man figured. Which gave him all night to come up with a plan. He hurried down off the roof and headed for the one place he thought he could find an ally.

• • •

Wan Chur was happy to see Raider until he told her what he wanted.

"A disguise?" she said disappointedly. "But I thought . . ."

Raider shook his head. "Maybe later. Right now I got to come up with a way to look like a sailor. And it's got to be good. If Ulysses or Gilmore knows who I am, then I ain't got a icicle's chance in the Mojave."

Wan Chur pouted for a little while, but when she realized the seriousness of Raider's request, she set to work with her best intentions. Raider put himself in her hands, reckoning that she had known enough sailors in her time to make him look authentic. He balked when she started to shave his head, but he gave in finally. His mustache came off as well.

"You've got scars on your head," Wan Chur said, grimacing. "You don't look like yourself anymore."

Raider picked up a hand mirror. "You're right—I don't. Hell, my noggin' looks like somebody's been after it with an ax."

Wan Chur smiled at him. "You look ugly, but somehow it's exciting. Maybe we could—"

"Later. What's next?"

She mixed up a concoction of iodine and whiskey to stain his skin to a darker color. Sailors spent a lot of time in the sun, so he had to have some sort of tan. When the skin dye had dried, she used red and black ink to make a tattoo on his right arm, a Chinese symbol that she said meant "Killer of Hateful Fools." On the left forearm, she drew an anchor with a serpent coiled around it.

Raider studied her handiwork. "Not bad."

"I used to make real tattoos before I went to work for Madam Wu." She pulled his face toward her and frowned at him.

"What's wrong, honey?"

"Those black eyes of yours," she replied. "We've got to cover one of them. I'll have to make you an eyepatch."

Raider squinted at her. "That's kinda obvious, ain't it? I mean, what would Doc call it? A clitch?"

"A cliché," she corrected. "Yes, it is, but it's better than having someone recognize you. Don't you think?"

"I need both eyes, Wan Chur."

"I'll make a pinhole so you can see through it."

When the eyepatch was finished, she dangled something bright and golden from her fingers.

Raider stared dubiously at the bauble. "What's that?"

"If you want to look right, you should have an earring."

"No."

"Raider..."

He had to draw the line somewhere. "No earring. Just get me some clothes."

"I have some clean things..."

"Dirty clothes. I want to look like I'm down on my luck."

She pouted again. "All right. But when I get back, you have to fuck me. Is that understood?"

Raider felt a stiffening in his jeans. He grabbed her tight ass and swung her onto his lap. "I guess it's a sacrifice I'll have to make."

"You better keep your promise!"

When she came back with the clothes, Raider was more than ready to oblige the enterprising young lady.

In the loose-fitting, foul-smelling outfit, Raider appeared to have climbed from the bowels of a San Francisco sewer. As he staggered along the dock the next morning, he caught sight of himself holding the whiskey bottle to his lips. He flinched at the reflection in the storefront window of a fish market. At first he thought some bum was staring at him from inside the shop. But it was him, scarred head and all, cutting the perfect image of a salty dog whose luck had run out at birth.

The fishmonger rushed from the shop, waving a sharp knife. "Get your ass away from here, you damned rummy!"

Raider obediently staggered on, lurching toward the corner of the building. He slipped into the alley, watching the building a few doors down. When the Huntley warehouse was opened, he started toward the workers who were loading the crated rifles onto a clipper ship that had docked overnight. The *China Princess II* was ready to accept cargo.

Raider stumbled straight for two Chinamen who carried one of the large rectangular boxes toward the gangplank. The big man bulled right into them, causing them to lose their balance and drop the crate. Luckily the container did not break open, but the accident was enough to arouse the ire of the foreman, Ulysses.

"Why, you stupid baboon! Whyncha watch where you're goin'?"

He tried to cuff Raider's ears, a blow that the big man managed to avoid. Raider scuffled around penitently, reaching for the crate himself. The Chinese men tried to shoo him away, but he did not budge.

Ulysses grinned toothlessly. "No. Let's see if he can carry it by his lonesome. He made you drop it, now let him pick it up."

Raider positioned himself by the center of the crate. He hunkered down, lifting with all the strength in his legs. With one smooth movement, he raised the box and swung it onto his shoulder. When the crate was perfectly balanced, he carried it onto the clipper, depositing it on deck.

The Chinese men chattered among themselves, obviously impressed by the big man's display of strength.

Raider came down the gangplank, smiling dumbly. Ulysses was grinning from ear to ear. He clapped Raider on the shoulder.

"Now that's how a white man works," he said, leering at his Oriental crew. "What's your name, Leviathan?"

Raider shook his head, making animal noises, pointing at his mouth.

"A mute, eh. Can you hear me? Can you understand what I'm sayin'?"

Raider nodded, making a foolish face.

Ulysses slapped his arms. "You're a big one, all right. How'd you like to sign on with us? You'd make short work of this load."

Raider wrinkled his brow as if he did not understand.

"Work!" Ulysses replied. "Hire on. You're a sailor, ain't you? You've worked on a ship before. You . . . sailor? Cargo?"

Raider continued to play dumb.

Ulysses reached into his pocket and withdrew a dollar.

"Pay, Leviathan. Money. You work for money." He put the silver in Raider's hand and closed his fingers around the coin.

Raider laughed like an idiot, nodding his head, jumping up and down.

"Take her easy," Ulysses said, trying to calm him down. "You'll get twice that on payday. Now come on, we got work to do. I want you to show these runty little yellow savages how a real man works."

With Raider's help, they had the entire cargo of guns and ammunition loaded by noon. The big man figured they would set sail immediately, but instead of departing, the crew was sent into the warehouse to handle several other bundles that had to be loaded on the clipper. Raider detected a sweet, dark odor from inside the burlap-wrapped squares as they took them aboard.

He pulled one of the Chinese men aside and pointed to the bundles, asking without words what was inside them.

The man replied, "Poppies."

Raider squinted as if he did not understand.

"Poppies," the man said again, smiling. "Opium." He lifted an imaginary pipe to his mouth, drawing in nonexistent smoke. "Ha-ha. Opium. Good. Make you sleep. Have pretty dreams."

Raider grimaced, pulling away like he wanted no part of it.

Ulysses saw him backing off the gangplank. "Hey," he called, running up to them. "What's the matter, Leviathan?" He glared at the Chinaman. "Don't be scarin' him, Kwong Lee. Just leave him alone. We're gonna need him when we get to the island." Then, looking back at Raider: "Don't worry, mate. It ain't gonna hurt you. Go on, there's more work to be done."

By dusk, the clipper's holds were full of contraband. Raider wasn't exactly sure what else they were carrying, but he figured most of it was tainted merchandise. After the last crate had been loaded, Ulysses disappeared for a few minutes, only to return with Judd Gilmore leading the way. The little man inspected the cargo and then expressed his satisfaction with a job well done.

Ulysses singled out Raider, clapping him on the

shoulder. "I owe it all to me big man here. He does the work of three Chinkos."

Gilmore looked right at him. Raider felt his stomach turning cartwheels. If the little man recognized him, it was all over.

Gilmore nodded. "Well, just do whatever it takes to get this to the island by tomorrow morning. We don't want to be late. He wouldn't like it."

"We're casting off right away," Ulysses replied.

Gilmore turned and strode confidently away from them. He had looked right through Raider. To him, the big man from Arkansas was just another body to tote his burdens.

Ulysses reached behind a crate and pulled out a bottle of whiskey, which he tossed to Raider. "Here, Leviathan. Take a rest. You earned it."

Raider nodded like a Comanche with a jug of firewater. He was relieved that the foreman did not expect him to help with the sailing of the ship. He knew nothing about rigs or lines or navigation, so he was happy to lay back on the crates and pretend to get drunk.

As he swished the cheap liquor over his tongue, he wondered what island Gilmore and Ulysses had been talking about. No doubt it was the port of delivery for the hot cargo. As the ship swung out into the tidal currents of the bay, Raider wondered if he had made a mistake in signing on with the crew. Even though they were carrying contraband, it didn't mean that Doc was somewhere at the end of the voyage. But it was too late to turn back, so the big man told himself that he was at least finding out what sort of cards Judd Gilmore had up his sleeve.

CHAPTER 18

The sun rode up out of the east, throwing a dazzling orange reflection on the choppy, purple surface of the Pacific. A steady breeze pushed the *China Purple II* south toward the gentle green rise of an island shoreline. Raider stood on the bow of the clipper, peering toward the land that jutted up out of the sea. He had awakened earlier in the hold of the ship with his stomach tied in knots. The fresh salt air had revived him enough so that he was able to fight off the seasickness. If Ulysses and the others had seen him heaving over the side, they would have known immediately that he was no true sailor.

"Mutey! Hey, Leviathan!"

Raider turned to see Ulysses waving at him. He wanted Raider to come back and take the wheel. The big man shook his head furiously, grunting negative animal sounds from his maw, showing reluctance at the thought of taking responsibility for the ship.

Ulysses laughed. "Don't be afeared, Leviathan. You don't have to be the captain. Just hold her steady while I light a fire under these Chinkos."

Raider had no choice but to obey. He tentatively grabbed the wheel and held the *China Princess II* on course while Ulysses directed the crew for the inevitable mooring. A long pier extended from the beach of the green island, stretching into a narrow harbor. Raider wondered if the water was deep enough to accept the clipper.

Beyond the pier were two structures that became more apparent as the ship drew closer to the shoreline. A tall, white two-story house rested on the cresting bow of an incline, probably the highest point on the island. Closer to the beach, a circular stone tower rose up like a medieval turret.

Smaller boats sat on the sandy crescent of the beach, and another vessel, about one-third the size of the clipper, was tied to the pier, lapping in the water's undulations. When the *China Princess II* was in range, the boat at the dock casted off, chugging toward the clipper under the hissing power of a small steam engine.

Ulysses waved at the approaching vessel and then came back to take the wheel from Raider. "Right on time, Leviathan. I can't wait till the *Princess* gets her engine. Mr. Gilmore says we'll be on steam no later than September. I'll grow barnacles on me butt if he's wrong."

A steam engine for the clipper? Hadn't Sir Lionel planned to revamp the fleet in the same way? Gilmore claimed to have limited assets, but here he was planning to convert at least one ship in the outdated Huntley fleet. Raider felt excitement growing in him at the thought of learning more about Judd Gilmore's real operation. Even if it didn't lead him to Doc, he might be able to talk McCurley into reopening the Huntley case—if he turned up the right evidence.

Ulysses pointed toward the bow. "Get in front, Leviathan. Make yourself useful on the lines."

Raider nodded and headed for the bow.

The small steamer swung around, pointing its stern at the clipper. A Chinese man threw a line to Raider, who attached it to a cleat. The steamer then started forward, towing the *China Princess II* toward the pier where several Oriental men waited with hooks and lines.

When the clipper was securely moored to the pier, the steamer backed out again and headed east, disappearing around the curve of the island's shoreline. Raider watched it until a hand fell on his shoulder.

Ulysses turned him around. "No time for gawkin' Leviathan. We got work to do. Get your back limber. We got to empty this tub."

They began to unload the ship, carrying the crates of rifles and ammunition to a wagon that waited on the beach. A rutted path led up the slope, with two trails branching off, one leading toward the stone tower, the other going all the way to the white house. Stretching away from the tower, along a natural cliff, was a stone wall about five feet high. Raider wondered how long it had taken the builders to haul all the wood and stone from the mainland. It must have taken years to build two such impressive structures.

By noon, the wagon had made several trips between the dock and the stone tower. Raider wanted to get a look at the turret, but Ulysses kept him at the ship to lug the crates down the gangplank, along the pier to the wagon. When the last box was loaded, Raider started to pick up a bundle of the poppies that remained in the hold.

Ulysses stopped him. "Not yet, mate. You go back to the wagon and wait there. We're gonna need your strong back to get them crates into the tower."

Raider strode the length of the pier and hopped on the back of the wagon, anticipating the driver's shaking the reins to urge the big draft horse up the incline. For some reason, the driver hesitated, shifting in his seat so that he could peer out toward the deep water. Raider focused in the same direction.

Another clipper ship came around the corner, towed into port by the steam vessel. It took about twenty minutes for the second clipper to dock on the opposite side of the pier. Ulysses supervised the mooring, acting uncharacteristically nervous as he laid the gangplank for the multitude of men who came up on deck.

Raider counted them as they came off. Thirty in all. They trudged along the pier, quietly passing the wagon as they made for the white house. They had the look of hardbitten men, the scarred faces and rugged bodies of hired guns, mercenaries. Some were white, but most of them were Chinese. Raider squinted, rubbing his bald head. Why only thirty? They had unloaded enough guns to outfit a small army. Maybe these were just one platoon. Maybe there were more inside the white house. Something else he would have to find out about. What the hell were they doing there in the first place? Did Gilmore plan to invade the mainland?

Raider kept his eyes trained on the second clipper. Two more figures came down the gangplank to be greeted by Ulysses' nervous smile. Judd Gilmore was there with a second man who was clad in a black satin robe. A hooded cowl hid the second man's face. Raider figured to get a closer look, but the driver shook the reins as they started toward him.

The big man watched them as the wagon turned toward the tower. He could still see them as their backs headed away from him. Raider sat up straight, his eyes bulging. He almost spoke but then remembered that he was feigning muteness.

It was the emblem on the black robe that alerted him to a new danger. For embroidered on the silken cloth was a frightening pattern that was easily discernible, even at such a long distance. A large, curling white dragon leered hideously at him with burning red eyes. The White Dragon. Raider had found him to be entirely real. And he was definitely in league with Judd Gilmore.

As the wagon rolled around in front of the tower, Raider got his first glimpse of the improbable structure. The stone turret rose about fifty feet into the air. Some sort of lamp rested on the top, which meant that the tower acted as a lighthouse in addition to being a storage place for the arms. One thing the big man had not counted on was the row of artillery weapons that stretched along the stone wall. Six cannons and six mortars were angled so that they could shoot their projectiles over the wall at any sort of vessel that sailed into the island's harbor. The White Dragon needed heavy firepower to protect him.

The driver halted the wagon and hopped down out of the seat.

Raider climbed off and stepped toward the stack of cannonballs beside the first big gun. He lifted one of the iron missiles from the top, hefting it for a moment. The artillery certainly wasn't for show.

"Hey! You goddamn guy! Hurry, hurry!"

The driver was waving at him. They had work to do. Several of the other men had come up from the ship for the same reason.

On the front side of the tower was a small recess that looked like a cave. Through this alcove they gained entrance to the structure. On the back wall of the recess was a wooden door that led to a storage area where the others had already begun to stack the guns. To the right of the door, on the opposite side of the recess, rose a set of stone steps that spiraled up into the tower. An armed guard, also Chinese, stood at the base of the stairs to prevent anyone from going up.

Raider began to help the rest of the crew, hauling the crates by himself as the others doubled on the task. All of the crates had been stacked outside the storage room, which was a musty, dungeon-stinking enclosure. Not a good place for keeping guns, the big man thought. The moisture would eat them bit by bit—unless the White Dragon intended on using them soon. The whole room was stacked with munitions that had been brought on previous trips. It took them until dusk to fit the remaining boxes into the humid stone chamber.

As he wiped his brow, one of the men lit up a small pipe. Opium glowed momentarily in the evening shadows. The others, including the stair guard, crowded around to have a puff. Raider figured it was time to have a look at the top of the tower. He crept toward the steps, slipping quietly upward.

A faint sound reached his ears as he climbed. It was a low, mournful noise, like a lonely tree bough creaking on a windy night. When he drew closer to a second wooden door, he realized the sound more closely resembled the desperate tone of human beings in pain. Raider stepped to the door, gazing through the barred square that served as a window.

The White Dragon's captives, mostly women, were crammed into the stone turret like cattle in a holding pen. At first Raider figured the women were there to service the men who had come ashore. But then it hit him that they might very well be intended for other ports of the East. White slaves for the highest bidder. His eyes scanned the despairing faces until he saw the pearl-gray derby wedged between two brown-haired prisoners.

"Doc."

He said it so softly that the man from Boston did not even hear him. Doc had his eyes closed, leaning back against the stone wall. His right arm rested on the shoulder of the brunette next to him. Raider wanted to kick down the door right then, to drag his partner away from this awful incarceration. He hated Penelope Bloodsworth for delivering Doc to such a fate.

Suddenly he felt cold steel in the middle of his back. The man behind him uttered something in a harsh voice. Raider wheeled around slowly with his hands up. He began to babble incoherently in his mute performance.

The Chinaman led him back down the stairs, where Ulysses was waiting.

"Leviathan," he said, shaking his head. "What the devil were you doin' up there?"

Raider aped around, grabbing his crotch, smiling and drooling.

Ulysses laughed. "Drop that rifle off his back, Chinko. He was just lookin' for some relief from one of them doxies we got up there."

Raider nodded frantically.

"Don't worry, boy," Ulysses assured him, "we'll be lettin' you get it wet before we leave this island. But you better come back to the ship now. We don't want you gettin' in any more trouble."

Raider had wanted to get a look inside the white house, but it was clear that the hired help didn't venture past the front porch. How many men did Gilmore have in there? What the hell were they planning?

He followed Ulysses back to the *China Princess II*. At first he thought he might be able to have a look at the second clipper, but a burly guard stood by the gangplank with a rifle. The White Dragon wasn't taking any chances. Raider had to go back down into the cargo hold to rest on a burlap pallet.

Ulysses tossed him a bottle of cheap rotgut. "Drink hearty, Leviathan. I'll see you in the mornin'."

With that, the captain left the big man to his own devices. Raider immediately leapt up and looked out a small porthole. The sun was sinking on the western horizon, showing only the last tip of an orange circle. It would be dark enough for him to move in a few minutes. He'd have to be careful with all the guards around.

There was only one plan of action. Free Doc and get to one of the smaller boats on the beach. Then they'd have to row all the way back to the mainland and tell somebody about the White Dragon and his arsenal. There was no way the two of them could fight off so many men. It would be suicide to even try.

Raider considered leaving by himself, which would be a hell of a lot easier. But he finally decided to take the risk of breaking out his partner. He couldn't leave Doc in such a mess. It just wouldn't be right.

Raider lifted the whiskey bottle to his lips and took one last pull to bolster his courage. Then he started on his way.

CHAPTER 19

With the armed guard stationed between the two clipper ships, Raider knew he would not be able to leave the *China Princess II* by way of the gangplank. The only other alternative was to slip quietly over the starboard rail, dropping into cold, purple drink. Swim to the beach, hoof it to the tower, take out the sentry, and then free Doc. They could grab one of the smaller boats from the narrow strip of sand between the tower and the harbor. Doc knew all about boats. He'd have no trouble getting them to land, where they could enlist the aid of the marshal or the Army or the governor, or anybody else who might be able to help them.

As Raider eased through the shadows of the clipper's belly, he wondered how it was going to sound when he told someone about the standing militia on the White Dragon's little island. Who the hell would believe it? A tower full of guns, a row of artillery, and a barracks full of soldiers. Raider wouldn't have bought the story with found money. They'd have to hurry, to get back quick before Gilmore shipped out the guns again—if he planned to ship them out.

Raider's bald head bobbed up above deck into the cool night air. He peeked over the port rail, looking at the guard who dragged on a thin, glowing pipe. All of the White Dragon's men seemed to be juiced up on opium. That could come in handy in the right situation, Raider thought.

When the guard lowered his head, Raider slipped onto deck, hitting his belly, crawling through the dark to the opposite side of the ship. In one graceful motion, he rolled over the rail, hanging on with his hands for a moment while his feet dangled in the lapping water. It was going to be frigid, the kind of cold that brought on the croup and rheumatism. Raider let go of the rail and entered the water with no more sound than a wave against the hull.

The swim was easy. After a few strokes, he hit a rocky bottom where sea plants and moving sea creatures squashed under his bare feet. Raider waded up onto the beach, stopping immediately to take his bearings in the moonless dark. In front of him, fifteen or twenty feet high, rose a steep cliff that ended at the stone wall adjacent to the tower. It wasn't necessary to climb. He only had to step to his right, taking the beach to the wagon path.

As Raider approached the tower in the shadows, he made as much noise as he could so that the sentry on duty would hear his arrival. When he turned the corner of the stone wall, the guard lowered an old single-shot Army rifle at him. Raider made animal sounds so that the guard would know immediately that he was the tall mute with the strong back. Raider played the ape, begging the man not to shoot him.

The guard nodded but then tried to shoo him back to the ship. He figured Raider had come for the women. But the big man went into his hasty pantomime, cupping his hands, indicating that he had something to smoke, a pipe to share.

The guard smiled, lowering the single-shot. As he came toward the big man, Raider turned away, coiling his body for the strike. He swung upward, catching the sentry's un-suspecting chin. The man buckled and fell flat on his back. Raider picked up the single-shot and applied the rifle butt for good measure. He didn't want the guard to wake up anytime soon. He searched the man's pocket until he found a single key on a leather thong. There were also five rifle cartridges, which he slipped into his pocket.

The single-shot preceded Raider as he mounted the stone steps to the dank prison. He clung to the wall, stopping when he saw a light glowing above. Had they stationed another guard at the top of the stairs? He listened for signs of movement but heard only the low groans from the tower's dungeon. Best to push on and meet any challenge with a round from the rifle.

An oil lamp flickered by the door. For a moment, Raider wondered why the Chinese man had left the lamp up there. But when he looked back, he saw the flickering shadows on the wall and realized the guard had been watching the dark shapes that performed in the slight breeze of the night. Opium could make a man do things like that.

The key fit perfectly in the lock. It turned a little rough, but the mechanism finally clicked and the door swung open. The lamp glow spilled into the dark cell, falling on the pearl-gray derby. Doc sat up, shielding his eyes from the sudden intrusion of light.

Raider went in and knelt beside his partner. "Come on, Weatherbee. Let's get the hell out of here."

Doc grabbed his partner's arm. "Raider! Is it really you? I'm not dreaming?"

Raider shook his head, chortling. "Blabbin' all the golldanged time, even when we're shit deep in trouble. Come on, Doc, we ain't got much time. There's a whole lot of bad shit fallin' in this place. We got to find somebody who can shovel it out before the stable gets full. I'm afraid it's a damned sight too big for us to handle."

Raider tried to make him stand up, but Doc resisted. Instead of hurrying along, the man from Boston turned to his right, nudging the woman who slept next to him. "Wake up, dear girl. Raider's here. I told you he would come."

The woman groaned and started to roll over.

Raider shook his partner. "Leave her, Doc. She's only gonna slow us down. We'll come back for all of 'em when we raise some kind of posse."

Doc was insistent. "I won't leave without her."

The brown-haired lady sat up in the light.

Raider gaped at the recognition of brown eyes and full mouth. "You!" he cried. "What the hell are you doin' here?"

Penelope Bloodsworth gaped right back at him. "Raider! Doc said you would come. I didn't believe him."

The big man stood up, glaring down at her. "You ain't comin' with us, Penelope. Not after you sold Doc into this mess."

Doc put his arm around her, holding her close to him. "No, you've got it all wrong. We were captured together after we left the doctor's office. A carriage full of Gilmore's men nabbed us before we had walked a block."

Raider grabbed Doc's shirt, pulling the shorter Pinkerton to his feet. "Don't you see what she's done? They used her to get to you. Now that she's sprung the trap, they're leavin' the bait to rot with the animal. She's stayin' right here, Doc. You hear that, Penelope?"

Doc pushed him away. "She's not Penelope Bloodsworth," he insisted, helping the distraught woman to her feet. "Raider, allow me to introduce Rebecca Huntley, daughter of the late William Huntley and sister of the deceased Theodore Huntley."

Raider scowled disbelievingly at both of them. "Kiss my ass!" he cried. "Is that what she told you?"

Rebecca looked at him with soulful eyes. "It's true. I am Rebecca Huntley. I don't care if you believe me."

"Well, I don't," Raider replied. "You're lyin' so Doc will pull you out of here. Gilmore left you to rot after he was finished with you."

"No," she said softly. "Please listen to me."

In a weak, gentle voice, with Doc's help, she explained how she had come west to San Francisco after her brother's murder, hoping to learn the truth on her own. At first, she suspected Sir Lionel and Gilmore of being in league together, trying to take over her family's business. Since Gilmore knew her, she decided to infiltrate Sir Lionel's operation. She feared Gilmore might try to kill her the way he had killed her brother.

When she answered Sir Lionel's advertisement for a personal secretary, she figured Strang would prefer a woman from his own home country. Rebecca dressed accordingly and feigned a British accent. The Englishman hired her on the spot, giving her access to all his private records. Once inside the operation, she quickly learned that Strang was innocent of any wrongdoing that concerned her brother's demise. She also learned that Strang and her brother had indeed completed the transaction that would have allowed Sir Lionel to assume half ownership of Huntley Shipping. However, proof of the deal was stolen from Strang's office, and since he had paid in cash, Sir Lionel had no proof that the merger had been consummated. Gilmore had bilked Strang out of a great deal of money, as well as blaming him for Theodore Huntley's death.

Raider squinted at her. "Why didn't you just tell us the truth from the beginnin'?"

She broke into tears, leaning against Doc. "I didn't know who to trust. For all I knew, you were working for Gilmore. You wouldn't believe me when I told you Sir Lionel was innocent. You seemed to be protecting Gilmore. Doc and I fought the whole time. I wanted to tell you, Raider, but I just couldn't. I was also afraid of facing Gilmore. I knew he would want me out of the way. Then he saw me at the funeral. I didn't think he recognized me with my veil, but he did."

"And he decided to abduct us," Doc broke in. "Treachery that has no limit. And I was too blind to see it coming."

Raider exhaled, shaking his head. "Yeah, I reckon Gilmore was the one all along. But I'm here to tell you that I've seen the White Dragon, Doc. He's real, and he's on this island. That's why we got to get the hell out of here. He's got an army that's ready for trouble."

Doc's brow wrinkled. "My God, I'd no idea the political climate was so bad in California. You don't think he intends to invade the mainland?"

"I don't have the slightest notion what he's got in mind," Raider replied, taking Rebecca Huntley's arm. "Come on, if we're all goin', let's get down them stairs. Hell, these others are startin' to notice what we're doin'. We can't take 'em all."

Stirring on the floor were Doc and Rebecca's cellmates. They might get too excited if they thought they could get away. Raider had to lock the door again before the others made a disturbance that would be heard outside the tower.

As they started to turn for the door, Rebecca lost her balance and stumbled.

"She's weak, Doc."

The usually dapper Pinkerton looked bedraggled and exhausted, but he lifted her into his arms. "I can't leave her. I love her too much for that."

"Well, let's shake a leg. I don't want to . . ."

Something strange caught the big man's eye. The lamp was rising on its own, the flame flickering above the stone floor. Raider started to raise the single-shot, but the metallic chortle of three rifle levers stopped him short. He knew then that they weren't going anywhere.

Raider dropped the single-shot, lifting his hands to the sky. The three riflemen framed the doorway. They were Chinese, just like the majority of the men on the island. Judd Gilmore moved between them, holding the oil lamp in front of him.

"Fox in the henhouse," Raider said sarcastically.

Gilmore tipped his hand to the rough-hewn detective. "Mr. Raider," he said in a hatefully triumphant tone, "I must congratulate you on your ingenuity. You had me bamboozled with your disguise until I heard you talking just now. I suppose you Pinkertons really are as good as they say. If you hadn't made your move during the change of watch, we might never have caught you."

Raider shrugged. "My bad luck." He glanced at his partner. "See what happens when you leave me alone, Doc. I mess it all up. You wouldn't have missed a detail like that."

"Such stirring loyalty," Gilmore offered.

Doc turned away, helping Rebecca Huntley back down to the floor of the cell. He sat next to her, stroking her hair. She put her head on his chest, sobbing quietly.

Gilmore smiled horribly, shaking his head. "Touching. Just look at the lovebirds, Raider. Such a pitiful sight. Oh well, at least I won't have to kill her the way I killed her brother. Aren't you happy to hear that, Rebecca?"

Raider scowled at the little man with a lamp in his hand. "Just gonna sell her into white slavery, huh?"

Gilmore nodded. "She's pretty. Someone will pay my price. A pity that Weatherbee can't afford to buy her."

Raider leaned back against the stone wall. "You're somethin', Judd. You killed ole Teddy and made it look like Sir Lionel was to blame."

Gilmore winced, like a hangman who had just been given a compliment on the way he pulled the gallows lever. "It had to be done. Strang would have jeopardized my entire operation."

"What's the matter?" Raider offered. "Teddy figure out that you were usin' his ships to smuggle guns and opium?" He gestured around him. "Not to mention slaves."

Gilmore frowned hatefully. "The fool. I was making more money than Strang could have imagined. But Teddy wouldn't listen. He insisted on making the operation legitimate. Said he wanted to make his father proud of him."

"You kill his daddy, too?"

Gilmore laughed. "No, William was considerate enough to die for me. I rejoiced when Teddy left for Boston. I ran the company to my own preference, until Strang showed up, offering to buy in for half."

Raider smiled confidently. "I can pick it up from here."

"By all means."

"You made Huntley demand cash from Strang," Raider said. "Then after the deal was struck, you killed Teddy and robbed Sir Lionel of his papers. You stole the money out from under him and kept the company for yourself. It happened just like Sir Lionel said."

Gilmore nodded, a sick expression of satisfaction on his face. "Just like he said. Only no one believed him."

Raider's eyes narrowed. "I did. At least until I saw the gun in his hand at your office. How did you fake it, Gilmore? You managed to make it look so damned real."

Gilmore waved the lamp at him. "I won't tell you—figure it out for yourself."

Raider sighed deeply, thinking about it. "I been mullin' this one over for a long time. I remember how calm you were that day when we finally settled the plan to draw out Strang. You knew we wouldn't be able to see you when Sir Lionel came into your office. When he stood in front of your desk, Sir Lionel was in our way."

Gilmore turned to the three riflemen behind him. "Did you hear that?" Then, back to Raider. "Commendable. Can you speculate as to the rest of it?"

Raider shrugged. "Maybe. Try this on. You were waitin' with a gun when Sir Lionel came in. You asked if he had a weapon, and when he said yes, you made him take it out of his coat, real slow-like so he couldn't use it and we wouldn't see it right away."

"Bravo," Gilmore rejoined. "Keep going."

Raider glared at the loathsome man. "You made him unload his pocket revolver so he couldn't defend himself. Then you made him turn toward the window with an empty gun, forcin' him to close the curtains like it was his own idea to shut 'em. That gave us a look at the gun. It seemed like he pulled on you when it was really the other way around."

"Splendid! Splendid!"

"You had to work fast then. You made Sir Lionel throw his gun on the desk and you picked it up, putting one bullet in the cylinder. Bang, you plugged Strang in the head. Then you turned and shot a hole in the wall behind you, makin' it look like Sir Lionel had shot at you."

Gilmore grinned appreciatively. "Exactly as it happened. Did you know all along?"

"I had my doubts from the git-go," Raider replied. "The powder burns, the small shot coming after the loud one. Strang's gun was at his feet where you threw it after he fell. But you did too good a job, Gilmore. Nobody would listen to me. It was almost perfect."

Gilmore enjoyed a hideous chuckle. "It *is* perfect now that I have the three of you."

Raider pointed at the little man. "I ain't finished. There's still the murder of Madam Wu to answer for. And the attempt on Strang's life at the cathouse. You were behind both of those, weren't you?"

"I'm afraid I can't take credit for either one," Gilmore replied. "The Tong arranged the woman's death. They had to stop her from telling you about the White Dragon. They also wanted to take out Strang, but unfortunately, he was too quick."

Raider turned his shoulder to Gilmore. "Get on out of here. You can kill me and Doc tomorrow. Just let me spend some time with my friends before you do it."

"Oh, Weatherbee won't die. Not here anyway. After the girl leaves with these other Shanghai brides, your partner will be shipped east as well. He'll probably die in a Chinese coal mine."

"Doc always did like adventure."

Gilmore grinned. "Be as flippant as you like. You're the only one who's going to die. And it will be a slow, torturous death. The settling of an old score, if you will."

Raider squinted at Gilmore, saying they had never had any truck between them in the past. Gilmore kept smiling, telling the big man it was high-time that he was reacquainted with an old friend, someone who couldn't wait to see him. Raider started to protest until the riflemen moved in to take him away.

"So long, Doc."

But the man from Boston just sat there in silence, his arm wrapped around the shoulder of the weeping girl.

CHAPTER 20

Judd Gilmore and his three riflemen led Raider down a dark, narrow corridor in the white house. Dim gaslights illuminated the bare plaster walls and wooden floors just enough for them to find their way through the barren palatial structure. The trio of rifle-wielding Chinese men pushed Raider through an archway at the end of the hall, throwing him to his knees in a rather large parlor. They hovered over him with the same kind of single-shot breechloaders he had taken from the sentry at the tower. Gilmore remained close by with the lantern and a Colt .45 that he had picked up along the way.

Raider looked up at the wall in front of him. Incense bowls hung low from the ceiling, smoldering lazy clouds of jasmine into the air. Between the bowls rested a huge thronelike altar draped in red silk and satin. Over the throne, stretching the width of the wall, hung a large, ornamental dragon that had been forged and beaten from white metal. Raider realized it was white gold.

A weak, garbled voice came out of the deep shadows around the throne. "Hail, the big Pinkerton. The infamous

Raider. What would your colleagues say if they could see you in such a lowly state?"

Raider squinted into the dark. "You got the edge on me, partner. You see me, but I can't tell you where you are. Why don't you step out where I can get a look at you?"

The man on the throne clapped his hands twice. Instantly one of the riflemen moved to the far wall, cranking a lever that brought up the gas lamps, making the room brighter. Raider regarded the man in the black robe, trying to catch a glimpse of his face. His captor's features were hidden by the black cowl. Raider still couldn't recognize him.

"Gilmore said you got business with me," the big man offered. "How come I don't remember you?"

An evil laugh from the oval of the hood. "Because you are a fool, Pinkerton. Because you are so careless to think that once you kill a man, he remains dead. You thought you could kill me once before, but you were wrong. I have lived to exact my revenge."

Raider glared up at him. "Tried to kill you, huh? Sorry. I reckon I must have meant it, though. I usually don't try unless I mean it."

"Spare me your homespun wit," the White Dragon replied. "Bind his hands and feet!" he said to Gilmore.

Gilmore complied, using thick jute to strap Raider's wrists and ankles together. Raider cursed him in a whisper as he worked. Gilmore just kept smiling with his self-satisfied expression.

With his hands tied behind him, Raider had to fight for balance. He barely managed to stay upright on his knees. A stiff wind would have knocked him over in hurry.

The hooded man got up off his throne and came down the steps of the altar toward Raider. He came closer to the big Pinkerton, studying him the way a man would look at a dangerous captured animal. Raider sensed fear in the White Dragon. He kept trying to find the man's eyes in the shadows of the cowl.

"Who the hell are you?" he demanded.

The White Dragon lurched forward, grabbing Raider's hair, jerking his head back. "You will pay for what you did to me, Pinkerton!"

"Just tell me what I did so I'll know what I'm dyin' for!"

The White Dragon pulled back the cowl, revealing his hideously scarred face. Raider could see where the moniker had come from. Skin that had once belonged to a Chinese man now resembled the mottled hide of a white reptile. The layers of scar tissue had come from a burn, Raider thought. Nothing else could do that to a man's face.

Raider's stomach turned over, but he still didn't know the man in front of him. "Tell me who the hell you are!"

The White Dragon replied through a hole that had once been his mouth. "Galveston, two years ago. You blew up the *China Princess,* you and your partner. You made a bomb, a torpedo that destroyed my beloved vessel. A man named Stalmaster was arrested, but the authorities believed that I went down with my ship."

Raider's mouth hung open and his eyes grew wider. He recalled everything in one rush of memory. The Chinaman he had stopped once before: "Lin Ching!"

Lin Ching slapped Raider, toppling him to the floor. He hovered over the big man with a bony finger pointed in his face. "You could not kill me, Pinkerton. I have lived for this day. Now you will know the torture and pain that I have endured for two years. That is how long I will take to kill you. And you will pray many times for death before it finally comes."

Raider rolled over on his side and peered up at the disfigured countenance of Lin Ching, the White Dragon. "It was all a game, Lin Ching. You knew the risk. You broke the law when you traded them coolies for Texas women. We destroyed your ship because it was our job."

"And I will destroy you because it is my pleasure." He lifted the hood back over his head, retreating into the anonymity of shadows. "Take him below. We will begin tomorrow."

Gilmore cut the ropes that bound Raider's feet so he could walk again. The riflemen got him up and pushed him back through the corridor. At first he thought they were going to take him back to the tower, but instead they brought him to the rear of the house.

Gilmore opened a door. "In here."

"This must be below," Raider offered.

Gilmore struck him in the back of the head and then pushed him down a flight of wooden steps, delivering him into the deep, dark bowels of the White Dragon's lair.

Raider figured his torture had begun a little early.

They trussed him up in the dark cellar, hanging him from a beam with his arms tied overhead. The rope was fixed so that Raider's tiptoes could barely reach the dirt floor. He could put pressure on his toes for a few minutes until they began to cramp. Then he would have to hang by his arms again, feeling the pain and the threat of separation in his shoulders. No matter which position he was in, it was only a few seconds before the pain set in. Not a restful way to spend the night.

But Raider kept up his balancing act, trying to prevent his arms from coming out of the sockets. When they finally came to start on him, he was going to try to goad them into killing him right out. He might even run if he got the chance. Better to die with a bullet in the back than to let the demented Chinaman spend two years making him wish he was dead.

As a clock struck three somewhere in the huge house, the door above rattled with a key in the lock. The door closed quietly and soft footsteps came down the stairs into the dark cellar. Torture for the day was about to begin, Raider thought. He tried to get angry.

"Piss-ant bastard!" he cried. "Cut me loose and I'll tear your head off!"

No reply from the shadows. Raider could hear the figure moving, coming closer. His nose detected the strong scent of jasmine over the darkness of the basement. They were really trying to get to him. Did they figure the perfume would make him think of women? Did they think it would make his gut ache? They were right.

"Son of a bitch. I'm gonna kill all of you if I get the chance. Do you hear me?"

The rasping strike of a match. Flame to candle. The swell of an orange circle of light. She had on a black nightgown.

"Hello, Raider."

His eyes opened wider. "Goldie?"

The blond girl from Madame Wu's came closer, smiling with a thick, sultry mouth. "I don't remember that I ever told you my name."

Raider grimaced, dropping down to his tiptoes. "You didn't. I asked about you the last time I was at the parlor."

She touched his face with her soft hand. "Aw, that's sweet."

Sweat poured down into Raider's eyes. "Wan Chur said you run off with a rich man."

She frowned, nodding dolefully. "I reckon I did. I didn't want to, but I did. I can't say I'm happy about it."

"Gilmore?"

She shook her head. "Lin Ching. Old Lizard Head himself."

Raider laughed until he felt the pressure on his shoulders. "Goldie . . ."

"Came to the parlor one night," she continued. "Looked over all us girls and then decided he wanted me. I coulda refused to go with him, but he would've just had me killed. What else could I do?"

"You can cut me down. Ow!" He muttered several curse words under his breath. "Cut me loose, Goldie. I'll get you outta here."

She started to walk around him, giving him the eye. "I might. If you promise to do something for me."

"Anything."

"You have to hump me," she replied, setting the candle on the floor.

Raider exhaled, becoming impatient. "Goldie, I ain't in no mood and I ain't in no shape to do that. Now cut me loose!"

"Let's see if you're in shape."

She pulled down his pants, immediately taking his cock into her mouth. Raider realized he was ready for her. His member stiffened between her lips. Goldie came up, stroking his length.

"Even when you're hanging by a thread, you still get hard."

Raider grunted. "Cut me down. We'll get it over with."

She reached up with a blade that reflected the candle-light. Raider hit the floor on his back. Goldie didn't even give him time to recover. She lifted her nightgown and straddled him, guiding his prickhead toward the wetness between her thighs.

Raider hung on for the ride, trying to forget the burning in his feet and shoulders. As he neared release, he felt the pain subsiding a little. He managed to roll Goldie over on her back, finishing his climax on top of her. She heaved and moaned, bucking off the dirt floor like a raw bronco. He drove his cock deep into her, discharging, making her body shake with her own orgasmic sensations.

Her face was covered with perspiration. "Thank you, honey. You don't know how good that felt."

He squinted at her. "Lin Ching ain't takin' care of you?"

She shook her head. "He's crazy. It even embarrasses me to think about the things he wants me to do. I don't want to talk about it."

Raider rolled off her, pulling up his pants. He got to his feet, maintaining his balance, stretching to work the kinks out of his body. He had felt worse in his life. At least he had a chance now.

Goldie stood up as well, putting her arms around his neck. "When I heard you was here, I waited until old crocodile face was asleep. I had to get down here to see you."

"We gotta get outta here, Goldie."

She sighed, burying her face in his chest. "Not me, Raider. You go. If you come back with the law, you can take me away. But for now, I got to stay here. If I leave, Lin Ching will know I was the one that set you free."

She had a point.

Raider pushed her away from him, holding her arms. "You got to tell me a few things, Goldie."

She nodded. "Anything."

"How do I get out of this basement?"

"Not by the stairs," she replied. "There's nobody by the door, but the place is crawlin' with Lin Ching's soldiers."

Raider kissed her on the cheek. "Good. That's the kind of stuff I need to know. How many men has he got here?"

Goldie shrugged. "With the thirty that came in today, I'd say sixty or seventy. They mostly stay upstairs, so I can't get a real good count."

"What's he need them for? Is he gonna try to take over California or somethin'?"

"I don't know," she replied, "I think it's got something to do with something back home. In China."

"Then he *is* gonna ship out. That means I got to get Doc out of here and make a run for the mainland. If we don't hurry, he might be gone by the time we get back. Goldie, you got to show me the way out."

She picked up the candleholder. "Come on. There's a hatch that opens to the outside. I've seen it from the yard."

She led him under the house, to the outside door that opened into the cellar. It was locked, but only from the inside. Raider felt the cool night air on his face as he swung it open. The moon was also in the sky to light his way.

"Cowboy!"

He looked back at Goldie. She had dropped her nightgown to the dirt floor. The moonlight shone on her white breasts. Raider felt the urge as it ran through every cell of his body.

"Honey, I can't."

"Just hug me one more time before you go," she pleaded.

Raider stepped back, wrapping her in his arms. She was warm and moist and fragrant. Her erect nipples pressed against his chest. Her hand went for the swelling at his crotch.

"Put it in me one more time," she whispered. "You don't even have to come. Just let me feel it inside me."

"Honey..."

"We can do it standing up," she offered. "I'll take it from behind. Please, Raider. It may be the last time for both of us."

Raider figured she was right. Besides, it was easier to do it than to fight her off. They exacted the position necessary for their final coupling. Raider hoped that Goldie wouldn't drain the last ounce of his energy. He had a feeling he was going to need all his strength to get away from the White Dragon and his hateful little island.

CHAPTER 21

Raider stole away from the house, running across the backyard toward the beach. He wanted to approach the tower from the water's edge because it would give him a view of the tower and the pier. As his bare feet made impressions in the coarse sand, he wondered if Lin Ching had put extra men on guard duty. Raider's appearance had stirred things up around the White Dragon's headquarters. He fell beside a wooden boat and studied things in the moonlight.

Sure enough, there were five men now guarding the twin clipper ships. That meant more than one man would be guarding the tower. Raider leaned back against the boat, trying to figure a way to get into the tower without making too much noise.

He felt the boat behind him. Maybe he should just row away and hope for the best, try to get help by himself. But they'd kill Doc if he left him. Raider couldn't sacrifice his partner to Lin Ching. He had to free Doc if he ever wanted to see him alive again.

The big man rose up, moving around the bow of the

boat. He stumbled over an anchor rope that lay coiled in the sand. Raider picked up the line and followed it until he found the hook-shaped iron at the end. He hefted the weight of the anchor, thinking it might be just what he needed.

Stepping back to the cliff, he swung the anchor, launching it upward. The hook clinked on the stone wall that ran along the ledge. Raider began to climb hand over hand until he felt the wall beneath his feet. He rolled over the wall and landed next to the mortar at the end of the row of artillery. Hesitating in the moonshadows, he peered toward the tower, trying to see how many guards had been stationed at the dungeon.

There were two sentries, and they had both heard him. One of the tower guards was already coming to investigate. Raider quickly crawled to the mound of cannonballs between the big guns. He lifted one of the iron orbs from the stack and heaved it over the side of the cliff.

When the ball hit the ground, the sentry immediately ran to the stone wall and peered downward. Raider lifted the anchor and jumped to his feet, rushing straight for the guard. The Chinese man was turning with his rifle when Raider hit him. His skull caved in under the force of the anchor. Raider sent him over the wall to land with a dull thud on his back.

The second guard came running when he heard his partner hit the earth below the tower. Raider swung the anchor over his head, twirling it like a lasso, feeding out enough rope to catch the man as soon as he was near. The line wrapped around his neck until the anchor smashed into his face. Raider jumped him and finished the job by hand.

As the sentry breathed his last, Raider looked up, anticipating some clamor from Lin Ching's men. But no one was stirring in the house, and the five sentries between the clippers were quiet. They hadn't heard a thing. Raider went back to the body and searched for the keys to the dungeon. The dead man didn't have them, which meant that the man on the beach probably had them in his pocket. Raider didn't have the time or the inclination to climb back down the rope. He picked up the single-shot and started for the tower.

The oil lamp flickered at the top of the spiral stairs.

Raider picked it up and held it next to the barred window in the door. Doc and the woman were leaning back against the cell wall, sound asleep. Raider knocked until Doc opened his eyes.

"Get over here, Weatherbee!"

"Raider. But how. . ."

"Never mind that. We got to get this door open. And I ain't got no key."

Doc came up next to the window. "Blast it open with that rifle."

"Too much noise. Stand back. I got a better idea."

He jacked the cartridge out of the single-shot and put the slug between his teeth, twisting the shell casing until the lead popped out. He spat the slug away and tilted the cartridge toward the lock, emptying the black powder into the keyhole.

Doc was quickly catching on. "You think one will be enough?"

Raider reached into his pocket and withdrew the five slugs he had taken earlier that night, during his first rescue attempt. He repeated the process five times, biting off the bullets and pouring the powder into the lock. The big man hoped the trick would work. He didn't want to arouse the sleeping army under Lin Ching's roof.

"Stand back, Doc. Cover your eyes."

The flame from the lamp ignited the powder, setting off a fiery stream of red-hot sparks from the lock. The heat melted the inner mechanism clear through, enabling Raider to open the door with his shoulder once the powder had fizzled out. Doc was standing next to Rebecca Huntley, trying to lift her off the floor.

"Get her and come on," Raider urged. "We probably don't have much of a chance, even if we do make it to the boats."

Doc lifted Rebecca to her feet. "What about the others? They'll be able to escape now that you can't lock the door. They'll give us away."

"It don't matter," the big man replied. "Not now. Here, let me help you with her. I'll get the other arm."

They dragged Rebecca toward the stone steps. Raider figured they could climb back down the anchor line to the beach, although the woman would have to be lowered on the rope in her condition. One of the small boats could ride that tide away from the island. Once Lin Ching discovered they were gone, he'd just crank up the steamer and come after them. It was a slim chance, but they still had to try.

As they came away from the tower, Doc Weatherbee stopped dead in his tracks. He released his grip on Rebecca, moving down toward the line of artillery weapons. Raider hung on to the half-conscious girl, gaping at his partner.

"Are you loco, Doc? Git on back here. We got to bring somebody to this island who can stop all this shit!"

A strange inflection crept into Doc's voice as he studied the big guns. "We can stop it, Raider. You and I."

Raider hesitated, looking down the row of cannons and mortars. "What are you thinkin' about, Doc?"

"Twelve guns," replied the man from Boston. "Four on the house, four on the clipper ships, and four on the tower. We could aim them and then fire all twelve weapons at once. Lin Ching wouldn't even know what hit him."

Raider lowered Rebecca Huntley to the ground and moved next to his partner. "It's crazy, Doc. I don't even know how to load one of these things."

"I do. We just need powder and wadding."

Raider gestured back toward the tower. "In the storage room there. Big kegs of powder."

Doc took off his coat. "We can use our clothes for wadding."

"We could blow up the whole storage room with a good torch."

Doc wheeled toward him with a demonic look in his pale blue eyes. "Let's wreak havoc on them, Raider. Let's kill them all."

Raider tried to keep his wits about him. "Doc, if we start shootin', how the hell are we gonna get out of here?"

The man from Boston pointed toward the harbor. "The steamer is anchored out there, away from the pier. We could shoot our barrage and then take one of the smaller boats out to the steamer. In the confusion, no one will see us until we're well on our way."

Raider had to laugh at the thought of firing all twelve guns. "Hell, that would put a burr up Lin Ching's ass."

Doc glared at his partner. "Lin Ching?"

"The White Dragon is our old buddy."

"Galveston!" Doc said. "We stopped him from selling coolies to the railroad company. Stalmaster is still in prison."

Raider nodded. "And now Lin Ching wants to even the score."

Doc rubbed his hands together. "Let's kill them, Raider. Let's blow them off the face of the earth."

"Not a bad idea, Doc. If we work fast . . ."

"I know we can do it. I can load these guns in less than an hour. You stand watch in case anyone comes."

"I don't know."

Doc pointed a finger at him. "If we don't do this, Lin Ching will remove everything from this island as soon as he learns that we're gone."

"I can't deny that."

"What will it be, Raider?"

The big man had to smile. He was too scared to do anything else. "You know something, Doc? It just might work."

While Doc rigged the artillery, Raider cleared out the dungeon. He led the wretched captives across the yards, all the time fearful that someone would see them. When they reached the shoreline, he told them to hightail it along the beach to the other side of the island. Doc was loading the seventh gun as the big man made his way back to the tower.

Raider nodded to his partner. "How long?"

Doc wiped his brow with the back of his hand. "No longer than fifteen minutes. I've had another thought. Instead of aiming four guns at the tower, we can aim one into the arsenal. There's enough black powder in there so that one good burst should set the whole thing ablaze."

Raider had never seen Doc so enthusiastic about wanton destruction. He peered nervously at the house. Everything was quiet. Their movements had not been discovered as yet.

The big man sighed. "I hope Goldie is all right."

"Goldie?"

"I'll tell you later. You got all the stuff you need?"

Doc took a deep breath. "Some fuse line would make it

easier. I don't necessarily require it, but . . ."

"I'll take a look."

Raider headed for the tower and the storeroom. He had been able to force the door open without using the powder trick. The oil lamp burned in the threshold, illuminating the musty enclosure. He had to keep the flame away from the ammunition to prevent a premature explosion.

Inside the dim chamber, Raider searched for the fuse, sifting through the boxes until he found a coiled spool of line. He took an extra moment to look for dynamite, but unfortunately he couldn't find any. A few sticks of red might give them an edge in a tough fight.

Doc was happy to get the fuse. "Perfect. Five minutes and we're set."

Raider nodded and went back to the storeroom. He needed a few things himself. Breaking open one of the crates, he armed himself with an Army Colt .45. The cartridges were in the same box with the pistols. Raider loaded up, wishing that Lin Ching had seen fit to buy some repeating rifles. Gilmore had only been able to get the single-shots. Given a choice between a six-shooter and one rifle shot, Raider would take the handgun every time. He put the Colt in his belt and turned toward the door.

As he started out, something caught his eye. He moved closer to a narrow box about five feet long, reading the black stenciling on the crate. It was just what he needed. Raider hoisted the crate on his shoulder and stepped out of the tower.

Doc was loading the last cannon. He looked up at Raider and frowned. "What's that on your shoulder?"

"Nothin', if we don't need it. Maybe a little insurance if we do. You about ready?"

Doc gestured toward the doorway of the storeroom. "Bring me the lamp. I'll need it to light these fuses."

"Get it yourself," Raider called over his shoulder. "I got to lower this crate to the beach. Then I'm gonna climb down and check on the girl."

They had already used the rope to lower Rebecca over the wall. She waited for them in a boat at the water's edge. Everything was set. All they had to do was torch the fuses and launch the boat. The big man wondered if they could indeed pull it off.

. . .

Doc picked up the lamp and hurried back down the row of big guns. He started at the far end, lighting the fuses that gradually decreased in length as he came down the line. He had calculated the time of burning as closely as possible, so it was a reasonable assumption that most of the guns would go off at the same moment.

Five of the cannons were aimed at the white house, one straight into the storage room. The six mortars were trained on the clipper ships below. Doc wasn't sure that all six volleys would reach their targets, but it didn't matter as long as each ship caught at least one of the round missiles. Doc was sure that Lin Ching had purchased exploding charges.

As the last fuse sparked to life, Doc went over the wall, climbing down the rope to the beach. Rebecca and Raider were waiting for him. The two Pinkertons cast off the small vessel, climbing in when the boat drew water. Doc grabbed the oars and began to row as quietly as he could for the anchored steamer.

Raider looked back at the tower, holding up the Colt. "How long before it goes?"

"Soon."

Rebecca pointed toward the clipper ships. "Look, on the pier. They see the sparks from the fuses."

Four of the clipper guards hurried along the pier, making for the wagon trail. One man stayed behind to stand watch on the vessels. Someone rang an alarm bell somewhere in the night.

Rebecca slumped down in the boat. "That's the end of it. They'll catch us for certain."

Doc pulled hard on the oars, making for the steamer. "They won't reach it in time to stop those fuses."

Raider glared up at the tower. "You sure about that?"

Before Doc could answer, a rifle exploded from the pier. A slug whizzed hotly over their heads, making them duck. The man on the pier had heard the oars, and there was enough moonlight for him to see what he was shooting at. Quickly he moved to reload the single-shot.

Raider looked back at the pier, shaking his head. "I'll never get him from here with this pistol. He's out of range."

The rifle came up again, sending a slug into the side of the boat, splintering a hole just inches from Rebecca's head.

"We're dead," Raider said in a soft groan.

But then the cannons and the mortars erupted, embellishing the night with fire and thunder and chaos.

CHAPTER 22

The tower explosion was the most impressive display of fireworks that Doc and Raider had ever seen. When the cannon blast triggered the stored munitions, the stone turret virtually disintegrated, raining down powdered rock and large chunks of mortar. Doc, Raider, and Rebecca huddled together in the boat, turning their backs to the sky. The tide had caught them by this time, sweeping them to the farthest edge of the falling debris.

Raider peered up over the side of the boat. "Damnation, Weatherbee! It worked. Look. The house is on fire too."

Doc looked up at his handiwork. "My God!"

All five cannons had found their mark. The white house burned in every section. Flames licked out of windows, claiming the roof, conquering the whole second story. Men poured out of the doors and casements, but many of them could not escape the fire. Raider had to wonder if Goldie and Lin Ching had escaped the inferno. He felt bad for Goldie, even though she had made the choice and had stuck with it.

Rebecca gaped at the pier, toward the clippers. "Only

one of them is burning! They'll catch us!"

Doc grabbed the oars. "We're almost to the steamer. Once we get the engine started, we'll head straight north, into the wind. They'll never be able to overtake us then."

Raider kept his eye on the dock. The men who had gotten away from the house had come down to fight the fire on the first clipper, the one Raider had arrived on. A separate crew hurried to cast off Lin Ching's ship before the fire reached over the pier. Another explosion erupted in the hold of the first ship, sinking it where it lay. Raider thought the fire would get Lin Ching's vessel, but the crew managed to unhook it from the mooring just in time.

"Doc, they're swinging out that clipper."

Doc looked back over his shoulder. "We're almost there."

Raider touched the crate that lay next to him in the boat. He was going to need it. He wondered if the weapon would be enough. His black eyes peered back toward the shore. Some of Lin Ching's survivors were launching the smaller boats from the beach. Raider kicked himself for not crippling the lesser craft when he had the chance.

"Doc, there's more of them on the way."

A rifle puffed in the distance. The slug dropped harmlessly a few yards behind their boat.

"They're shooting again," Rebecca cried. "Doc, what are we going to—"

The bow of their boat bumped into the stern of the steamer.

Doc reached for the rail of the steam-powered vessel. "Abandon ship!"

Raider stopped him from jumping over the rail. "Me first." He lifted the Colt. "In case there's anybody who wants to fight."

Doc deferred. Raider leapt onto the steamer with an agility born of natural skill and sheer terror. He pushed the Colt into the face of a frightened, ratfaced man with his hands in the air.

"We don't want no trouble. Just . . . Whoa!"

Without a single sound, the rat-faced sailor went over the side into the harbor. Raider didn't even bother to watch him swim away. He turned back and looked down at Doc.

"Rebecca's coming up," his partner said.

Raider shook his head. "The crate first."

Doc started to protest, but Raider pointed back toward the beach. The clipper was free now and jockeying into a position where the tide would take the ship straight for them. Doc quickly hoisted the crate up to the big man. Rebecca came next, followed by the man who loved her.

"I'll start the engine," Doc said, ducking into a forward compartment.

Raider gazed off the stern. Lin Ching's men had caught the tidal flow. The smaller boats swung around the clipper, making straight for them. The big man leaned the crate in front of him, banging with the butt of his pistol to dislodge the top.

Rebecca watched him as he quickly assembled the bizarre-looking weapon. Her eyes flipped back and forth between Raider and the approaching armada. She counted six vessels. The clipper was starting to move as well.

"Raider, they're coming."

He rested the assembled weapon on the rail. "I'm way ahead of you, lady." He dropped the gravity clip into the notch at the top.

"My God," Rebecca said, gaping. "What is that?"

"A Gatling gun."

Raider pulled a mechanism that allowed him to open fire. He waited until the slugs from the smaller boats began to tap against the stern. Below, the steam engine started to chug and clang. Raider cranked the Gatling and chopped the water in front of the onrushing horde of pirates.

Doc's head jutted out of the forward compartment. "I can't get it to go. I've never seen one like this before."

"Have you got steam?" Rebecca asked.

Doc looked dubiously at her. "Well, yes, the gauge is in the red."

Raider dropped in another gravity clip, this time slicing through several of the men in the lead boats. "Will you two quick jawin'. That clipper looks like it's gonna keep comin'!"

Rebecca started forward. "Let me have a look at it."

Doc gaped at her. "But what do you know—"

"I've been around ships since I was a baby," she replied. "Get the hell out of my way."

She brushed past Doc, sliding into the engine chamber.

Raider dropped the third clip, ripping apart the boats that were now in close range. The men who hadn't been hit leapt from the craft to escape the barrage of lead. Raider chased them back toward shore, stopping a few of the ones who could not swim fast enough.

He saw the clipper starting to gain on them. "Get that damned engine goin'!"

Doc looked out again. "Cut the back mooring line!"

Raider cranked the Gatling a half turn, splitting the line into two pieces. The steamer's bow started to swing around, away from the clipper. Raider adjusted his aim and kept firing at the bow of the oncoming ship. If he could just cut a hole big enough, then a hot bullet might ignite something in the forward hold. He reached back to find he had three clips left.

"Doc, you better get that engine goin'!"

"Cut the bow line!"

Raider turned the Gatling, repeating his unorthodox procedure for weighing anchor. The steamer floated free in the current, heading straight for the mouth of the harbor. Raider peered toward the landmass ahead of them. If they didn't get control of the boat, they'd run aground in a hurry. The bow was aimed right at the shoreline. He looked back at the clipper. "They're gonna ram us, Doc!"

The engine came to life in the stomach of the ship. Doc backed out of the compartment, followed by Rebecca, who had grease smears on her pretty face.

"She did it!" Doc cried. "Is it any wonder that I love her?"

Rebecca glared at him. "Just get us out of here!"

Rebecca wheeled the barrel of the Gatling to aim again at the clipper. "He's comin' fast. That bow is knifin' through the water."

The crew had also raised some sails. The wind was behind them, at least until the steamer cleared the mouth of the harbor. Doc turned the wheel, steering away from the landmass ahead of them.

"Damn that clipper!" Rebecca shouted.

Raider dropped in another gravity clip. "Let's see how it likes this."

He emptied the clip and then another one. The clipper just came on. The steamer was running well now, but the steam pressure was still too low for Doc to open it up. The clipper was only fifty yards behind them. Men with rifles stood on the bow, waiting to come into range.

Raider picked up the last of his ammunition. "I'm gonna set them bastards on fire."

Doc looked back quickly. "Wait. Rebecca, take the wheel!"

Rebecca assumed command of the vessel as if she had been doing it all her life.

Raider hesitated on the Gatling, his eyes burning with anger. "Damn it, Doc!"

A slug from the clipper's rifles slammed into the stern.

Doc rushed on deck dragging a large barrel of kerosene. He needed Raider's help to heave it over the side. The keg floated behind them, lapping in their wake.

"Blast it!" Doc cried.

Raider obeyed him, destroying the barrel with a quarter turn of the Gatling. The oily liquid began to spread over the surface of the harbor. Doc rubbed his hands together, smiling.

"It didn't explode," Raider said.

"It wasn't supposed to. Wait."

"But Doc—"

"Wait, damn it!"

Raider held his breath.

"Now!" Doc cried. "Shoot the water!"

Raider cranked out the cartridges, shooting straight into the oil slick. A fire erupted and began to spread over the water. The clipper sailed straight into the fire, which quickly found its way up the sides of the vessel. Flames licked at the holes Raider had made with the Gatling gun.

"Fire in the hole!" the big man cried.

"They're still coming," Rebecca shouted, looking back over her shoulder. "They're going to ram us!"

"Goddamn it, she's right!" Raider howled.

The men on the bow of the clipper were taking aim with their rifles. Raider lifted the Army Colt, emptying it harmlessly at the marksmen. Rebecca swung the wheel, trying to veer to the port side. It appeared the clipper was going to hit them on the aft-starboard section of the boat.

All three of them were perched to go over the side when the bow of the clipper exploded. The riflemen flew away from the deck, into the dark harbor. Raider watched the creaking vessel as it lurched in the harbor like a stunned gator. The bow sank about thirty yards off their stern, sizzling as it was claimed by the purple water.

Doc reached back for the wheel, turning the steamer out into the ocean.

Raider just shook his head, staring back at the island.

For a while, they all watched the clusters of flames that illuminated the narrow strip of land. But then it became unreal to them and they turned away, looking north into the darkness. Doc gave a quick blast on the steam whistle and then steered the bow of the boat into the wind, making for San Francisco Bay.

CHAPTER 23

Police Captain Charles McCurley sat behind his desk with one hand folded over his protruding girth and the other one stroking his thick red mustache. Doc and Raider had just finished relating the improbable tale of their encounter with Lin Ching and Judd Gilmore. McCurley tossed the facts around in his head, wondering which details to believe and which ones to chalk up to exaggeration. The captain knew from experience that Pinkertons usually reported the events of their investigations with an eye for complete accuracy. He did have a few questions, however.

"You say all this happened night before last?"

Raider nodded. Doc backed him up. Both of them wondered if McCurley was going to buy their story. It did sound farfetched, like a lot of their cases. Could the captain bring himself to believe that Doc and Raider were really that good, or that lucky?

McCurley sighed, leaning back in his chair, eyeing the Pinkerton tandem. "Why'd you wait until today to come tell me all of this?"

Raider expected Doc to say something, but when the

gentleman detective just stared off into space, the big man had to speak up. "We motored in from that island yesterday afternoon. Took us all day to get here. Hell, it was Sunday and you wasn't around. We didn't feel like chasin' anybody down. Needed a bath and some rest, some food. Besides, we didn't figure there was any rush. We took care of everything before we left. Ain't that right, Doc?"

Mr. Weatherbee glanced at his partner. "I beg you pardon?"

It was the woman, Raider thought. Doc couldn't get her out of his head. Rebecca had left them after the boat landed. Doc hadn't seen her since then. And he was grieving about it.

McCurley frowned, shaking his head dubiously. "Well, I happen to know that you boys are tellin' the truth."

Raider sat up in his chair. "Yeah?"

"How fortunate," Doc said blankly.

"The Navy saw the fire on the island," McCurley continued. "They had a ship out there. They went to take a look, but you were long gone by then. Some captain brought in a couple of bodies today. One of them was Judd Gilmore. They found him floatin' in the water, drowned."

"Did they find Lin Ching?" Raider asked.

McCurley smiled diplomatically and shrugged. "There were bodies all over the place. They did find them pilgrims you set free, and a woman who claimed to be Lin Ching's mistress."

Raider was glad that Goldie and the other Shanghai brides had made it to freedom, but he hadn't gotten the answer to his question. "What about Lin Ching, Captain? They would have known him if they found him. He had a face like a Gila monster."

McCurley's face stiffened into an expression of disapproval. "Let it rest, cowboy. The Navy man said there were bodies all over the place. Nobody really even knows what happened."

Raider corrected him. "Except us. Me and Doc and that girl. We all know what happened."

The captain shook his head. "No, Raider. Not even you."

Raider scowled at McCurley. "Whoa there, bluecoat. Me and Doc put this one in a sack and drew the string tight. We mighta had some luck along the way, but we proved Strang innocent of killin' Theodore Huntley. Gilmore killed that kid. Lin Ching was usin' the shippin' company for contraband. Girls, opium, guns for his own private army. Hell, the Tong was even steppin' to the White Dragon's fiddle. He had 'em goin' after Strang and Madam Wu. The Tong got their backs up."

"Not now," the captain replied with a smile. "The Tong'll settle down with Strang and that Dragon fellow out of the way. Wouldn't you agree, Weatherbee?"

Doc was still thinking about Rebecca. "Agree with what?" he said absently.

Raider shook his partner's shoulder. "Damn it, Doc, he's saying we ain't gonna get no credit for stopping Lin Ching."

Doc shrugged, grimacing impatiently. "It's over, Raider. There was never any threat to the California mainland. Gilmore's body has been brought in. I doubt if Lin Ching survived the fire."

"Everyone wins," McCurley added with a smile.

Raider grunted. "Ever'body but Sir Lionel. He's six feet down because nobody would believe him."

McCurley leaned forward, playing the politician. "Look, I'll have the record changed. Strang's name will be cleared. Gilmore will be listed as Theodore Huntley's killer. Officially, Gilmore will have been shot while trying to escape custody."

Raider still wasn't happy. "We almost die, and nobody gives a tinker's damn."

"Aw come on, Raider," the captain said good-naturedly. "I'll see to it that your boss knows what a good job you done. You'll be paid for all your time, includin' the stuff you did on your own when you was chasin' after Gilmore. I might even rustle up a medal from the citizens' committee if you—"

Raider came up out of his chair. "Stick that medal where—"

"Raider!" Doc was glaring at him. "Sit down!"

The big man eased back into his seat.

Doc took over. "No medals will be necessary, Captain. Simply report to our superiors that we performed the required task and saw it through until the end. That will suffice. Raider and I will take care of reporting the details."

"Good enough, Weatherbee."

Raider exhaled disgustedly.

McCurley eyed the tall Pinkerton. "What else can we do for you, cowboy?"

Raider mulled it over. "Maybe a few lines in the local newspaper, tellin' how Strang is really innocent and all."

"The Navy wants it kept quiet," McCurley replied. "And I can't say that I blame them. We got enough trouble here in California without madmen like this White Dragon to think about. Let it rest, Raider."

Doc glanced up and asked curtly, "Are you quite finished with us, Captain McCurley?"

The big policeman threw out his hands. "As long as you write your report."

Raider started to say that Doc was good at stuff like that, but before he could offer words of encouragement, the man from Boston bade them good day and exited in a hurry.

McCurley squinted after him. "What's his rush?"

"Woman," Raider replied. "The Huntley girl."

The captain nodded appreciatively. "I wish him luck."

Raider stood up, tipping his Stetson to the copper. "So long, chief. I'd like to say it's been a pleasure, but to tell you the truth, it's been a hell of a lot like work." He turned and started for the door.

"Raider!"

He looked over his shoulder. "Yeah?"

McCurley shrugged. You could always drop a wreath over Sir Lionel's grave."

"You know somethin', Mac. I might just do that."

It was a good day for visiting graveyards. Overcast, gloomy, cool, and damp. Raider bought a wreath and then rented a horse. He rode out to the cemetery where his late friend had been interred.

The tombstone that Raider had purchased read, SIR LIONEL STRANG, UNKNOWN—1879, COMMENDED TO THE EARTH IN PEACE. The man who carved the stone had insisted on the fancy words. He hadn't charged any extra for chiseling the lofty sentiment.

Raider's eyes grew wide as he bent over to drop the wreath on Sir Lionel's final resting place. It wasn't the tombstone that caught his eye, but rather the small leather pouch that hung to one side from a rawhide thong. Raider grabbed the pouch and opened it to find two letters inside. Both of the letters were parchment sealed with wax. One bore Doc's name, the other was intended for Raider. The big man unfolded his parchment. The handwriting belonged to a woman.

"Raider, I knew you would come to Sir Lionel's grave. Please give the other letter to Doc for me. I'm sorry I left without saying goodbye. I'm going back east to Boston. Please let me thank you for all that you have done for me. I will never forget you, or Doc. Sincerely, Rebecca Huntley."

Raider stared at the letter intended for his partner. It sure as hell didn't look good for him. Raider considered throwing the parchment away, but then he figured that, either way, Rebecca Huntley's message would settle the whole thing once and for all.

When Raider knocked on Doc's door, the Boston-bred Pinkerton shouted for him to come in. Doc was pacing back and forth, puffing on an Old Virginia cheroot. The brandy bottle was on his nightstand, close to half empty. Maybe he already knew what was in the letter.

"I can't find Rebecca anywhere," he said anxiously. "Do you know, she's already sold Huntley Shipping to a group of Sir Lionel's former partners from back east. They gave her a wonderful price. It seems they also believe in Strang's ideas about connecting the East and Pacific routes."

"Doc, maybe you should—"

"I tried that doctor again. He said she had been by to see him yesterday afternoon. I suppose she's at one of the hotels. She'll send for me as soon as she's settled. I know it."

Raider held up the letter. "Better read this first." He slapped the parchment into Doc's hand. "I hate to be the one to tell you, but she's on her way back to Boston."

Doc stared disbelievingly at the letter. "No!"

He broke the wax seal. "My Dearest Mr. Weatherbee,

Words cannot adequately describe the way I feel about you, especially after the adventure that we shared together. Your courage and stamina were astounding. I will always feel a special bond between us because of the dangers we faced together. I can truthfully say that I love you and probably have since the first moment I met you."

Doc looked up, glowing. "She loves me! Do you hear that! She says that she truthfully loves me!"

"Keep readin'."

Doc started again, out loud. "Listen: 'I could spend hours delineating your good qualities, Mr. Weatherbee. But finally, you are a man of adventure. Since my brother's death, I have experienced enough adventure to last me the remainder of my natural life. For this reason, I can no longer be in your company. We must never see each other again.' What!"

There would be more, Raider thought. In matters like this, there was always more pain on top of the initial hurt. Love didn't really leave time for much else.

"She's gone back to Boston!" Doc cried.

"That's what I told you."

"She says that we could never be together because I would be bored with the quiet life she's seeking. She tells me not to follow her. Right here: 'It is my wish that you make no attempt to find me or to follow me east.' Damn!"

Well, Raider saw what was coming so he excused himself and hastened to the nearest establishment that sold good bottled whiskey. Then he went back to the hotel and made arrangements to have food sent up to the room at regular intervals. He had no idea how long it would take Doc's misery to bottom out. Somehow, the big man felt he owed it to his partner to help him through it. They would have to get drunk, though. Doc needed to because he was hurting, and Raider had to so he could stand Doc.

The man from Boston was staring out the window when Raider came back. Raider popped a cork, and the long bout of drunkenness began. They just sat there, talking about everything but women, particularly Rebecca Huntley. They drank well into the next day and night. Only then, when the whiskey had numbed him, did Doc choose to talk about his beloved.

Doc sighed, holding his face in his hands: "I love her.

She's everything I could ever want. Intelligent, brave. Look at the way she came out here to find her brother. On her own! Damn courageous."

"She purty, too," Raider offered drunkenly. "Fills out her dress just fine."

In his stupor, Doc took the remark to be Raider's version of a compliment.

"Decide what you want to do, Weatherbee. We'll have a new case comin' in soon. We'll have to go back to work."

"I feel dead without her." He looked up. "I want to go after her, Raider."

"Shit or git off the pot."

Doc threw out his hands. "She told me not to follow her. She thinks that it's hopeless between us."

Raider stood up, teetering soddenly. He lifted a finger toward the sky. "It has been my experience with women ...that what they say and what they want can be *egg-zactly* the opposite of what really is. I leave you with that pearl of wisdom. My duty is done."

He staggered for the door.

"Raider?"

Looking woozily back: "Yeah, Doc?"

"You're right. I'm going after her!"

The big man from Arkansas wanted to cheer, but instead he reeled in a circle, fell backward, and passed out on the floor, beginning an inebriated rest that would last well into the next day.

CHAPTER 24

Doc Weatherbee paced back and forth on the rail platform, waiting to board a train and begin his journey back east. He was all decked out in a new tricot suit, complete with silk vest, pearl-gray derby, and Melton overgaiters. They were both going to take a month's leave of absence while Doc straightened out his head. Raider watched his partner, thanking Providence that he wasn't the one in love.

"You're gonna wear a hole in this platform, Weatherbee."

Doc stopped, trying to get a grip on himself. "I can't help being nervous. In addition to looking for Rebecca, I'm going back to my hometown for the first time in more than a decade. I can't be sure how I will be received."

Raider remembered Doc's story about his early years, how he had left home and messed it all up between him and his family. "You gonna get in touch with your brother while you're there?"

Doc blushed and lowered his eyes. "I hope to. Although I wouldn't blame him if he refused to see me."

"Don't be so hard on yourself, Doc. Just tell him

you've been a detective all these years. And a damned good one at that."

He looked up. "Raider..."

Doc got that tone in his voice, like he was going to say something sentimental and stupid. Something that didn't have to be said. But he wanted to say it anyway.

Raider had to head him off. "Save the mush, Weatherbee. You can tell me all about it when you get back from Boston. Hell, you'll be back here, draggin' that little filly behind you. Set up house and then we'll start in again, business as usual."

"What if I don't come back?"

"Shut up, Doc. The train's comin'."

The executors of Sir Lionel's rail company had furnished a private car for Doc's trip home. They were impressed that Doc and Raider had cleared Strang's name. Raider helped load the bags onto the apron of the compartment car.

"Fancy," the big man offered. "Travelin' like a gent."

Doc still had that hangdog look on his face that meant he was going to cut loose any minute. "Raider..."

He wanted to get away quickly, but Doc wasn't going to let him.

"Raider, you're a titan. A Herculean figure. You've saved my life a hundred times. I can never repay you."

Raider hesitated on the platform, looking embarrassed. "You don't owe me a goddamn thing, Doc."

"Raider, back there in Nevada, when I said you killed Judith. I didn't mean it. And I'm sorry I said it."

"Hell, I know you didn't mean it, Doc."

"Maybe it's better that I go now," said the Boston-bound gentleman. "I felt I was losing something there at the end. An edge. I may not be back. But I don't care. 'They also serve who only stand and wait.' Milton."

Raider shook his partner's hand and stepped down off the apron. When he was on the platform, he turned back and smiled up at Doc. "You know, Weatherbee, I always said you had poetry in you."

Doc brushed a tear from his eye. "Thank you, Raider."

"I hate poetry."

The train whistle blew.

Raider turned and walked away without even looking
back.

The big man decided to begin his month's leave in
Stockton, where he knew a married lady that belonged to a
California rancher. He rode the stage from San Francisco
and checked into Stockton's only hotel. He expected to
play the game with Lorinda the way they always played it.
Raider would send word to her that he had arrived. Lorinda
would wait until her husband was asleep, and then she
would slip out and drive the buggy into town. It was an
easy rendezvous since Lorinda and her husband slept in
different rooms.

The game went on as long as Raider was in town. A
few well-placed silver dollars made the hotel help agreeable. The townspeople knew about their affair, but no one
seemed to care. Lorinda's husband had a mean nature and
wasn't too popular with the local folk. So far the husband
had never found out about Raider's visits.

Raider sent word to Lorinda, but to his surprise, she
arrived at his hotel in broad daylight. She sashayed into
Raider's room wearing a low-cut black dress that left no
doubt as to her buxom endowments. Her lovely round face
was covered by a black veil.

Raider slammed the door behind her. "Lorinda, are you
loco? What if your husband saw you here?"

She pulled up her veil, revealing big blue eyes and a
smile on her lips. "Buried Henry a week ago Sunday.
Dropped dead on me without any warnin'. Doctor says it
was natural causes." She winked at him. "We was in bed at
the time, if you know what I mean."

Raider wasn't sure exactly how he should feel. "Well,
Lo, I'm real sorry about that. If you want to be alone, I can
hightail it out of here."

She moved closer to him, wrapping her arms around his
waist. "Raider, I got a buggy out front. Why don't you
drive me back to the ranch? I'd be happy to welcome you
for as long as you'd like to stay."

So that was the way it had been for nearly a month.
They lived as man and wife. Raider shared the chores and

her bed. He worked the place like it was his own. The hired helped even accepted him as the new boss, a fact that spoke to the deceased husband's unpopular nature.

At first the big man thought it felt good to work hard all day, sit down to a hot supper, and languish in the arms of Lorinda all night. She was a healthy woman in most respects, a bit older than Raider, but the wear set well on her. Her disposition was naturally friendly, and her sense of curiosity had led to more than one surprise in bed.

But by the end of the third week, the awe and wonder of domesticity had begun to wear thin with Raider. It was time to find Doc, climb into the saddle, and get back to the work he did the best. He was a detective, and he was ready for a new case.

He hoped Doc had settled the thing with Rebecca Huntley. Lorinda had been dropping hints about marriage after the second night they shared her bed. She wanted another man in her life on a permanent basis. The marriage talk signaled leaving-time. But it had to be subtle. He couldn't force it or he would mess up their arrangement for future visits.

On the Monday of the fourth week, Raider insisted that he take Lorinda into town so she could buy a new dress. Naturally, she figured it was for their wedding. While she shopped, Raider slipped down to the Western Union office to send a telegram to Chicago. He told Wagner where he was and that he was ready for another case, with or without Doc. He gave the operator a dollar to bring the reply to Lorinda's ranch as soon as it arrived.

That night, the big man was able to enjoy his status again, knowing that a new case assignment would be arriving the next day. But the wire never came to his rescue. In fact, he had to sweat through the rest of the week and then clear into the middle of the week after. Lorinda was setting the date for their bethrothal when the postal rider knocked on the front door, delivering a packet from the Pinkerton Agency.

Raider breathed easier, although he let on like he hadn't expected it.

Lorinda eyed the packet with a miserable frown. "What is it?"

Raider leaned back at the kitchen table, nursing a good

cup of coffee. "Go on, you read it. It might be bad news."

She opened the packet and looked inside. "There's two things here. One from a Mr. Wagner and the other from a man named Doc Weatherbee. Hey, ain't that the handle of your partner?"

Raider nodded. "Keep readin'."

"Well, it says here that Doc didn't know where you were so he sent the letter to the agency. It's addressed personal for you. That's why Wagner says he didn't open it."

Raider's heart was pounding. He figured it was bad news. He told Lorinda to read Doc's letter. It would make her feel important and spare him the trouble of wading through Doc's wordy prose.

Lorinda sighed. "Well, he married that girl and he ain't comin' back."

Raider shook his head, feeling lower than a gopher's supper. "Damn it all. I reckon I knowed he was gonna stay. What else?"

Lorinda read a few more lines and then translated: "He says you're the best partner a man could have and that he's sorry he ain't comin' back. He says not to take it personal. He thinks your new partner will learn a lot from you."

Raider chortled disgustedly. "My new partner, huh?"

"Wait, there's somethin' here about his brother. Says they made up and that Aaron never got his letter a long time ago. Says the brother's been searchin' for him all these years. Look here, there's a newspaper clippin'."

Raider watched the joy come into Lorinda's face as she perused the story.

"Aw," she said softly, "they had a big weddin', Raider. All of Boston society turned out. Rebecca was well known because of her brother, who's dead. But he was big doin's before he went. And your partner's gonna work in his brother's bank. She plans to teach school."

The big man grimaced. "She's probably already tellin' him what to do."

Lorinda slapped his shoulder. "What's that supposed to mean?"

He held up his hands. "I surrender. Is that all it says?"

"Just some stuff in the paper story about ever'body who came to their weddin'."

Raider gestured to the other letter, the dispatch from

Wagner. "What's the other one say?"

Lorinda had begun to pout. "Don't say nothin'. You gotta read it."

"Well, go on."

She read it and slammed it down on the table. "Says you're supposed to be in Albuquerque by the end of next month."

Raider grunted. "Hm. Take me that long to ride there. Reckon I'll have to buy a horse."

"Then you're goin'!" she accused.

He stood up. "Yep. I can go now or I can go tomorrow. Whichever one you want."

"Go now!" she cried.

Raider reached for his hat, which was hanging by the door. "So long, Lorinda. If I'm ever back this way..."

She sighed. "Tomorrow. You can leave tomorrow."

"I'll have to go into town and buy a horse this afternoon."

"I'll sell you one of mine."

He put his hat back on the peg. Lorinda broke into a smile. She wanted to go to bed before supper—and after supper, too. She said she'd keep him up all night and then again before breakfast. Lorinda wanted to send him away exhausted, so Raider wouldn't easily forget her. She wanted him to think of her when he was swaying in the saddle as he rode through a rainy night. She wanted him to feel as miserable as she felt when he left her.

Raider slid his arm around her shoulder and promised her that he would.

Epilogue: Shadow
of the Cougar

Raider rode slowly into Albuquerque, towing the corpse-slung mare behind him. Men stopped to look, women covered their faces, children gaped in awe at the site of a dead man. Raider just stared straight ahead, oblivious to their wide eyes and furtive comments. Albuquerque was starting to think of itself as a respectable town. The citizens didn't see many dead men these days. They really didn't like being reminded of a wilder time, when killing occurred on a regular basis.

Raider guided his chestnut filly in front of the marshal's office. As he dismounted, the marshal came out onto the sidewalk. He frowned when he saw the body of Billy Mel Peters, a robber and killer of wide reputation in New Mexico. It had taken Raider almost a month to catch him.

While the marshal was happy to see Peters apprehended, he was not glad to see him dead. "He ain't breathin', Pinkerton."

Raider untied the body and rolled it off the saddle into the street. "Well, partner, it was either me or him. So I decided it better be him."

The marshal sighed. "We'll never find that gold now."

251

Raider gestured to the body. "It's on him. You boys just have to pick it off." He grinned at the marshal. "Now it don't matter if he's dead or not."

Raider started for the saloon across the street.

The marshal stopped him. "Big man, there's been a fellow around here lookin' for you. Fancy-pants kind, talks real proper."

Raider's jaw dropped. "Doc! You know where he is?"

"Last I seen him, he was over to the saloon."

Raider turned and hurried across the street, expecting to find that his former partner had come back to work with him. He knew the Boston society routine would grow old. The gentleman Pinkerton had returned to action.

When he went into the dim saloon, a man immediately stood up at the bar. He wore a freshly pressed suit and sported a new Stetson. Doc had finally given up on the derby.

Raider went toward the man, extending his hand. "How you doin', you old son of a gun? Did you bring the little wife with you?"

As the man's face eased out of the shadows, Raider saw that he was not Doc. The gentleman still shook his hand, offering a warm smile. He said he was Jimmy Heller, Raider's new partner.

The big man dropped his hand and frowned. "New partner. Boy, you ain't old enough to shine my boots."

Heller stiffened indignantly, his young face blushing red. "I'll have you know that I'll be twenty-five next month. I've been with the agency for a year. Are you familiar with the Dudley case?"

"No."

"Well I solved the Dudley case along with Stokes. You've heard of Stokes, haven't you?"

Raider nodded, trying not to laugh at Heller's banty-rooster posture. "Yeah, Stokes is good. 'Course, I'm better."

"Mr. Pinkerton insisted that I work with you," Heller continued. "He sent me here to find you. We're supposed to investigate a number of killings up at Medicine Bow."

Raider nodded to the bartender and ordered a bottle of whiskey. "Medicine Bow's pretty in October. Should take us till then to ride there."

Heller's smooth brow wrinkled slightly. "Ride? Isn't there a train or a stagecoach that runs up there?"

"This ain't Chicago, Jimmy. If you can't take it, git on back to the boss and have him put you on train duty." Raider uncorked the bottle and took a long drink. "Whiskey?"

Heller shook his head. "No thank you. I refrain from liquor and tobacco. I find it dulls my senses."

"Sometimes you want 'em to be dull." He glared at the kid. "You really want to work with me, boy? It gets pretty dangerous. Maybe you oughta pack up and head east."

"I resent that!" Heller replied. "I'm as qualified as any agent on the job. And I'm not afraid of anything."

Raider chortled derisively. "Man with no fear is a dangerous man."

"I've come to work with the great Raider, but I'm beginning to think he's a myth."

Raider grabbed his lapels. "Watch your mouth, boy. I'm flesh and blood just like you. I'd send you packin' if . . ."

Heller gaped at the big man. "If what?"

Raider let go of his new partner's coat. "If you didn't remind me of a pain in the ass Yankee from . . . where the hell do you come from, anyway?"

Heller smiled. "New Hampshire."

Raider grimaced. "I knew it," he groaned. "I'm really in trouble now."

Heller straightened his suit. "Shall we get under way?"

Raider laughed. "So we're gonna work together. God Almighty. You know how to use a gun?"

"I'm an expert marksman with pistol or rifle."

Raider drew his Colt, coming up fast, poking the Peacemaker on the tip of Heller's nose. "You're slow, Jimmy. You gotta work on that." He dropped the Peacemaker back in his holster. "Still want to come along?"

Heller nodded, looking a little green around the gills. "I'm sure I have a lot to learn. But I'm ready. I suppose I should buy a weapon, however."

Raider reached for his saddlebag, taking out something that had been wrapped in oil cloth. "Here. Take this. It's a .38 Diamondback."

Heller unwrapped the cloth and hefted the weapon. "Thank you. I don't know what to say."

"Just take care of it," Raider replied. "It belonged to Doc."

"Doc Weatherbee?"

"One and the same."

Raider was going to show him how to load it, but Heller quickly broke down the weapon, examining all its working parts. "Not bad," the big man said. "At least you weren't lyin' about knowin' guns."

Heller replied that he had heard many stories about Doc Weatherbee and he was proud to own his pistol.

Raider decided to straighten out a few things right away. "Okay, Jimmy, I ain't gonna squawk if the home office thinks you're ready to work with me. But we got a few rules to live by."

Heller nodded nervously.

"Main thing in this kind of work is keepin' your back covered. Careless won't bury you, but it will sure get you ready for the box. I move fast when I'm goin' somewhere. First time you can't keep up, you're gone. Sometimes I do stuff that would make Pinkerton and Wagner shit prickly pears, but I don't never tell nothin' I don't have to. You think you can live with that?"

Heller agreed that he could.

"Then one more thing," Raider said. "You are now the official writer of all reports. Send a message to Chicago, sayin' I caught Billy Mel Peters and brought him back. Say I recovered the gold and that the marshal is happy with what I done. Then go over to the marshal and tell him to write a letter sayin' the same. You got it?"

Heller had been busily scribbling all of the information on a little notepad. "Get the marshal to write a letter saying the same."

"And make sure he mails it."

Raider picked up the bottle of whiskey and started away.

"Hey," his new partner called after him. "Where you goin'?"

Raider looked back over his shoulder. "Well, you don't drink or smoke. I'm guessin' you ain't big with the ladies either."

Heller straightened proudly. "I'm engaged to my sweetheart back in St. Louis. We're to be married in the spring."

Raider turned again for the door. "Well, I'm about to go get married for a couple of hours. You meet me back here in the mornin'."

Heller frowned. So there it was, the booze and the whoring. Tales of Raider's debauchery were as true as the exploits of his bravery and daring. Heller had to grin, however. Since he had joined the agency, he had dreamed of working with one of the great detectives. When Doc Weatherbee resigned, it took Heller almost two weeks to talk Wagner into letting him partner with Raider. Now he had his chance, and he knew he would prove himself worthy of the task.

Heller looked down at his notes. Best to do just what Raider said. No need to get him riled. Jimmy had no intention of getting on the wrong side of the big man from Arkansas.

Raider figured that heaven's streets could not be any prettier than Medicine Bow in autumn. The reds and golds of the changing leaves made it seem like he was riding straight through sunshine. He urged a gray gelding along the base of a yellow mountain, where only the evergreens disturbed the solid rise of pure gold.

"Ever seen anything like this before, Jimmy?"

Heller rode behind him on a mule, his face grimacing with pain. Jimmy was just getting used to the saddle. He had been riding trains for too long. Still, Raider had to give the kid some credit—he had kept up, and he had not complained once. The only aversion he had shown was to eating snake, but Raider figured he'd catch on when he got hungry enough.

"God's own country," Raider warbled. "I love it."

Heller just grunted, trying to keep his backside off the saddle.

They rode to an old silver mine that had been purchased from a mining company by a speculator named Franklin Greeves. He met them on the porch of the mining office, waving a friendly hand. A man of fifty, Raider thought, lots of dark hair left, hawkish nose, clear brown eyes. He seemed to have a good nature and an amiable disposition.

"Been waitin' a while for you fellers. Come on in and have a cup of coffee."

Raider and Heller followed Greeves into the cabin. The place was run down and smelled of mildew. Raider sat at a small table, taking the tin cup of steaming liquid that Greeves set in front of him.

He handed another cup to Heller. "Sure you won't sit down?" Greeves asked the young man.

Heller rubbed his backside. "No thank you."

Raider eyed the lanky gentleman. "S'pose you tell us why you had to hire a couple of Pinkertons, Mr. Greeves?"

"Man comes to the point. I like that. Killin', gentlemen. Two of my oldest friends. We bought this mine from the company. They said it's drier than a popcorn fart. But Zack and me and Johnny figured there's another vein, further up the mountain. We looked for it till Zack and Johnny was killed. I'm the only one left."

Raider leaned over his cup of coffee. "Who you think killed 'em?"

Greeves stood up, rubbing his pointed chin, pacing back and forth. "It was a cougar what done it. Leastways, that's what it looked like."

Raider frowned. "We ain't hunters, Mr. Greeves. Unless it's men you want hunted. Then we could oblige you. But if you want a cougar killed, you should stir up some of the local trackers. There's a few of them still around."

Greeves shook his head as if something had squirmed into his brain. "It wasn't right, mister. It didn't fit."

Heller had become interested. "What didn't fit?"

"Zack and Johnny. They were attacked, I know that. I heard the cat screamin'. But it was the way they were killed."

Raider squinted at his host. "We can't read your mind. Just tell it how you see it."

Greeves settled into the chair, gazing across the table at the big Pinkerton. "The cougar chewed their throats out. That's all. No marks anywhere else. Just cleaned out their gullets. Didn't even use its claws."

Raider leaned back. "That don't make sense. A cougar claws and bites anything it grabs. And a cat that would attack a man is usually old or hurt. Unless the man walked up on his lair. Where'd the attacks take place?"

"Right out behind the shack," Greeves replied. "Zack was choppin' wood while me and Johnny was up at the mine. The time Johnny got it, I was at the mine by myself. I've been stickin' close to my shotgun, I can tell you."

"Any sign of the cat?" Heller asked.

Greeves shook his head. "I've heard him in the mountains a couple of times, howlin' like he wanted me to leave."

Heller frowned. "I don't know much about the behavior of mountain lions, but it does seem odd that a wild animal would come so close to a human habitat. And such an animal would not simply bite the necks of its victims."

"Unless it was trained," Raider offered.

Heller stared at his partner. "My God. That's brilliant!"

Raider sighed, looking straight at Greeves. "Sir, I'd like to help you, but like I said, we ain't hunters."

Greeves lowered his head disappointedly. "Won't even have a look?"

Raider shrugged. "You direct me to a telegraph station, I'll wire the home office and ask if we should continue on the case. I'll abide by their decision. That fair enough?"

Greeves nodded. "I can live with it. You boys are welcome to bed down on the back porch if you want."

Raider was about to accept his offer when a shrill cry rolled down out of the mountains, chilling them where they stood. It was the high, witchlike howl of a mountain lion, screaming back in the trees.

"I'll take the first watch, Jimmy. You can stand the second."

Heller nodded, his face slack with apprehension. But when he saw that Raider did not appear to be frightened, he straightened himself and asked for another cup of coffee. The young man from New Hampshire was determined to prove himself in his partner's eyes.

Raider stirred in the cool morning air, climbing out from under the fur blankets that Greeves had given him. The big man sat up, expecting to see Heller on the steps, holding Doc's old .38 Diamondback. But his young partner was no longer there.

Raider got up and moved toward the smell of bacon and pancakes. Greeves was fixing breakfast. He offered the big man a cup of coffee. Raider sat down at the table, wiping his eyes.

"There's a boy about three miles east that'll take a message to the nearest wire," Greeves offered. "Or he'll ride with you if you don't know the way."

"Good enough." Raider glanced toward the front of the shack. "Where's my partner? I'm gonna chew him out for leavin' his post."

Greeves pointed up toward the mountain. "Said to tell you he was goin' to have a look for himself. He'll be back before . . . hey, where are you goin'?"

Raider was out the back door, picking up his '76 Winchester before he started for the mountain. Heller hadn't waited long to pull his first stupid stunt. The big man hoped he found him before anything happened.

His gut churned for the first time in months, the old raunchy feeling he got when he knew something was bad wrong. He found Heller's footprints in the soft earth of the trail that rose into the autumnal forest. A brown cat could hide in that stuff like he was invisible.

Raider climbed all morning, following his partner's ascent. Shortly before noon he heard Jimmy's voice echoing through the slopes from above. He peered upward, searching for the Yankee greenhorn. He was going to send him back after he found him. No more partners.

Raider caught sight of a waving arm between the trees. Heller was standing on a high ledge, in front of cave. He pointed into the cave, yelling that he had found something. Raider hollered back for him to sit tight.

The big man started to climb, but he never reached his partner in time. A cougar screeched from inside the cave. Heller turned, drawing the .38 Diamondback, but he never got off a shot. Raider saw the cat leaping from the shadows and sink its teeth into Heller's throat.

He raised the '76, but the cat was too far away. The shots scared it back into the cave, but it was too late for Jimmy Heller. When Raider reached the young man, he was lying in a pool of his own blood. His throat was gone, just like the others.

Raider spun toward the cave, looking for the cat. He started forward with the '76 in front of him, anticipating the cold eyes and the silent leap. But there was no cougar inside the dim recess. The animal had escaped from a back entrance, a hole that opened to another spot higher on the mountain.

Before he dragged his partner down, Raider studied the hard ground for cat tracks. There wasn't enough loose dirt to make a print. It was going to be rough finding the cougar, but he had to now that his partner was dead. The cat had to pay for killing a Pinkerton.

Raider went outside and looked down at the body. They had sent him out while he was still too damned green. The big man wondered who would tell his fiancée. He'd write a report that stated Heller was killed in the line of duty. He wanted to make him seem like a hero, if possible. A dead hero.

He picked up the body and carried it over his shoulder until he saw Greeves coming toward him on the path.

Greeves shook his head. "The same." He helped Raider with the burden.

When they were back at the cabin, Raider began packing food into his saddlebags. He also got his canteen and a bottle of red-eye.

Greeves watched him with a concerned look on his face. "What are you gonna do, big man?"

Raider slung the saddlebag on his shoulder. "I'm goin' back up on that mountain and kill me a cat. Maybe somethin' else if I'm right."

"Right about what?"

"Just bury my partner," Raider replied. "And wait for me to come down."

He started back into the mountains. Greeves hollered after him, saying that two hunters had already failed to find the cat. Raider said it didn't matter—he was going to let the cat find him.

If you waited long enough for something, Raider thought, it would eventually come to you. He had been sitting for three days, perched over the entrance of the cave where Heller had been killed. He had seen all sorts of wildlife—deer, squirrels, a wolverine, racoons, a coyote, two foxes, and a bull snake—everything but a cougar. Still, the big man had a theory, and he wanted to sit it out. On the morning of the fourth day, he was proven right.

His eyes opened to the low growl of a big cat. The dull purr resounded from the entrance to the cave, growing louder as the cat came on. Raider thumbed the hammer of the '76 and dropped into position.

The mountain lion moved slowly out of the cave, into the morning light. It was a beautiful animal, lean and muscular, sporting a shiny, golden coat. Raider took aim from above, hesitating only when he saw the collar on the cougar's neck. A leash was attached to the collar and to the arm of the man who stepped out beside the big cat.

Raider had said it earlier—the cat had been trained to kill quickly. The big man did not wait for the cat-man to turn around. He fired the '76, sending a slug through the animal's heart, dropping it with one shot. It almost hurt him to hear the beast's pitiful cries as it wallowed in its final agony.

He cranked another .45-caliber cartridge into the chamber of the Winchester. "Don't move, hombre, or you get the same."

The man's face was turned up. He wore Indian buckskins and had the broad features of the Blackfoot tribe. When he realized his cat was dead, he slipped the leash and dived back into the cave.

Raider dropped from above and looked back into the recess. He heard scrambling as the cat-man scurried through the back entrance. The rifle barked again, but the Indian was gone.

Stepping back into the cave, Raider hesitated at the other opening. He knew better than to follow through the narrow hole. Instead, he took off his Stetson and sailed it into the circle of daylight. A hand dropped a knife as soon as the hat flew by. Raider lifted the Winchester, firing two bursts that caught the Indian's forearm. The man fell back into the cave holding his wrist.

Raider put the rifle in his face.

"Let's go, boy. You got a lot of explaining to do."

The Indian seemed to understand, although he did not reply. He got to his feet, stumbling for the mouth of the cavern. Raider stayed behind him with the rifle pointed toward the middle of his back. When the Indian saw the dead cat, he knelt beside it, stroking its fur.

"You trained him from a cub, didn't you?" Raider asked.

But the Indian did not reply. Instead, he rolled the body of the cougar off the ledge, watching it as it tumbled to the forests below. Raider started to urge the man back down the hill, but the Indian had other ideas. He screamed and leapt off the ledge himself, following his pet to his death.

Raider flopped down, shaking his head, staring at the golden forest until Greeves came up the trail.

"Heard a commotion," the miner replied. "Came to see."

Raider told him about the trained cougar. After he described the cat-man, Greeves said it sounded like a man named Injun Willie, who hadn't been heard from in a couple of years. He also remarked that it was damned smart to train a cougar from birth, but why had Injun Willie trained it to kill?

Raider gestured back toward the cave. "Take a look. Climb back up into them trees. See what Injun Willie was guardin'."

Raider waited almost an hour for Greeves to come back.

The miner nodded his head. "It's the vein we been lookin' for. Injun Willie had him a dig back in there. I guess he wanted all the silver for himself."

Raider stood up. "I guess he did."

They went back down to the cabin.

Greeves had buried Heller out back. All of his belongings were tied up in a neat sack. Raider thanked Greeves and said he had to be on his way.

The miner sighed deeply, his face slacked in a lonely frown. "I reckon I got my silver. I ought to be happy, but I ain't. I wish Zack and Johnny were here to share it with me. I had to lose 'em to find it."

As he swung into the saddle, Raider caught sight of the fresh cairn on Jimmy Heller's grave. "Ever'body lost on this one, old man."

He spurred the gray and started for Denver.

The key operator for the Western Union office in Denver looked up to see a grizzled, scowling cowboy staring straight at him. The man swallowed, wondering if he was going to get robbed. "Yes?"

Raider slammed a dollar on the counter. "I want to send a wire to the Pinkerton Agency in Chicago."

The man nodded and started to hand him a pencil and a piece of paper.

"I'll tell it, you write it," the big man said.

The key operator was happy to oblige him.

Raider dictated his message. "To William Wagner. Pinkerton National Detective Agency, Chicago, Illinois. I caught the killer of the men in Medicine Bow. He killed Jimmy Heller before I was able to stop him. Franklin Greeves can tell you the same if you bother to ask him."

The operator looked up, scribbling away. "Is that all?"

"No." Raider took a deep breath. "Send this. I, Raider, do hereby resign from the Pinkerton Agency as soon as you get this wire. Send my back pay to the Western Union office in Denver." He looked at the piece of paper under the operator's hand. "You get it all?"

The man nodded. "You want me to send you any money that comes in?"

"Just hold it," Raider replied. "Keep that dollar against any charges that might come up."

With that, the big man turned and headed out of the office. He wanted a bath and some food. And when that was taken care of, he planned to buy a bottle of whiskey and then spend a week in a whorehouse. After that, he figured he would have to look for a new job.

The buxom woman tapped Raider's shoulder, trying to wake him. They had been together for three days, enjoying each other when they weren't sleeping or eating. Raider had paid a special rate so he could stay overnight at the cathouse. They knew him there, so they let him get away with it.

"Raider, open them black eyes."

The big man stirred, groaning at her. "Leave me be. We'll do it later."

"You don't understand. There's a man downstairs to see you. Says his name is Wagner."

Raider sat up. "What?"

"Says he's your boss."

"Hell, I don't work for him no more."

"He says he wants to see you."

Raider climbed off the bed, searching for his pants. Who the hell did Wagner think he was, interrupting his sleep? Apparently he hadn't taken the resignation seriously. Raider planned to settle it once and for all.

Wagner stood up when Raider strode bare-chested into the parlor. "Hello, Raider. It's good to see you."

The big man from Arkansas pointed a finger at him. "What the hell are you doin' here? Didn't you get my message?"

Wagner nodded, removing his wire spectacles for another nervous cleaning. "I got it. But I believe you owe me an explanation. That's why I came all the way out here to see you. I wanted to hear what you had to say."

Raider exhaled, finding that he was no longer angry. "Yeah, I reckon you got the right. Dottie, make us some coffee. What time of day is it?"

"Eight in the morning," Wagner replied.

"Get us some breakfast, too."

They ate in silence. Wagner knew Raider wouldn't talk until he was ready. Finally, over the second cup of coffee, the big man sighed and shook his head.

"It ain't the same without Doc."

Wagner felt some sympathy for his rough-hewn agent. "I understand. We'll let you pick any partner you want, Raider. Anyone from the agency."

Raider hung his head. "That's just it. I don't want another partner. Look what happened to Heller."

Wagner raised an eyebrow. "You didn't go into much detail about Heller's demise. Would you care to elaborate?"

Raider told him the story.

Wagner leaned back, sighing. "Heller's own fool-headedness got him into trouble. You can't blame yourself."

"I don't. But it's always going to be the same. Anybody that rides with me will end up in the ground. I'm too set in my ways. Doc was used to me, and he was damned smart. Pretty tough, too." He looked into the cold coffee. "No more partners for me, Wagner. I'm finished."

Wagner was not ready to give up. "What if we let you work alone?" he offered with a sly smile. "You don't have to take a partner. We won't give you any assignments that you can't handle by yourself. And if you ever need reinforcements, you can feel free to ask the agency to send as many men as you need to back you up."

Raider squinted at his former boss, not sure he had

heard Wagner right. "You'd do that for me? Let me work alone?"

Wagner nodded.

"Why?"

"We don't want to lose you, Raider. We need a trouble-shooter. Hell, you practically solved the Huntley case by yourself. Mr. Pinkerton and I feel you can handle it alone. What do you say?"

Raider grimaced. "I don't know. I was thinkin' of look-in' for other work."

"Like what?" Wagner challenged. "Are you going to clean stables? Or drive a stagecoach? Perhaps you could become a sheriff or a marshal. I happen to know, however, that you have always harbored an intense hatred of local law enforcement officials. You've always found them lack-ing in detective skills."

Raider pushed away from the table, avoiding Wagner's stare. "I got to think on it."

Wagner stood up. "Very well. I shall be in Denver for another day. You may contact me at the Sundowner Hotel. Room three."

Wagner started out of the parlor. He paused at the threshold, looking back at Raider. "If I don't hear from you, Raider, I just want to say that you've done a good job for the agency. Mr. Pinkerton has always been rough on you, but I know he respects you deep inside."

"Okay," Raider replied.

Wagner tipped his hand and started to open the door.

"No!" Raider cried. "I mean, *okay*. Yes. *Sí.*"

Wagner's brow wrinkled. "What?"

"Do I have to hit you over the head?"

Wagner took off his spectacles. "I still don't understand what you're trying to tell me, Raider."

The big man from Arkansas kicked his feet up on the table. "I'm tellin' you that you're right, Wagner. I been thinkin' about it, and I can't really come up with any other kind of work that I want to do. If you let me work by myself, I'll stay on with the agency."

Wagner came back toward the table. "Splendid. It just so happens that I have an assignment for you."

Raider grinned his coyote expression of friendly con-tempt. "Is that so?"

Wagner knocked his feet off the table. "Now that you're working for me again, it's time you started to show some respect."

"No offense," Raider replied. "What you got for me, boss? Another chicken-pickin' trail drive?"

Wagner shot him a cool glance, but then opened his notebook and said, "Now, here's what we want you to do . . ."